By
THE LORD OTTER

The Shadow of Twin Moons
Steel & Stormbright, Vol. #2
Published by: Alcaron Publishing
Cover by: NeutronBoar
Map by: The Lord Otter
Illustrations by: NeutronBoar & Frederic Guimont
Special Thanks to: Inkarnate Pro

This book is a work of fiction. Names, characters, places, organizations, and events are either products of the author's imagination or used fictitiously. Any resemblance to actual events, places or persons, living or dead, is entirely coincidental.

First Edition, 2025

ISBN: 979-8-9892148-3-9

A Time of Trouble

Taken from their home as slaves, young Serithas and Zolan were forced to survive under the Ilgrathians, deep at the heart of the Alcaron Empire.

Wearily they worked and starved at the hands of their captors. All hope was lost when their father, Kolthan, was taken from them. It was then that the astromancer, Aedas, recognized the brothers and their torment. Evidently, their father was alive, even after two years of imprisonment. With the Slave Pits having taken their toll on the youths, Serithas became Steel, and Zolan, Stormbright. They fought towering beasts and through armies of voracious demons. As mercenaries, they crossed into the nation of Divnarost, escaping their old lives while their commanders and "comrades" were slain about them.

Thence taken as prisoners of war, Steel and Stormbright found a new reason to go on living. Striking an alliance with King Telinor, the king of the mysterious star wraiths, they formed a last stand against the encroaching empire.

The battle was hard-won, but victory came at a cost.

With newfound determination, the brothers wandered north in search of Kolthan. Little do they know, however, that an old enemy has sworn vengeance against them.

This is...

Table of Contents

To Leslie. In my darkest moments, you have given me care and counsel; for that I cannot be grateful enough.

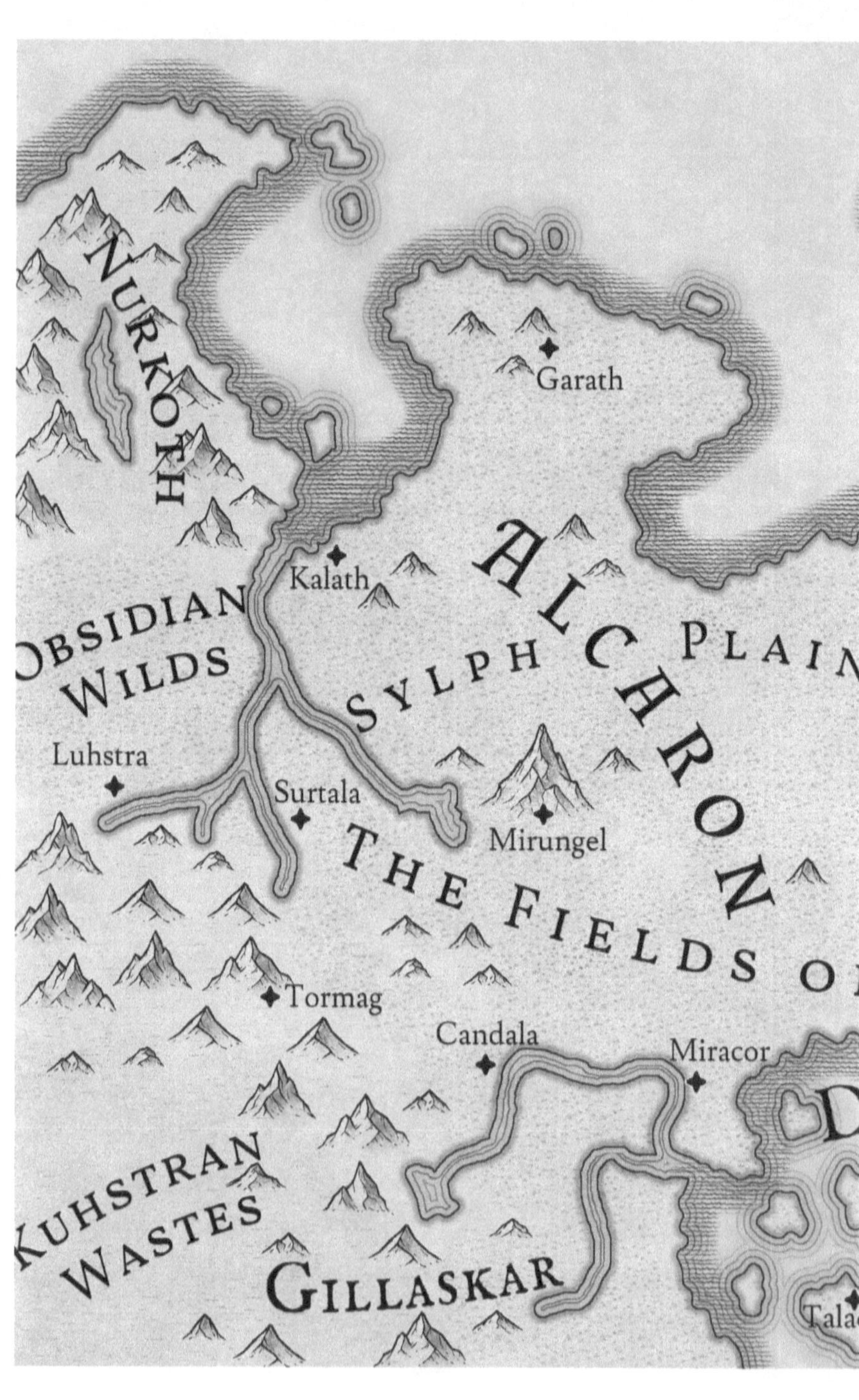

NURKOTH
OBSIDIAN
WILDS
Garath
Kalath
ALCARON
SYLPH PLAIN
Luhstra
Surtala
Mirungel
THE FIELDS OF
Tormag
Candala
Miracor
KUHSTRAN
WASTES
GILLASKAR
Tala
D

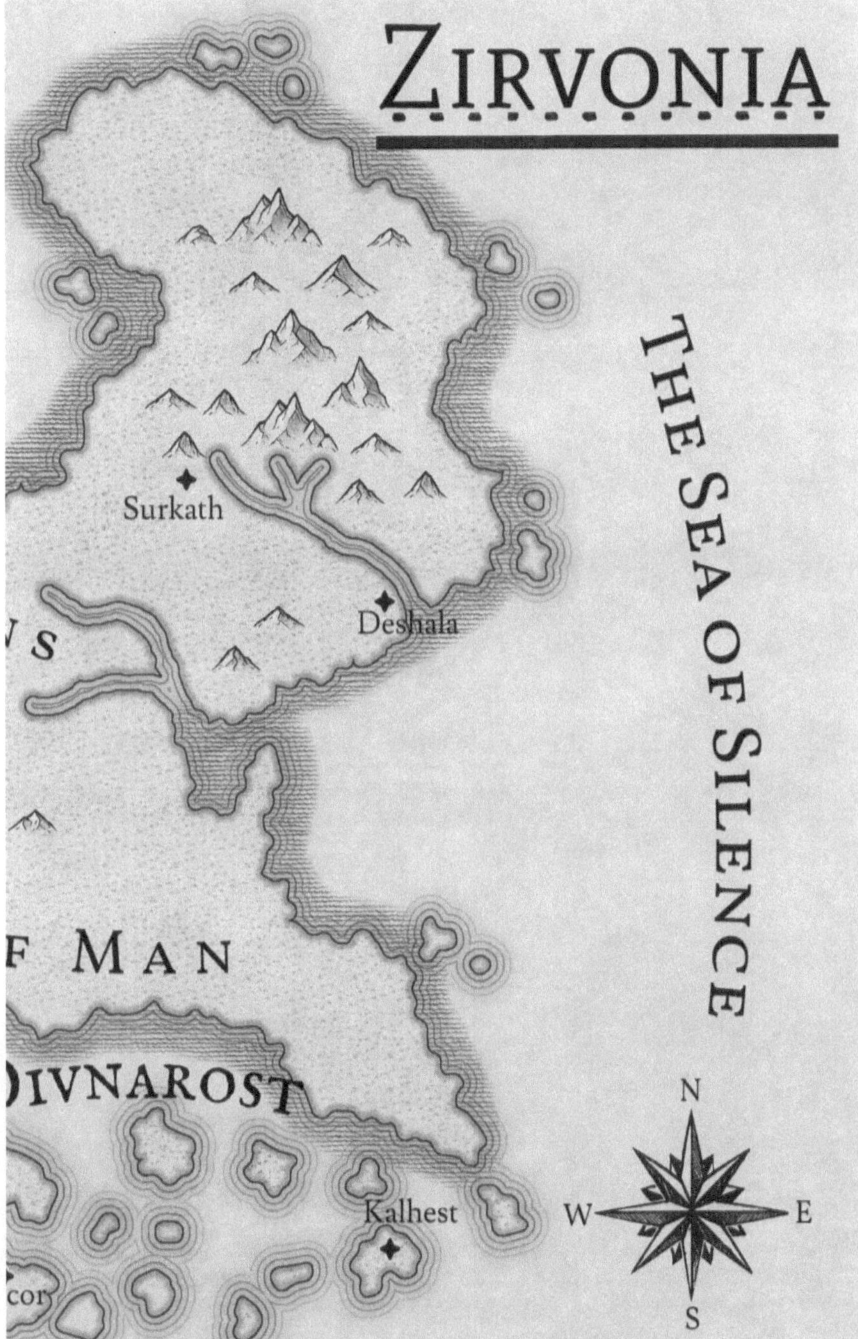

ZIRVONIA
THE SEA OF SILENCE
Surkath
Deshala
...S
F MAN
DIVNAROST
Kalhest
...cor
N
W
E
S

THE SILKEN DOVE
HIGH-TOWN
THE FEATHERLE...
ILGRATHIÉ TEMPLE
LOFTY TOWER
HOLY DISTRICT
ANCIENT'S HOLD
THE GO...
QUINN'S APARTMENT
HELVIA MANOR
BIXBY'S WARES
CANDALA BARRACKS
ROGUE'S APARTMENTS
THE SILVER HEARTH IN...
TEMPLE OF THE ANCIENTS
LINDRA...
MERCHANT'S CORNER
LOW-TOWN
TWILIG...

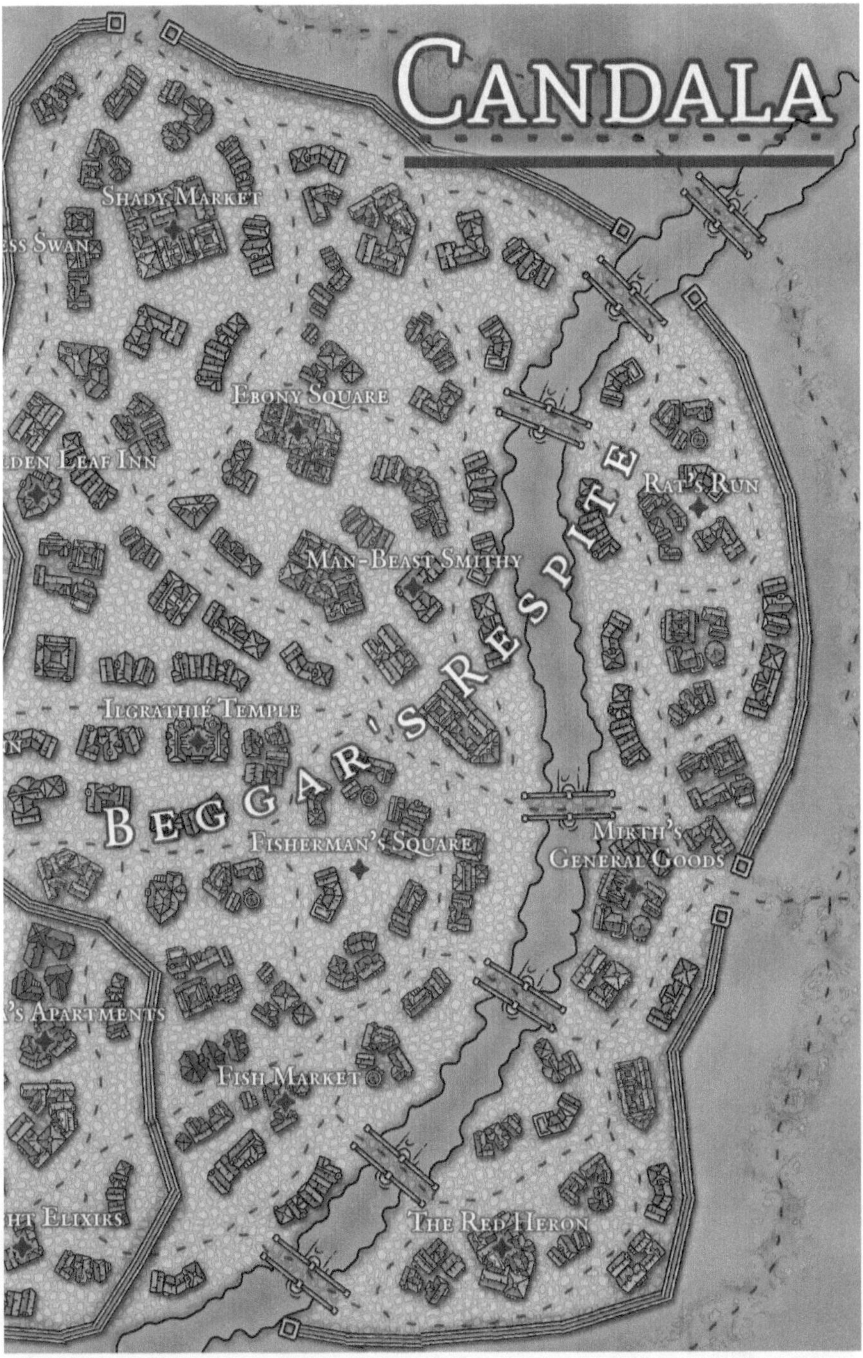
CANDALA
SHADY MARKET
EBONY SQUARE
RAT'S RUN
MAN-BEAST SMITHY
BEGGAR'S RESPITE
ILGRATHIÉ TEMPLE
FISHERMAN'S SQUARE
MIRTH'S
GENERAL GOODS
FISH MARKET
THE RED HERON

Prologue

Heavenly lights danced in swirls over the wide, golden halls. From many censers fumed a heady incense, and angelic rays caressed the smoothed stone with their warmth, tinged with aromatic spices and herbs, promising dreams of sweet ecstasy—pleasure and pain. Brief intervals were punctuated by a scream as the goddess lounged on Her throne. Her mind darkened with discontent, whereas a rich, golden hue spilled to all corners of the chamber, bathing the palace in Her divine aura.

Despite Her slaves' efforts, who tried to comfort and please amidst their drugged stupor, Ilgrathié pursed Her lips. Their hands passed over bronze skin and smooth curves, forming Her divine, alluring figure. A thin arrayment of chains cascaded down Her supple figure, barely covering whatever was necessary, so as to provoke one's inner lasciviousness.

Still, the goddess made no response to Her slaves. The spirit-like sylphs weaved in grand patterns above—those ethereal beings of the wind—dancing their malicious dances, as each action was followed by a chill *swoosh*. To the onlooker they would have appeared much like maidens of beauty, with flowing hair and semi-transparent ribbons trailing. The sylphs shared their doubts, cries manifesting as a disturbing combination of howl and groan. A pair of the creatures had well separated themselves from the rest, singing their songs while close to a decrepit old man. With each sonorous note, the goddess beheld him scratching and tearing at his own flesh, his body writhing and convulsing.

Hours passed with the slave's horrified screams as entertainment. Each bout of mutilation grew more pronounced than the last. Despite this distraction, Ilgrathié sank further into boredom.

The golden halls dampened with Her mood. Shimmering lattices and mosaics of silver, ivory, and lapis lazuli grew duller along the walls. All was quiet, save for the large double doors opening wide. Stepping inside was a hooded man who appeared exceedingly frail. One might have expected the figure to stoop like a crone, just as one might emerge from a fairy tale. Instead his posture was upright, gait steady, as he beheld the tortured thing kneeling twenty cubits distant, the divine carpets stained with dried streaks of blood.

"You are just in time." A slight smirk dawned on Ilgrathié's lips. The radiance shimmered from Her magnificent form, and the room beamed with holy light. This was contrasted by another cry for help, as the poor human tore into an eye socket. An issuance of blood and jelly-white liquid streamed from his mangled face. With a signal from their master, the sylphs ceased their torturous games; the slave crumpled to the floor. "Are you aware why I've summoned you here?"

"That I am, Your Radiance." He bowed low while averting his gaze. Such was the case for any human who was summoned. Aedas' forehead touched the floor as he prostrated himself before the Ilgrathian goddess. Keeping perfectly still, he continued: "Many weeks have gone since we've heard from General Caerst. I have seen into the future, Your Radiance, and the omens speak ill."

Ilgrathié frowned where She sat. "Then it's as I expected. Are you certain the siege was a failure, that my most esteemed Falconer has gone missing?"

"Aye, I am certain of it. I have meditated these many weeks, and each night I have beheld visions of the Falconer abandoning her post. We astromancers may be few in number, but we have all seen the same. The siege is lost, Your Radiance." He bowed his head even further, his nose pressing against the polished marble.

Prologue

Rising, the goddess emitted the faintest of sighs. "My esteemed Falconer has failed me twice, both times having pained me most grievously. Judging from our armed forces' silence, I must assume you are correct. Perhaps it is time I took stricter measures with my lieutenant, astromancer. A deed such as this shall not go unpunished."

"Do you think it's possible she perished in the battle?"

"It is a possibility, yet I have my doubts. Nay—I sense much worse. This Falconer is more resilient than most. She is strong and capable, but perhaps her loyalty isn't what I had believed. At this point, one can only speculate she has strayed from the path."

"Caerst might have abandoned her post, though surely she would not betray our cause. I know her too well, Your Radiance."

"Would you stake your life on such a claim?"

The astromancer did not answer.

Her servants recommenced their efforts, doing their best to pleasure the being they so admired, yet the goddess ignored them as She ruminated. "I fear the worst for my Falconer, Aedas. Perhaps it is time I sent one to learn of her whereabouts. You have served me well these many years, especially for a human. I ask that you locate General Caerst and bring her back to me. If she is dead, you will return her corpse. If alive, well, there is the potential you will have to subdue her."

The astromancer stirred where he knelt. Ilgrathié perceived his trembling, but whether that was because of Her presence or the nature of his task, She was not certain. He lifted his eyes to the base of Her divan, a supreme honor for one so wretched as he.

"If what you say is true, and General Caerst has gone rogue, in what manner shall I bring her to you? I am an astromancer, Your Radiance; my duty is studying the past, present, and future with my magicks. How could *I* subdue a Falconer?"

Ilgrathié gave a light chuckle. Gesturing to one of Her slaves, a naked man scampered near, his hands closed over a small, hidden object. A

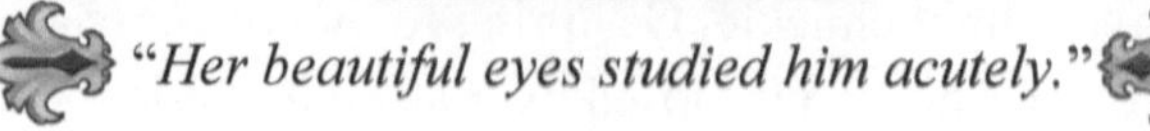

"Her beautiful eyes studied him acutely."

peculiar luminescence beamed between bony fingers, changing from soft tones of scarlet to jade, jade to violet, violet to azure, and so on.

Pacing down the wide series of steps, the man opened his palm to the astromancer.

"It cannot be," Aedas gasped. "This is… It isn't every day one is given Dreamstone of such quality."

"I see you are familiar with it." Her beautiful eyes studied him acutely. "I trust you will not handle such weapons lightly. I give this knowing that you will use it in good faith."

Indeed, Aedas knew well that Dreamstone wasn't an ordinary crystal. It was true that it could augment one's magical ability, and the fact it shaped reality at a whim was nothing short of wondrous. However, using such a stone came with a cost, and judging by the stories, none of them were at all pleasant.

"Aye," he replied. "It is like oneiromancy."

"It *is* oneiromancy," She interjected. "And it is greater than any sorcerer alone." Her voice resumed its regular tempo. "I assume you will do your utmost to ensure General Caerst is captured?"

"I will," he replied. "If I may ask, Your Radiance, where did you procure such an item?"

The goddess smiled, regarding the frail human with affluence. "It was found in the depths of a city known as Candala, in a labyrinth holding a formidable monster. This is but one of a few we possess."

"I understand," said Aedas. "Forsooth, the Ancients have proven most ingenious with their artifacts, forgotten race though they may be."

"Undoubtedly so." Ilgrathié pondered as she nodded her approval. "You may depart with my blessing. On the morrow, you will venture south with my most loyal Ilgrathians. I expect your return within a month."

The astromancer bowed once more, interweaving his fingers diagonally in the holy salute. She waved a hand in dismissal. With quivering knees, Aedas rose to his feet, leaving the hall with the two giant doors slamming behind him.

So the goddess lounged in Her divan, a hint of relaxation stealing over as the sylphs prodded what had been their source of entertainment. The slave was dead.

"Bring me another," said Ilgrathié, motioning to one of Her servants who frightfully scampered off.

Among the streets of Mirungel, minstrels sang and soldiers reveled in various pleasures. The poets recited their verses; flowers rained from the high roofs above; the revelry in drink and song and sex was blossoming in full. Unlike many humans they owned, the Ilgrathians were exceedingly beauteous, with bronze skin and statuesque figures to match. Their faces were lean and fair, their silken hair a pleasing gold, silver, or jet. Their laughter was boisterous and musical, and their revelry unchecked, as their thirst for vices was unequaled.

Within that crowd of lecherous drunkards, aloof artists, and boisterous warlords, Aedas walked alone.

The astromancer wove a path through streets of white stone and gilded brass. For a human, steeling one's nerve was everything in a city where Ilgrathians deemed themselves his superior. A lone soul would pass him a glance; thus he wrapped his hood tighter about him.

He revealed himself to a pair of guards. The two nodded their approval, opening a thick stone door. Aedas' surroundings grew warmer. Leaving the Igrathian paradise behind, the tunnels dimmed. A crimson hue permeated the air, warping his sense of vision.

Then he heard the screams.

Around were the cries of humans; a line of shifting hempen bonds, flanked on either side by Ilgrathian soldiers. He spotted the unfortunate souls who had kindled the Ilgrathians' wrath, malice, and lust; anything which justified their torture. Chains rattled as humans were dismembered, raped, and bled dry. Those with luck died in minutes of arrival. Alas, many were goaded into rejoining their fellows, being handed a pickaxe, shovel, or other tool. The astromancer pondered the two brothers. A sharp pang of guilt followed as he considered the urgency of his task. By the gods, if there was a chance at redemption, this had to be it. The low, rhythmic *tink tink* of the mining rang in the dark—an unseen toiling which continued ad infinitum among the endless haze of misery—mining which would never stop, not until their inevitable death and passage into the Great Beyond.

It came as a rush of stifling heat and emotion, and thus Aedas remembered how much he hated this place—the real Mirungel that lay underneath the surface.

His head lowered instinctively. The tunnels smoothed into corridors of mortared stone. The astromancer was like a shadow, his gait soundless as a cat.

Rounding a stony corner, he came to a halt. An Ilgrathian guard wandered along the narrow corridor.

"I see you've returned," said the man with cool malignance. "If you want to speak with him, I trust you are willing to pay the price."

"But of course." Aedas tugged at the purse strings to his side, dropping a few drakons into the man's palm.

The coins clinked as the guard counted them individually. He eyed one with curiosity before biting.

"It's always a pleasure," he purred. "I still don't understand why you protect the man. What is he to you, a lover or some such?"

The astromancer shook his head. As much as he hated it, he was the only individual the prisoner could rely on. He had made a promise; and what was worse, the old giant's condition was worsening with each day.

"The man has information," he replied. "I must find what is locked within that old brain of his. It's little help that the Soul Cistern has destroyed his mind."

The guard shrugged. "A pathetic excuse. You should be proud of your station, astromancer. As for my two parcels, I know you're going soft on him." The Ilgrathian handed the astromancer a rusted key, pacing down the corridor as he left the hooded man alone. "I'll be back when you're finished." His voice echoed along the halls. "If you need anything, just give me a shout."

Aedas shrugged his shoulders. He inserted the key and twisted until a staccato *click* was heard. The door creaked open in front of him. Darkness permeated the room. Aedas took a single step forward.

A rotten bench hugged the wall, and close by was a bed of mildewed hay. Next to his boot rested an old tin plate, its surface caked in dried slop. His eyes followed these details, resting on a disheveled figure which lay curled in a fetal position.

"I've returned, Kolthan." He kicked what passed as food to one side, along with a rat the size of his foot, as he produced a few pieces of jerky and tossed them to the prisoner. Kolthan scarfed the foodstuff, quickly as one could manage. "Damn that guard! I told the fool you were to be treated properly." His face twisted in a scowl.

He spied the meek, frightened prisoner.

His rage lessened.

"I am sorry, my friend." The man flinched as Aedas took another step. The astromancer slowed, his countenance almost soothing. The sobbing lessened. A knot formed in Aedas' stomach as he knelt an arm's span away from the giant.

"What," Kolthan stammered. "What… here for?"

The astromancer grimaced. "I'm here to find your sons." The prisoner exhaled sharply, muttering until Aedas gripped him by the shoulder, gentle yet firm. "We are going to meet them, and you are coming with me."

The astromancer noted Kolthan's surprise. "Alas, I have heard very little from them as of late. Only the briefest glimpses in my visions have hinted at where they are. Your sons are in danger, Kolthan. I shall need your help if we're to meet with them."

The scrawny giant mumbled incoherently. The man was doubtful.

Aedas breathed softly. How he wished to have released this man alongside his two sons; yet the result would have been too obvious for someone joining his progeny as a fellow sellsword. Although he harbored the best intentions, every alternative for sneaking Kolthan out was too risky; after countless years of subjugation, he knew how Ilgrathians thought and behaved. Short of the astromancer taking him along personally—an act that would be closely supervised, no less—there was nothing to be done.

That was, until now.

"Do not worry, my friend. Our departure from Mirungel is nigh," he said, his other hand digging at a pouch along his waist. Aedas situated a number of ingredients; sprinkling powders here, tracing patterns with a piece of chalk there, his voice emanating a low, rhythmic hum.

He realized Kolthan hadn't stirred one cubit from where he sat. That was good. The spell was taking effect, and it would be some time before the ritual was complete.

Among the ingredients, he produced a myriad of incense candles. The astromancer gripped the Dreamstone in his pocket, his words taking on a deeper resonance. By the time everything was prepared—the magic circle drawn, candles lit, and the small bowl situated at its center—Kolthan was fast asleep. Aedas approached the basin, lighting a flame underneath its suspended base. Within it he placed a smattering of plant leaves, a pinch of mugwort, a dash of dried lotus seeds, and a preserved moonflower. Taking the mortar and pestle, he ground the mix together until it resembled a fine powder. A pungent aroma tickled at his nostrils.

"This will take but a moment," he said, kneeling and lying beside Kolthan, taking a calloused hand in his own. The fragrance spread, and Aedas' senses slipped. He cradled the Dreamstone in his palm, honing his attention. He would have to exert himself most carefully, for being too forceful with a Dreamstone would yield a bevy of risks. The stone would exact its toll from him, but fractures of the body and mind—even the soul—were avoidable.

"Now, I will enter your dreams," he said absently, "then we will find your sons. *Sangua Ligius Somnio Quar...*"

The words spoken, his surroundings blurred in a thick haze. Fire rushed through his veins as the Dreamstone drew in energy. That, too, faded as Aedas concentrated. Closing his eyes, all feeling, sound, sight, or taste was lost. The singular impulse which led him, in fact, was the heady scent wafting through the cell. The lone risk was the Dreamstone's magical torment, reduced to a dull ache in his subconscious.

Suddenly, there was light and color and shapes; taste and texture and knowing! A haze of colors engulfed Aedas as he plunged deeper. He imagined this was what comprised Kolthan's thoughts—a hazy jumble of memories which he imagined were the nearest and dearest to this man. In this, Aedas felt as Kolthan felt; he laughed and loved and wept and fought; his memories were Kolthan's, and the giant's were his!

The astromancer pondered how much time had crept by. To him, this realm seemed eternal. Yet even in the throes of passion or in the deepest sorrow following Tana's death, Kolthan's most beloved, he realized they were illusions—mere distractions from his goal.

He must go deeper.

Then, as he plundered through nameless abysses of consciousness and raw emotion, the chaotic visions parted. Yes! It was the blood! The same blood connecting relatives across time and space, the blood that bound souls and divined the whereabouts of those who shared it.

The image became more substantial. He was on the edge of a forest. A solid wall of trees lingered close by. He surveyed his surroundings, seeing the area was quiet, calm, and peaceful. Upon gazing down, he realized his body was Kolthan's. That shouldn't have surprised him at least, what with the spell at work.

A peculiar presence drove him forth. It was the blood, guiding him to a cave out of view.

He moved out of instinct, espying the two brothers he had freed all those months ago. One was situated at the cave's entrance, having tried and failed to keep a close watch for pursuers. Their slumber seemed light and unfulfilling, fraught with nightmares and paranoia. They were battered and exhausted, chased from one night to the next with little rest.

Aedas was familiar with the tactic; such was the nature of the hunt.

The astromancer exited the cave, his steely muscles tensing with each stride, as he maneuvered at peak condition. He crested a nearby hill. It was like he observed a hundred leagues out, for not so distant was General Caerst and her warband. Their numbers were few, he surmised, though they appeared none the worse for wear. A pair of scouts led the way, and he spotted the Falconer roaming about their company; an awful hatred swelled inside of her, an emotion which remained unseen, yet was felt by the astromancer.

By this time the truth dawned on him. Focusing, he rejoined the two brothers.

Kneeling at their side, the twain stirred to a sitting position, seeing that Kolthan's specter was speaking to them. They almost pictured their father visiting from the grave, having passed from his mortal vessel into the Great Beyond. Yet it was the bonds of blood that anchored him in reality, granting him the very aspect of a ghost. Oddly enough, Kolthan spoke with Aedas' voice, the man who had freed them.

Aedas had little time to explain, for his power was fast waning.

"You must travel to Candala," he said, each word stabbing like a needle into his subconscious. "Flee into the forest. Do not worry, your father and I shall meet with you shortly."

His vision faded as the landscape parted in clouds of ivory. The astromancer awakened. He and Kolthan were back to their original selves. Weakness overtook him as the Dreamstone was cradled in his palm.

To his side, he saw tears streaking down the giant's face. After their joined mental state, Aedas knew of his strife—his atrophied muscles, his failure to protect the life and joy that were his sons, his inability to speak.

The astromancer stood up.

"The time is very soon, Kolthan. Once the morning sun breaches the sky, we will make our escape. Assuming we survive," he drew in a deep breath, "our destination lies south."

I

Driftwind

Dawn's rosy hues bled over the horizon. In the hollow of a small hill, Steel and Stormbright stirred as their father faded in the fire's embers. The image fled once they awakened. They were alone and cognizant of how they had failed at keeping a rotating watch. Pushing through their exhaustion, the realization shocked them greatly.

"Brother, was that…?" Stormbright stammered. He swept aside a stray golden lock, azure eyes studying the embers. "It was so strange. As if Father were speaking to us."

"So you saw it too," said Steel, wincing as he rose. "No, I don't believe it was Father. It didn't sound like him."

"Now that you mention it, I think it was the astromancer's voice. Could there be such kinds of sorcery in this world?"

"You're the sorcerer, you tell me." His brother shrugged. "Besides, our little friend knows more than either of us. You heard what he mentioned about fleeing through the forest, right? That we should be heading to…"

"Candala!" they said in unison.

Stormbright rose to his feet, observing the hollow's interior as he ruminated. Roots hung suspended from the ceiling, and a distinctive clay smell clung to the back of his throat. "They've been chasing us ever since we left Miracor. It's like they've had a plan to wear us down from the start. Still," he said, "I'm not sure whether going into the Caprian Forest is our best option."

"What other choice do we have, Zolan?"

The sound of Stormbright's real name was harsher than usual. Ever since their enslavement at the hands of the Ilgrathians, they had scarcely referred to one another by their true identities. Serithas had become Steel, quick in battle and cold as the polished metal. Zolan, on the other hand, had assumed the moniker of Stormbright, a vague reminder of his encounter with Calamtu. That was so long ago, yet it had changed their lives forever.

"We know it's the bronze bitch who's after us," said Steel. "She isn't going to stop until we're both dead. She'll keep pursuing us, night and day, if that's what it takes for her to succeed." He spat, recalling what the Ilgrathian had done to them weeks ago—the grand siege, the murdering of Kitala, the same woman who was Miracor's Queen and his lover.

The recollection stabbed like a hot needle in his chest. With a deep breath, he calmed himself. "The Caprian Forest may be our best option after all."

"Perhaps you've a point, Serithas," replied Stormbright, placing a hand on his brother's shoulder. The young sorcerer saw anguish, but he couldn't dwell on it. They needed to keep moving.

Steel's lips widened into a smile. His fingers combed through a mop of brownish hair, which had been ruffled and unkempt since their departure. "Thanks, Zolan."

Stormbright didn't react, as he was lost in his own thoughts.

"What is it?"

"I don't know. The forest doesn't sit right with me. I want to be certain we're not getting into something worse than what we're in right now."

"Zolan…"

"No. You're right," he sighed, "it seems our best course of action is to go west. As much as I hate to say it."

"Don't tell me you're getting scared," Steel cajoled.

"No, it's just..." How could Stormbright describe the presence? Perhaps it was superstition, considering he hadn't detected any traces of magic through his wizardly *inner sense*. Even so, something felt off about the Caprian Forest, as if danger were waiting around the next corner.

"Come on. We're losing precious daytime. If we stopped every time you doubted yourself, we would both be dead."

Stormbright shrugged. "Very well. Lead the way, Serithas."

Thick pines loomed over them. The brothers were surrounded by trees, interspersing as far as the eye could see. The earthy scents of decaying leaves and fresh oak filled the air. How long had it been? Was it the fourth day or the fifth? It was difficult to tell as the boughs covered everything but a trickle of light, leaving them in near total darkness. The landscape rose at a gentle angle, and each step was met with a crunch from hundreds of pine needles and twigs. Stormbright's stomach twisted with unease. He could tell Steel was less confident than usual.

That night as they camped, a plethora of glowing pupils stared at them from the shadows—watching and waiting. A wolf's howl echoed at a short distance. Everything was pitch-black; naught was visible other than their weapons and bags of supplies. They shivered upon hearing a monstrous roar, a beast neither of them could identify. The creatures fought and struggled, lasting well into the late hours. The sounds of killing, whimpering, and dying shook the brothers to their very core.

"We should never have come here," said Stormbright, wrapping himself in his linens, chilled to the bone. Steel had warned him earlier that starting a fire would give them away to larger animals, though even in the dark it seemed likely they would be discovered.

"Are you sure we can't build a fire?" Stormbright took a bite from a squirrel they had managed to hunt, kill, and skin. Between the two of them, the meal was hardly a morsel, and being uncooked, the stuff tasted rather bland and slimy. Nevertheless, the driving force of hunger overrode his disgust.

Steel objected, his voice a whisper. "Just so long as we stay quiet and alert, we'll be fine. I'm certain we can handle wolves."

"What about the monster they're fighting?"

His brother didn't answer. Stormbright knew Steel was afraid. He said little more on the matter.

The hours crept by. Their sleep came in short spells as Steel would toss this way and that. The young sorcerer lay perfectly still, afraid to make a single sound for fear of attracting what was out there.

Eventually, his eyelids grew heavier. He drifted off into a light slumber.

When they awoke, their surroundings were black as ever. Stormbright gave a weary glance towards Steel, and the thief returned it.

They journeyed on. To their vast relief, thin rays filtered through the boughs above. What began as hours in darkness transmogrified into a gray, hazy morning. The woods flanked them on all sides; what was worse, they recognized the debilitating fatigue. Steel did not falter, surveying every corner and peering underneath any branch that might have housed a dangerous animal. Stormbright dragged his feet at some distance behind, his body on the verge of sleep.

"Are you sure we're heading west?" Stormbright asked, irritated beyond belief.

"Guess," said Steel tersely, a hint of agitation rising in his voice.

"What's that supposed to mean? We've been traveling for days and there's no end in sight." Stormbright clenched his fists, the anger spreading from the pit of his stomach to his outermost extremities. "We can see nothing!"

"Then we keep moving, Brother. We're wasting time by talking."

"We're also wasting time if we're heading in the wrong direction."

"What do you think of this?" Steel indicated the light around them. "It seems to me we're getting close!"

Stormbright scoffed. "You don't know that, Serithas!"

"Oh, keep quiet!"

"No, you keep quiet!"

Steel retaliated with his fist. The shock was enough to snap Stormbright from lassitude, but not enough to deter him. The youth shot back with a punch. The thief dodged, but knowing his brother well enough, Stormbright extended a foot, tripping him off balance as he landed another swing.

"Ow, all right! This isn't getting us anywhere!" Steel grabbed his brother's fists until Stormbright could do naught else.

"Let go of me!"

"Not until you lighten up."

"You started it!"

"And I'm ending it," Steel said as he maintained a firm grip. "Do we have a truce?"

Stormbright grimaced, relenting. "Aye. I guess so."

Steel grunted as he rose. He hadn't realized until now, but something was off.

"Can you smell that?" he asked.

The sorcerer sniffed the air.

"It's smoke," Stormbright replied.

"Help me up." Steel approached one of the trees. The trunks were smooth; Stormbright gritted his teeth as he hefted his brother up, the latter catching hold of a branch and hoisting himself higher.

Steel struggled as he climbed, maneuvering from one branch to the next in a precarious perch. Scanning past the trees, he spotted a column of smoke stretching high into the heavens. The thief wasn't quite sure what to make of it, but the sense of foreboding was unmistakable.

He was still pondering this mystery as he felt his way back to the ground.

"What's going on?" asked Stormbright.

"It looks like a battle."

"Is it the Ilgrathians?"

Steel shrugged.

Stormbright paced away from his brother, honing his *inner sense*. The chirping birds, swaying grass, and various aromas of the forest blended as his senses were heightened, his awareness expanding past their usual limits. Stormbright's mind traveled outside of his body, venturing along the forest floor, and out past the trees. He saw, touched, smelled, and tasted as if it were the slightest extension of will.

The youth sat at the base of a trunk until his eyes parted open. "It's a village," he said. "I am almost certain it was burned to the ground. As to who would do such a thing, perhaps it was Ilgrathians."

"No." Steel shook his head, denying what his brother was about to suggest. "We stay the course."

"For how much longer, Serithas? Food isn't exactly plentiful around here, and I would like to eat something cooked for once."

"No."

"But Serithas…"

"I said no."

Stormbright was tempted to swing, only catching himself at the last second.

Steel shook his head, arriving at a stream that bubbled and swirled with crystalline waters. Slaking his thirst, the thief realized how empty his stomach was. There had been no food along the path, not a solitary thing aside from a squirrel. That had done little to sate their hunger. No rabbits dared reveal themselves, nor did he sight any stags. Supplies were limited;

"The thief wasn't quite sure what to make of it..."

apart from his spear, dagger, shortbow, bedroll, and some simple leather armor, Steel carried little on his person. Stormbright held even less, with a shortsword and some basic camping gear accounting for most of his belongings.

Stormbright was sulking by the time his brother wandered close.

"Fine—we'll check out the village. We wait until nightfall. Do you understand?"

Stormbright sat, giving a warm smile. "Aye, Brother."

Steel and Stormbright maneuvered to the clearing's edge. Their anger was replaced with a vague notion of alarm. The spindly branches of pine trees stretched over their heads until they caught glimpses of the clearing beyond. Out in the vast opening were clusters of hills, with tall, swaying grass and a cool breeze which brought goosebumps. Farther along they spotted the outline of buildings, houses, and an all-encompassing wall near one of the larger mounds.

They waited crouched among the hills, biding their time until the sun was nearly devoured by the space between earth and sky. Light blues changed to a darker shade of cerulean. The sun's ochre hues flared late in the third hour, bathing the village like a second fire.

This faded once the fifth hour was upon them.

At this point they followed a dirt road which led directly into the village. In earnest, they expected an ambush. A pair of ravens cawed overhead; this caused Stormbright to raise his hands, lightning trickling along his fingers. Realizing his mistake, he relaxed.

Turning swiftly back to the path, Stormbright collided with his brother. "Ow! Steel, what are you-" He paused, noting the thief was peering headlong at the entrance. Flames and smoldering rubble littered the area, yet the village was deathly still.

"What happened, Serithas?" asked Stormbright.

"It's like you said—the Ilgrathians happened." Steel recalled how their own village had been massacred two years ago—how brutally their people were slain, corpses strewn without care. Such malice, as he learned, proved common in Ilgrathian raids.

They spotted no bodies as they neared the wall, heading through the entrance with a sign reading "Driftwind". Steel's words were low and disquieting, "Either they were captured or everyone fled."

"Something's not right." The young sorcerer reached with his *inner sense*, his vision dimming as his consciousness drifted among the streets, searching for any hints of magic.

Steel paced forward. The horrid burning flesh assaulted his nostrils. Around them, the buildings were razed, what with the occasional scorched arm jutting between jagged pieces of rubble. A few structures were intact, yet he did not doubt most of the denizens had perished. Where were the rest of them? The few remaining corpses were burnt to a crisp. There weren't any traces of blood. Save for the burning ruins, the area had been wiped clean.

Steel looked back; Stormbright was coming out of his trance.

"Did you find anything?"

"Nothing," he replied. "There's no recent tracks either. I can't understand how these people might have gone missing."

"Then we'll have to keep searching. Personally, my bet's on them being captured. Let's split up and see if we can scrounge up any food."

"Right."

Steel wandered alone, idly kicking aside bits of debris as he went. The village's layout was simple enough, being built around the crest of a hill, with a narrow pathway winding from an eastward direction to a northerly one.

Dusk settled into night. Overhead the twin moons Taldriath and Bruann gleamed in silent beauty, their paths almost crossing, but for the fact one moon was closer, they remained separate. The streets were bathed in silvery luminescence, a cool, pleasant chill worming its way in the night air.

The thief's gaze shifted to his right, identifying the largest structure in town. The tavern had been heavily damaged, as its roof was caved in on the second floor. The first appeared to be well intact, though light smoke issued from its interior.

Taking special care to mind the building's integrity, he stepped inside.

As this happened, Stormbright walked among the smaller dwellings. Most had been burnt to a crisp, and an awful stench permeated the area. He stifled his nose. The smoke cleared, and he glimpsed a hut standing before him. Remarkably, this structure showed no signs of burns or damage. Nostalgia rushed over him as he entered. Save for it being constructed of wood instead of stone, the interior reminded him much of home. Here he uncovered his face, detecting the wild scents of lilac, juniper, and summer berry. Although the occupants were long gone, the comforts of his old life seemed remarkably close.

"Alas, if things had been different…" Tears welled along his eyes. Wiping with his sleeve, he began searching the area. "I'm sorry, whoever you are. My brother and I are in need of food." His words went unanswered as he pocketed whatever he could find, taking a bite from a fresh carrot as he went.

His attention settled on a charm hanging over a single bed—a woven symbol which piqued his curiosity. The image was that of two crescent moons intertwining, akin to a lovers' embrace. That it was a charm of some significance he didn't doubt, although Stormbright had never seen anything quite like it.

He shut his eyes, feeling through with his *inner sense*. Yes, there was something about this charm. It was a presence of some sort…

"Is there anything nice in here, Zolan?"

Stormbright flinched as he snapped out of his trance. He realized Steel was shouldering a sack full of supplies.

"It's nothing," replied Stormbright.

"Then what are you looking at?" Steel asked as he bit into an apple.

Stormbright regarded the symbol, seeing it as mundane and inconsequential.

"I'm not entirely certain. It just seemed beautiful."

"Well, while you were busy gawking around, I found this." The thief held up a half-scorched banner. Its insignia was unmistakable. "Apart from a trapdoor that led me to food, everywhere else was abandoned."

"Was this General Caerst's doing?"

"I guess it's possible, though that would mean she's ahead of us. Last time I saw, they weren't riding by horse or rukh, so it's doubtful."

"That still doesn't explain what happened to everyone," said Stormbright.

There came a low scream. The sound was exceedingly faint, but given the emptiness Driftwind exuded—its winds howling like a phantom of the past—it registered as clear as day.

Steel and Stormbright froze, trying to place where the voice had come from. They listened intently as another scream echoed from the north path. The cry was for help.

Stormbright was about to run, until Steel caught him by the shoulder.

"This is none of our business."

"Let me go!" Stormbright spoke in defiance.

"Our survival is the only thing that matters."

Despite his brother's attempts to keep him still, Stormbright freed himself and bolted. The thief murmured a curse while making pursuit. The night reigned supreme, and though the heavens were largely clouded, the moons shone brilliantly as ever, illumining the landscape in their subtle hues. The young sorcerer rushed along the abandoned street, underneath the exit to the north, through fields of tall grass and grazing bays. A series of hills undulated in a gentle rhythm, lightly obscuring what lay beyond every few crests. From behind, Steel kept pace and gained ground, though it was much slower than he had hoped. He realized the horses were galloping past them, hooves thundering against the ground as another shrill cry pierced the air.

Steel's heart caught in his throat, the morbid shrieks terrifying him to the bone.

Stormbright halted, allowing Steel to catch up beside him. A path wound its way up the adjacent hill. He cast Stormbright a hard stare before the young magician parried with one of his own. As they breached the crest, their quarrel was forgotten as they spotted stony monoliths encircling a flattened stretch of land. The landmarks loomed at twice their height, with faint, archaic symbols being etched.

What frightened them most, however, was the horrifying aberrations. Fleshy blobs undulated with bodies that transmogrified into limbs, eyes, and tongues; anything to propel themselves to the pair of women they surrounded. Before anyone had reacted, a lady with brunette hair was being pulled, one of the things clamping down on her chest. The other girl cried for her friend, tears streaming as she tried to stop the abominable things.

"No! No! Please, Vana!" she wept.

Steel and Stormbright watched in horror as they readied their weapons. The ensnared woman screamed, thrashing as blood poured from her chest, neck, and shoulders. Abruptly, the sounds ceased. Her body snapped, twisted, and warped as the nightmare-kin shambled farther down, digesting what was left of the poor creature.

"Get away!" Steel cried, his rage granting him newfound energy. Two of the nightmare-kin made to intercept his mad dash forward; however, he feinted deftly to one side, striking with his spear whilst taking another with his dagger. Though his knees quivered, Stormbright didn't falter with his lightning. Strands of magic enveloped his arms, coalescing at the tips of his fingers. His hands stretched outward, and the air crackled blue.

"No, Vana… Vana…" Stormbright heard the girl muttering as they fought. It was like she had gone mad.

The young sorcerer knew her situation well. He saw one of the aberrations, its acidic flesh stretching in the form of unsightly limbs, ready to snatch her into fathomless oblivion. Lightning shot from Stormbright's fingers in an instant, his muscles aching with the exertion. By the time the woman had come to her senses, she realized a puddle of brown ichor pooled at her feet. It must have been instinct, for she acted with remarkable celerity.

She faced Stormbright directly, her dark eyes staring into his.

"Erm, greetings," he said awkwardly.

She didn't reply, merely giving a low and pitiful laugh before falling unconscious.

"Well, this keeps getting better!" shouted the thief, carving his way through half-a-dozen. He glanced at his brother. "A little help would be nice, Zolan!"

Stormbright snapped back to the present. Streaks of energy blazed through the horde of nightmare-kin, causing them to erupt into myriad balls of fire. The last two Steel dispatched himself.

"Are you all right?" the young sorcerer asked, facing Steel while lowering the girl to the ground.

"I'll manage," he said. "I'm not wounded anywhere. How about yourself?"

"Not a scratch," Stormbright smiled. His attention returned to the woman next to them. "What do we do with her?"

Steel shrugged. Looking closer, they discerned a few scratches, but the girl was unharmed. She couldn't have been younger than seventeen, Steel surmised, as he studied her well-shaped figure, heaving bosom, and flowing jet hair. Her clothes revealed a little too much in places, and her full lips were dyed a stark black. Her eyes were also shadowed.

In a way, she was like a reflection of the night, a nymph of darkness.

She came to. A visceral fear crept back as she breathed sharply.

"W-Where am I?" she asked. "We need to get out of here. Where's Vana?"

"We're sorry," said Stormbright. "We did what we could manage, but… we were too late to save her."

"I still don't get it," Steel interjected, quicker than she had time to answer. "How did the two of you survive when everyone else is dead?"

The thief noted her stark melancholy. She covered her face as she sobbed quietly.

"Please," murmured Stormbright, placing a hand on her shoulder. At this she flinched. He immediately withdrew, bewildered as to the girl's frightened reaction.

A moment later and her posture softened.

"I apologize," she said. "Please, if you would." She allowed him to comfort her. He sensed the tension in her muscles, though there was trust as well. Stormbright gaped at his brother, the thief responding with a shrug.

"What happened?" asked Stormbright.

"We hid ourselves underneath the bodies. We hid once they rode into town—burning, maiming, slaughtering…"

"Just calm down," said Stormbright. He felt her trembling subside. The sorcerer could only imagine what she must have been through. "Do you know why the Ilgrathians were here?"

She gazed up at him. "They were after an artifact—it's a relic our people greatly revere. A Moon Cup."

"And what is this Moon Cup?"

She swallowed. "I am aware it was forged of moonsteel, blessed by the Sacred Twins countless ages ago. It was kept here so it might bask in their holy light." She paused, a faint tremor registering in Stormbright's hand as it held her. He was confused as to what she meant by "Sacred Twins" until he followed her eyes, seeing the two moons hovering above them.

"They took it from us," she said, a hint of loathing in her voice. "They took it, and the nightmare-kin devoured the bodies. The Ilgrathians pursue its twin. Now all hope is lost."

"Well," Steel added, "I guess that answers one of our questions."

Stormbright ignored his brother. "What do you mean hope is lost?"

"The Great Equilibrium," she said. "It is coming, and already I've failed Taldriath and Bruann. My brothers and sisters have paid the price. All except for myself. I've failed my priestesses."

She hid her face within Stormbright's arm. To say he was baffled would have been an understatement. He glanced toward his brother, looking for an answer. Steel showed the same amount of confusion, as well as a dash of suspicion.

"Tell us your name." Although the command was simple, Steel's tone lost none of its edge.

"Aurora," she whispered. Her eyelids drooped as her lips parted subtly, as if she repeated a certain phrase. Stormbright was about to inquire further until she dozed in his arms.

"What did she say?" asked Steel.

"I don't know. She mentioned something about a... a leaf or some sort? What was it she said? I could almost hear it." He tried repeating the words she had spoken. "Gold- Gold- Golden... Golden Leaf?"

"What in the gods' names is 'Golden Leaf'?"

"I'm not sure."

"Are you sure that's what she said?"

"I'm almost positive," he replied. He pictured what the name might imply. "Brother, was she referring to an inn?"

"Perhaps with any luck it's close to Candala." Steel shrugged his shoulders. "It's a stretch, but it's worth a shot. That being said, something doesn't feel right about this."

"What do you mean?"

"I mean she could be bad news. Doesn't this seem a little convenient?"

"Not exactly," he replied. "Besides, you and I are capable on the road. We should at least take her to Candala, then figure out what we can do from there."

The thief sighed. "Fine. Don't blame me if we get stabbed on our way."

"Don't worry. I'll make sure we won't."

"I'll catch a few horses up the road. Many of them seemed docile."

Stormbright watched his brother descend the hillside, considering the girl who lay asleep in his arms. If they could save such an innocent damsel as Aurora, perhaps they had a chance in saving their father as well?

It was a stretch, but a hopeful one all the same.

II

A Path to Freedom

It was often said the souls of the damned dwelt below Mirungel. So thought Aedas as he stalked the darksome hallways. The screams of tormented men, women, and children faded behind him. What came closer were the howling voices in the Soul Cistern—unfortunate creatures tortured for so long they barely registered as human. The path loomed to his right, as being magically gifted himself, the sensation of what lay beyond terrified him to his core.

Aedas knew that most prisoners were never the same, as their essence was torn from their bodies for some greater, unknown purpose. Perhaps it was a form of arcane experimentation, or maybe they acted as an energy source? Either way, he was thankful to deliver one soul from this place— even if the damage was already done.

The frail man at his side trembled. Holding the hempen leash, the astromancer strode with the prisoner in tow. Aedas couldn't have picked a better candidate for the job, considering the decrepit slave was similar to Kolthan's height. All else would be brought into flux. The knowledge that this man was one of the Slave Pit's resident cannibals—not to mention committing deeds far worse—lessened his mental burden. On the other hand, condemning one to such fathomless horrors as the Soul Cistern should never be taken lightly; not even for him.

He rounded a shadowy corner, encountering the same guard he had met the day prior. The Ilgrathian greeted him with a smirk.

"Who is it you've brought with you, Aedas?" inquired the Ilgrathian, acknowledging the sorcerer's companion as they approached. It was sensible that the guard would take notice, for in mannerism and gait, the slave appeared as broken as Kolthan.

"He's a guest," quoth the astromancer. "Leave us be with the prisoner and we will be gone soon enough."

"Well, I suppose that's fair enough." The man shrugged as he was given a drakon, the faded gold shimmering in the wan torchlight. "I'll be back in an hour's time. Make sure you don't do anything too suspicious."

The Ilgrathian handed Aedas the keyring. Footsteps echoed along the corridors with a rhythmic staccato. The slave mumbled incoherently as the astromancer held the leash tight, unlocking and twisting open the door.

Kolthan stood before him. Although much weakened and disheveled, the giant seemed livelier than their encounter yesterday. The astromancer presumed it was excitement. Perhaps, after all this time, his body was beginning to heal?

The prospect was certainly hopeful.

"L-Leave?"

"That's correct, Kolthan. You will be leaving with me tonight. And this will be your replacement." He shut the door behind. "As much as it pains me to say, there's a few steps we must follow first. Do not worry, this won't take long."

He led the prisoner farther into the room. Sitting the man atop a rotting wooden bench, the astromancer gripped a pair of manacles that hung from the wall. The cuffs clicked over the man's wrists, and Aedas used a separate key to secure them.

"What... what...?"

"What am I doing?" Aedas exhaled. "A few alterations are needed to make the ruse convincing. I do not wish to scare you, Kolthan, but this must happen if you wish to see your boys."

He faced the chained slave, beholding the man's visceral fright. This was the best course of action, both for Kolthan and this broken prisoner.

Gods, he didn't even know the person's real name. Perhaps it was better that way.

Aedas held a vial, having the prisoner take a solid gulp. He brandished the Dreamstone in his palm, the chamber lighting up with its strange, vibrant glow. His other hand gripped the wrinkled forehead. The whining increased in volume and tempo. Aedas grimaced while the Dreamstone fed on his lifeforce. A wild bellow escaped the man's lips. The prisoner thrashed and struggled against his iron-like grip, against the magic which brought sickly fumes.

Kolthan scampered back to one corner. The slave resumed his struggle, though the manacles and sorcery held him in place. The poor soul wailed, eyes bulging, tears streaking down his face. The very outline of his head transformed, going from sickly and gaunt to a square jawline; hair changing its rough texture and hue; teeth regrowing where they had decayed long ago; right arm shrinking and deforming to naught but a stump at the elbow.

By the time Aedas relaxed his grip, the slave was nearly an exact replica of Kolthan.

"Unfortunately for us, no details can be spared. This man must resemble you in both aspect and voice. I've done all I can to ensure the vocal cords have been changed accordingly." He turned to the frail slave. "Can you talk?"

"B-B-Buh…" The man's words were incoherent, yet the baritone voice was unmistakable. Indeed, the prisoner sounded exactly like Kolthan.

Aedas produced a second vial from the folds of his robe. "Take this," he said. "It will give the impression you're inebriated. If it wasn't for this, I promise you the procedure would be far worse."

The giant mumbled as Aedas released the prisoner from his bonds, dragging him off to a far corner of the cell. Evidently the procedure had taxed the man to his limits, as the slave did not move a muscle.

"Please," Aedas indicated toward the bench, "have a seat."

Slowly, the giant acquiesced. The astromancer closed the manacles around his one wrist, fed him the potion, and allowed a moment for it to take effect.

"I warn you this won't be pleasant." Aedas revealed a folded gambeson and chainmail shirt from his robe, laying it beside him. He took a girdle from the set, holding it over the giant's mouth. "Bite down on this—for the pain."

Kolthan did so. Aedas held the Dreamstone, placing his palm on the giant's forehead as his body trembled.

What followed was indescribable to the seated human. Searing, scorching, excruciating agony, as Kolthan's jaw chomped down hard on the belt. Muscles heated and boiled under his skin, bones adjusting and realigning themselves. He struggled wildly, yet the astromancer's grip held firm.

Remarkably, the giant *felt* his right arm. What was severed from the elbow grew, little by little. The stump stretched into the semblance of a forearm, branching off into five small appendages which he recognized as fingers.

After an eternity of torment, the spasms subsided. The girdle fell from his mouth, as even the slightest movement proved a significant effort. Aedas walked with a similar weariness, although he tried his best to hide the fact.

Little had Kolthan realized, but to Aedas, he was the spitting image of an average Ilgrathian: a bronze complexion, fair hair, lean features, and a pointed jawline. What remained of his old visage were the eyes. What was more, he had a new arm gifted to him—a miracle of the Dreamstone and its magic. Kolthan grasped with his new appendage, admiring the muscles, bone, and sinew. He drooled in bewilderment, a wide smile tugging at his lips.

"I will have to make the change once more, though I shall save that for the end of our journey. Your alias from here on will be Menthus. You would do best to remember it well."

He discarded the manacles, and Kolthan fell to his knees, gasping and choking for air. The giant struggled to a sitting position.

Aedas unfolded the gambeson and chainmail shirt.

"I imagined this would be all you could handle for armor. You won't need anything elaborate to pass as a guard down here." The astromancer handed each piece to Kolthan. The process of donning the garb was dreadfully slow, but after a while Kolthan was moving around, albeit at a limp.

As expected, this was going to be difficult.

"Arm… armor… armor."

"I understand, Kolthan. The Soul Cistern has made you weak. I'm sorry this has to be how we escape, yet I can see no alternative." He reached out. "Here, allow me to help."

The astromancer shouldered the giant as he parted open the door. A low creak echoed down the halls. What was worse, the weight of Kolthan was far greater than he expected. For any muscle the man might have lost, he was still a beast.

They proceeded until the giant could firmly stand on his own. He strode several cubits in front of Aedas, his pace slow and hobbling.

Darkness loomed around them; Aedas removed a lit torch from its sconce, handing it to his companion. At this his fears were allayed, as Kolthan kept appearances as best a prisoner might.

A quiver in his legs brought him to a halt. Aedas was aware of his friend's hesitation.

It was the cries of tortured slaves.

Kolthan had nearly recoiled, yet Aedas held a firm grip over his arm. All the astromancer gave was a look, and Kolthan understood perfectly what to do. The giant grimaced as Aedas nudged him forward. They progressed past the mines and caves and columns of slaves; the cells, the hungering cannibals who slew and devoured their fellow man, and those who cried as their bodies were bent and broken on torture racks. Aedas imagined what his accomplice might be thinking, but thankfully the giant maintained composure. The iron, decay, and feces threatened to turn their stomachs; but they kept moving. Passing guards who lashed with the whip, the prisoner and his escort avoided hundreds of toilers who were worked to death.

The sights and sounds faded. Kolthan walked with renewed purpose, although his limp indicated he was exerting himself greatly.

A bump at the shoulder, and they were faced by a patrolling Ilgrathian.

"Watch where you're going!" he shouted.

"Please excuse us," responded Aedas, "I would be more careful if I wasn't caring for my dear friend."

"Is that so? Well if he's drunk, do not worry. I'll be sure to set him straight."

The astromancer held up his hand. "I would advise against that. He's being escorted by myself. Some type of disease or curse has been transmitted by one of the humans here. If I were you, I would keep my distance."

He knew his words had their effect, for the guard backed several paces.

"A wise man," said Aedas. "I believe it's under control for now, but you can never be certain until they're put to the test. Am I not correct?"

"Aye, if that be your cause, sorcerer." With a swift movement he collected himself, marching into the depths with a scoff in their direction.

Aedas motioned his friend onward. Ascending further along winding tunnels, they came to a stone door which was opened by a pair of guards. Walking outside, he saw the stars were out tonight, although Mirungel's lights obscured them greatly. Taldriath and Bruann were criss-crossing amidst their orbits, bathing the city in a silvery glow.

He cast a glance to his side, noting how Kolthan stared up in amazement. Aedas felt sympathy for the man, as many who were kept in the slave pits had forgotten the beauty of the sky and stars, of the summer heat and cool winds.

"Is he all right?" asked one of the guards.

"A bit too much to drink," Aedas replied, snapping out of his trance. "No no, I've got him." They approached a nearby wagon that had been assigned to the astromancer. A special cage was installed in the carriage's rear, with two pairs of shackles bound directly to the boards.

He called to his fellow Falcons—soldiers specially trained in the defense of Alcaron, the Ilgrathian bastion for Paradise—as they gathered about. With Aedas and Kolthan in tow, along with a succeeding wagon behind, they numbered over a dozen in total.

Aedas guided Kolthan onto one of the carriages. The giant's weight proved surprisingly difficult; yet when asked for help by a few querulous guards, the astromancer declined.

"What was that about? And who is this?" asked the Ilgrathian at the driver's seat.

"He's an old friend," replied Aedas. "Menthus is his name. I must warn you, he can be a little slow. He will be joining us until we arrive at Shadevale."

"What? Why?"

"He has business to tend to, and I'm inclined to help him. Begging your pardon, I caught the man when he had too much to drink. And if I'm frank, he's hardly coherent."

"I'll agree to that," the Ilgrathian gave a slight smirk. "He looks like he can hardly stand!"

"Nevertheless," said Aedas, "I agreed to take him with us to Shadevale, and I will hold to my promise."

"Couldn't he find a separate carriage to ride in? That or simply walk?"

"Are you implying I should be uncharitable to my dearest friend? The same person whom I've laughed and drank with for many years?"

The Ilgrathian groaned. "I suppose not." The two finished climbing aboard, and the driver grabbed hold of the reins. With a whipping he ushered the horses onward. "Hya!"

The wagons jolted as they were brought into motion, enough to disorient Kolthan who sat next to him. Aedas kept him upright, however. The driver cast them a sidelong glance that was hardly friendly.

The city walls flitted past, and before long they were riding into vast belts of gardens and orchards ringing the mountainside city of Mirungel. Soon enough they would reach the Fields of Man, and with any luck they would cross its furthest edge in a couple days.

The carriage rattled underneath. Aedas imagined Kolthan had slept soundly through the night, as he had awoken and eaten ravenously with the new dawn. Aedas was careful to give him but a single ration so he wasn't too conspicuous.

Regardless, discontented grumbles emerged from the Falcons. Given the man's broken speech, a few of them wondered at how he had become a soldier.

"Whoever this Menthus is, I'll be glad to be rid of him."

"We need not worry about him much longer," whispered another. "If my memory serves, we'll arrive at the village on the morrow."

As the guards voiced their displeasure, Aedas meditated. Channeling his astromancy, he ventured along the singular road of the past, the numerous possibilities the future might hold, and the ultimate convergence point of the present. Soon enough, he visualized what happened and what would likely transpire. Given how vague each future was, he would have to anticipate their probability. From there he could formulate a plan.

The twin carriages crested a nearby hill along the trail. Thick clouds shrouded the skies as it drizzled. What loomed ahead was a miserable little town, where the buildings were constructed of mud and crude stone. This proved to go much further than appearance, as not only were the structures rudimentary in design, the people were sickly and scowling.

Aedas knew the Ilgrathians hosted a barracks, yet he wasn't sure how well the guards would trust Kolthan. Thankfully, the astromancer had other plans. The dingy two-story building emerged into view, a rickety construction of wood lying at the center of town. The sounds of merriment and yelling were heard a good distance without.

This was the place.

The astromancer signaled for his company to halt. "We will stop here," he said. He and the giant dismounted and trudged along the hillock. A low doorway permitted one entrance. With a slight knock on the frame, a grille in the door slid to one side, where a dubious pair of irises glared at them.

"What is your business?" a feminine voice whispered.

"The same one would hope to find at any tavern, madam. My partner is looking for good wine, a fine woman, and some decent rest."

"Oh?" The eyes swiveled to the man at his side. "He's certainly handsome, but why is he so weak?"

"His time on the road has been long, madam, and unlike my fellows, his experience in the war was particularly grievous. As for the weakness, he was dealt a near fatal wound by star wraiths. They can steal one's life-force, you see. So my compatriots and I have brought him here. We're hoping to have him fattened and nursed back to health. Can your master do that for us?"

"Aye, of course." She unbolted the door, leading them into the main room. Her glower was more pronounced than ever. Her hair was curled blonde, spanning well below the shoulder line. Her lips were crimson and full, with each curve pleasing to the eye. Although her complexion was slightly wrinkled, she was no less a beauty.

"Please," she beckoned, "follow me. I will show you to Rabus right away."

She guided them past the seedy villagers who gave dubious glances, behind the bar counter, and in a room to their left. The woman opened the door with an air of courtesy. Aedas and Kolthan respectfully entered.

There at a small desk sat a morbidly obese human. A familiar cunning appraised the astromancer and the giant. Lips widened in a smirk. "Ah, Aedas! It's been some time, my friend."

"I would say that's an understatement," the astromancer replied. "Eight years is no short amount of time."

"Aye-aye, you have a point. But come! Sit, and we will discuss business."

Bearing a hint of reluctance, Aedas acquiesced. And with a nudge from their guide, Kolthan followed.

The obese man addressed his subordinate. "Tela! See that a room is prepared for our guests. A lazy whore like you can do that much, at least."

At this Tela scowled. "As you wish, Rabus." Her tone was equally venomous as she shut the door behind.

"Is that how you treat your workers?" inquired Aedas, facing Rabus directly.

"Just the ones who try to steal from me." He laughed. "You and your friend would do best to watch your coffers around here. Tela's been known to snatch up much more than what the lads pay for."

"You needn't worry about us," he replied. "Menthus hasn't a parcel to his name. I will be the one paying for his room."

"And what about you?" Rabus' eyebrows furrowed. "Aren't you staying as well?"

"Alas, I have business elsewhere. I'll be leaving with the rest of my compatriots, farther south to Candala."

"Really? After the years we've talked and drank together, this is how you treat your old friend?"

"I apologize," said the astromancer. "Alcaron's leash is a tight one."

"I would say that's an understatement!"

"Just so, but I should be going."

"Well, if that's how you see it," replied Rabus. "Ere your departure, I wanted to ask why you're helping this fellow." He leaned in a little closer, eyes narrowing on Kolthan. The giant wasn't muttering a sound, gods be praised. "Come on, Aedas, you can tell someone like me. We've known each other for so long."

The astromancer dropped a bag of drakons in front of him, seeing the avarice awakening in his friend. "Trust me on this one." He added a larger pouch for good measure, sliding them across the desk. "It's better you don't know until the job is finished."

The man contemplated the coins, his brow wrinkling, as he gave a low chuckle. "And here I expected you to be straight with me for once. Ah, well! I suppose I can take your extra coin. You know how to speak my language."

Aedas raised his finger. "Aye, but on one final condition," he said, "You must mention this to no one. Even your whores cannot divulge that he's aught more than a guest."

He chuckled. "Don't worry about them, I'll be sure they stay in line." He wagged a finger in Aedas' direction. "It's *you* who should be keeping your part of the bargain."

"Very well." Aedas moved to his feet. "I shall return by the end of the month, preferably with guests in tow. Until then—alas—I must bid you good-bye and farewell."

"Just a moment," said Rabus. "I require a password if you understand me. If anyone knows who this Menthus is, I can distinguish the truthsayers from the imposters."

Aedas pondered, hesitant to say more than what was necessary.

"Menthus' real name is Kolthan," he replied. "My guests know it well."

"Very well," said the fat man. "Always a man of few words, but when you talk you mean it. I always liked you for that, Aedas. You're cold and calculating when you need to be, though always amenable to a deal."

"I am what I am, for better or worse."

Aedas stepped towards Kolthan, noting the man's trepidation. He placed a hand over the giant's shoulder.

"Don't worry," he said. "Keep your head down and you'll be safe. I'll make sure they're brought to you. I stake my life upon it."

At this Kolthan calmed. Aedas smiled as he retired from the small office and main room. He closed the outer door behind him.

A cold wind and light drizzle greeted him in reply. The noise of villagers shouting and mud slopping underfoot served as a stark reminder of the town's miserly state. A strong gust of wind caused him to shiver. He said little to his band of soldiers as he rejoined them, the driver ushering the horses forward. Their carriage rattled as they gained speed along the wet road, the second trailing behind.

That was half of his plan finished, but now came the crucial step. He would have to locate Steel and Stormbright, wherever they might be.

III

On the Hunt

General Caerst led her men past endless trees. Dark leaves fell onto their heads and shoulders, the foliage blocking any semblance of light. The forest had taken more out of them than they anticipated.

The Falconer did not waver. As she and her scouts searched for tracks, they marched for the better part of the day. Weariness chipped away at their resolve, with some in the meantime falling due to starvation, or giving up entirely.

The Falconer slew the traitors herself, thus keeping the rest of them in line. Merely a hundred or so remained as they continued without rest.

A lone voice called from behind. General Caerst halted.

"Yes, what is it, Neto?"

"Are you certain this is the best use of our time, General?" As was typical for her lieutenant, his question was brash and to the point.

"We are making progress," she replied. "I'm certain we're close."

"Is that so, or is it what you want to believe?" He studied her, his words lowering to a whisper. "There hasn't been sight nor sound of them for several days. If you want to keep your subordinates in line, I suggest we find somewhere to rest. We are out of food, and this forest is wearing down even the best of us."

"But if there's a chance they are close, we take it. I will not retire for lack of conviction. If we're lost, then we rest here until we find the trail. We scrounge up any game and advance!"

Lieutenant Neto shook his head. "To be frank, General, you do not understand the gravity of our situation."

"Oh? And how is that?" Her nostrils flared wide.

"This is not a siege we are fighting; we are in a war of attrition. Do not be reckless. That's what cost us the Battle of Miracor."

Flaming hot fury awakened as she grabbed the Ilgrathian by the throat. Lieutenant Neto stood firm, sweat beading along his brow. Her feminine figure notwithstanding, General Caerst's grip was remarkably stronger than most men. Vicious insanity blazed from the depths of her soul. Neto knew well that her might was just one of a Falconer's gifts, along with enhanced beauty and cunning.

The Ilgrathian nodded, wanting to say more before catching himself. "So be it," he choked in reply. Her arm fell back to her side. The rest of the group watched on, apart from the scouts who had recommenced their search.

"Well, what are you looking at?"

Glum faces stared back at her. Hands strayed to their weapons as heartbeats quickened in tempo.

"We found something!" came a voice from the thickets.

One of the scouts had returned, momentarily distracting them from their violent moods. Accompanying the man, General Caerst and her men saw what appeared like drag marks at his feet.

"Have you found their tracks?" asked General Caerst.

"Take a closer look," said the scout. "Something slid along the ground recently and is making pursuit. The shrubbery around it is dead and rotting." The Ilgrathian halted his pace. "Ah, footprints! They are most certainly the brothers'."

On the Hunt

General Caerst grumbled beneath her breath, knowing the stories concerning these pursuers. "Nightmare-kin." She eyed her subordinates. "This is a blessing—a nightmare-kin will pursue its prey to the very ends of the earth. Which direction did they go?"

"North, General."

"Then we head north."

Walking into a glade of swaying grass, they discovered a wide dirt trail that led directly through a village. Most of it had been razed to the ground. A cursory search yielded little in the way of supplies to her scouts and soldiers, much to her chagrin. The sun rose and sank near the horizon. The hills grew taller as they turned west. Gray crags flanked the path on either side.

With a low series of commands, the Falconer instructed her men to fan out. Per their training, the scouts hastened with long strides, powerful legs tensing as they maneuvered the rocky terrain. To the rest, they were like stags bounding and loping. The heavy infantry and archers attended to their supplies while on the road. Their foodstuffs had been little from the outset, and now hunger was beginning to unman them. The Falconer heard her men groaning in protest, beholding their crazed looks as they regretfully obeyed.

A scout informed her of the situation. General Caerst spied a few of them atop one of the crags. She nodded towards Neto, indicating for the rest to stay put, whilst hiking up the escarpment. The climb would have been difficult for one wearing heavy armor, but as a Falconer she achieved it with ease.

Rising atop the summit, she regarded the view extending well to the horizon. The land before them snaked through a wide valley, fading into flat grasslands and the odd patch of hills.

Below them, perhaps a league or so away, lay a settlement. A river flanked it from the east, placing it directly within their marching path. Vast numbers of small, silhouetted figures darted among the structures, gathering around columns of smoke.

Following the example of her scouts, she pulled out her special looking glass. The view was distorted, yet it imparted a vital glimpse as to what was happening. "The town is under siege," she said, adjusting her lens and squinting. "It is difficult to discern much more. What else can you see from here?"

"It's difficult to tell," muttered one.

Another scout stood motionless. "Yes… that's it! It's our fellow Falcons!" He leaned in a cubit farther. "They seem to be battling with a group of humans."

General Caerst frowned. "In either case we advance. This battle is none of our concern."

"But General! If there are Falcons, perhaps we can help them. Who knows, they might grant us information and supplies."

The Falconer studied her men, seeing their hunger and fatigue. They spoke the truth: she was fresh out of leads on where Steel and Stormbright had gone.

"Very well," she said. "We march to our fellow Falcons."

The others nodded their approval, filing in line as they descended the cliffside. General Caerst rallied her men, and so the company marched forth with renewed vigor.

Fording the river proved easy enough, as the stream gave way to several shallow stretches. The town loomed closer, with the shouts and bellows of war echoing in their ears; the clangor of blades; the smoke and ash from burning huts; the thunderous drumming of feet. So entrancing was the effect that General Caerst's heart thrummed in her chest. Even without glimpsing at her men, she knew they harbored the same excitement.

Soon they were at the gates. The air sizzled with heat. The grounds were caked in crimson as corpses littered the area, most being Ilgrathian. Auxiliary soldiers, bearing the goddess' crest, greeted the unexpected reinforcements with confusion. Caerst couldn't determine who was in charge. And when prompted with the question, they responded by pointing in the town's direction.

"The siege is nigh at its end," said a lowly Falcon. "Captain Helvia has taken a group of her guards and attacks the city from inside. I can tell you little else."

She dismissed him and called for her troops to follow. Passing through the breached gates and along burning streets, they sighted soldiers razing buildings. The screams would have shaken the most devout of humans, but to Caerst it was euphoric. Houses, temples, shops, and stalls had been put to the torch. The surviving humans ran for their lives, the blood-thirsty Ilgrathians a footfall away.

General Caerst snared one who had nearly escaped. The young woman shrieked and struggled, though the Falconer's grip didn't falter. A soldier separate from their rank approached, tying her wrists as tears marked her face.

"My thanks for helping with this one," the Ilgrathian indicated the whimpering girl. He smiled. "I haven't seen you in Helvia's squadrons."

"That's because we are not. My name is General Caerst, and these are my Falcons. Please, if you would, show me the way to your leader."

"Aye," he said. "The last I saw of Captain Helvia was towards the main square."

"And what is Captain Helvia's purpose for being here?"

"Our Captain is searching for a relic that's revered in these parts. As you can see," he waved around them, "when we prodded their leaders with questions concerning the trinket, the humans got mighty defensive. They slew whoever dared to investigate, then fortified once we arrived for support. It's a crying shame. First Driftwind and now Thayden." He gave the girl a solid kick with his boot.

"Is that what this operation is about?"

"Why, it should be obvious," he said.

"Very well. You have my gratitude, soldier. May your conquest be fruitful."

At this the man smiled, sparing a malicious glance to the woman who wept.

Proceeding, the roads converged in a central square. A stone temple acted as one of the few surviving landmarks, stalwart among the blackened corpses. Its entrance was open and billowing with smoke. From it emerged an elderly man, who fell and rolled along the ground.

Pacing up from behind, the Falconer glimpsed two armored soldiers. Between them stood a slender figure: a tall woman with raven hair, handsome features, and a long chin. Her armor was light in make, being forged of silver scales with an embroidered vest displaying a black rose.

"Where is the Moon Cup?" The chaos around them notwithstanding, her words were calm. "Tell us, or there will be naught left of your precious town."

The Ilgrathian halted, crossing her arms as General Caerst approached. The captain's shock was evident. She smiled regardless.

"This is quite the surprise," she spoke. "I wouldn't have expected allies to join us in the middle of a skirmish. But Fate can be kind when it wishes."

"Is there assistance you require?" asked General Caerst, stepping so they faced each other.

"It is quite unnecessary." The woman frowned at the groveling human. "The gesture is appreciated, but we have everything under control."

They heard the man cackling.

"You fools! The time of the Great Equilibrium is nigh! The reign of Ilgrathié shall be brought to a quick and bitter end!" He clenched his teeth. Although his mouth was shut, laughter reverberated between his lips.

"What do you mean, old man?" said Captain Helvia.

"*You* are finished! You are *all* finished!"

Goosebumps rose as the Falconer smelled something worse than the rotting, burning flesh. Both she and her companion turned as the man laughed uncontrollably, seeing a horde of shambling figures moving along the streets. A chill ran up her spine as the amorphous things, slithering blobs with glistening tendrils lined with teeth, devoured whatever wounded lay in their path, be they human or Ilgrathian.

An Ilgrathian emerged from one of the streets. Perhaps it was Fate, for it was the same Falcon General Caerst had happened upon.

"Nightmare-kin! All over the place! We're being flanked from every side!"

"What happened to the girl?"

"Dead," he replied. "The swarm came upon us too quickly. They are everywhere!"

At their side, Captain Helvia pursed her lips. "It seems we may require your aid, after all. If you would be so bold as to join me, sister, I can promise you glory and a place to rest. Are you with us?"

"You needn't ask." The Falconer prepared herself as they charged towards the monstrous creatures. With surprising grace and dexterity she drew her rapier, piercing through abominations as they gibbered, bulbous arms swaying and dagger-like teeth gnashing. She kept out of reach, with the rest of her company maneuvering in behind and hacking at the fiends.

The roars of unholy anguish, of ravenous hunger, echoed in her skull. She did not relent; now was the time for just deliverance, to exact Ilgrathié's will through her divine gifted strength. Her heart hammered with excitement. Her arm thrusted, sending another aberration to one of the many hells. She didn't stop as the monstrosities leapt onto her men, devouring with sickening reverie. Her heart quickened, eyes going wide with a sort of madness, but no more.

A building sat close, burning and partially collapsed. Out of the entrance emerged several more horrors. One darted after a youth as a second chased a man that had caught fire.

This didn't stop the other monstrosity from snatching the burning man where he stumbled, the dying flames going still as the aberration fed.

"Save us, please!" The young man dashed behind them as the Ilgrathians advanced. More sickly beings emerged from street corners and balconies. Their horrific squeals resounded whilst they hungered for flesh.

The nightmare-kin were relentless, yet General Caerst fought on. As was the case for Falconers, she knew much concerning this spawn of Old Man Darkness, beings who entered their reality from the formless Great Beyond. All they desired was to digest and consume, to expand and corrupt like a sickness, until naught was left but their own twisted amalgam of "real".

She struck with her rapier, killing the abominations with ease as they bled profusely. Captain Helvia drew a long scimitar and slashed at an aberration. A dozen mouths lunged after her. The area surrounding them was largely on fire, buildings crumbling into piles of debris with loud, cracking jolts.

The monstrosities wailed as their bodies split and bled, melting into puddles of putrescent ooze. General Caerst and Captain Helvia swung their blades without slowing. By the time they were finished, scarce few of the nightmare-kin were left, and those alive were covered in hideous wounds, leaking black ichor as they fled.

"Well," said Captain Helvia. "I think that's the rest of them. Except for this one."

General Caerst knew she referred to the elderly man. The old priest had clearly fainted. His terror returned, however, once Captain Helvia shook him awake.

"Where is the Moon Cup?" she asked calmly.

No answer.

"I will not ask a second time. *Where* is the Moon Cup?"

With trembling lips, the man peered toward the old temple. Helvia issued the order and thus her soldiers departed. The flames by this point had died out. They re-emerged, one holding a carved chalice of astounding craftsmanship.

"We located a secret compartment," said the Ilgrathian. "No wonder we hadn't found it at first. The damned thing was nigh impossible to spot."

The woman studied the object with scrutiny. She scoffed, tossing it at the priest.

"The nightmare-kin were relentless..."

"Did you think I wouldn't notice this as a fake? After I retrieved a real Moon Cup, no less?" Seeing that the man didn't respond, she said, "I know much about your petulant order. Take him away, and make sure he is nice and talkative by the time I see him."

"No, you can't! I'm a holy priest!"

"A priest to heathen gods."

"No-no-no-no!" The man shouted as the Ilgrathians restrained him, dragging him to gods-know-where. General Caerst, meanwhile, sat beside her lieutenant. Neto had sustained a few grievous wounds, but these he shouldered with pride.

She smirked at his dry optimism.

"What is our plan of action, General?"

At this she tried to speak, but no response came.

Her eyes shifted upward. Standing in front of them was none other than the captain herself.

"The name is Helvia," she said. "In Candala I am captain of the city guard, not to mention an inquisitor on heretical matters."

The Falconer smiled. "My name is General Caerst. We were heading along the road when we happened across the situation." She was aware of how being here went against orders. How would this captain of the city guard react to her vengeful quest? She cleared her throat. "I suppose we were sidetracked."

"Wait. You mean you're *the* General Caerst?" She emitted a light chuckle, apparently unaware of her bluff. "I never thought I would be speaking with someone so well-renowned. You simply must come to Candala! I'm sure you and your men could do with some well-earned rest."

The Falconer considered the proposal.

"But of course," she shrugged her shoulders. "It's been a long day, and about time we took some rest."

IV

New Alliances

Little had the Falconer realized it, but their sojourn relaxed her more than she cared to admit. Although the trip to Candala was short, with its stacks of rickety buildings looming above lofty walls, passing through the gates was reassuring. Thieves, brigands, and cutthroats littered the streets in dense numbers, yet once they crossed into Helvia Manor, a profound sense of security washed over them. The courtyards were lavish, the architecture unusual, being constructed from a race of humans countless ages ago, or so the legends claimed.

The interior halls were most impressive. To describe it as opulent would have been an understatement. The sweet scents, spiced fumes, and sumptuous decorations served as a stark contrast after their many weeks of traveling.

The sensations of a hot bath and delectable meal proved most refreshing. How long had it been since Caerst experienced such pleasures? The water poured along her face and arms, her nerves relaxing with the soothing heat. The experience was indescribable, but she would not relax for long; rest was a triviality when compared to her revenge against Steel and Stormbright, the very same humans who had ruined her life at Miracor.

Come the end, she would see them torn limb-from-limb, their spirits shattered for daring to sabotage her glory. A burning hatred spread up her stomach, warming her better than any hot bath. Soon they would be hers.

Shortly afterward she was dressed in fresh clothes. The Falconer found this odd as she wore a noble's garments instead of her usual armor. The cuirass, as one servant told her, had been taken away to be repaired, cleaned, and polished. Her rapier, however, was permitted to stay on her person. As for the outfit, the light cotton fit snugly against her skin. She was warm and comfortable—both luxuries she could have scarcely afforded on the road.

What nearly broke her resolve, however, was the aroma of Candala's delicate foods. As she sat before the captain, Lieutenant Neto, and her fellow comrades, the servants revealed a variety of appetizing dishes. Among the foods were delicate fish; hardy venison; a great variety of steaks; assortments of fruits, salads, and breads. The meats were cooked to perfection, and the exotic fruits and vegetables complimented the meal to where their mouths watered. They ate with voracity, and even General Caerst had nearly forgotten her manners.

"You must have been on the road for some time," said Captain Helvia. "In truth, I'm not certain I've ever witnessed a group consume my stock so quickly."

Neto replied after clearing his throat, taking a long draught of wine for good measure. "The road has been most strenuous, and many of us were nigh on starving to death." His comment received several grunts of approval. The Falconer remained silent.

"So I see. And what was the nature of your assignment?"

None spoke as they were reminded of their defection. A few looked to their superior.

"We were granted a special mission," she said hesitantly.

"Oh?"

"It was spoken to very few of us. We are searching for a group of fugitives."

"Well, you will find no shortage of them here," Helvia chuckled, swirling a glass of red wine in her palm. "But tell me, what makes these fugitives so special? Why did Ilgrathié send you after them?"

The Falcons glanced uncomfortably in her direction, waiting for her reply. General Caerst sought for the correct words, saying nothing.

Their host donned a smile. "Perhaps I have inquired enough for tonight. My servants will escort each of you to the local barracks. We have plenty of room and a fresh supply of drinks if you're so inclined."

At this a number of servants entered and bowed, beckoning their guests to follow. Everyone rose from their seats and started for the door.

"Falconer," said Helvia. "A word, please."

"Of course." General Caerst seated herself. The servants and her men departed, and thus they were alone.

"I trust your meal was satisfactory?"

"Satisfactory is one way to describe it. I will be honest that you've saved us from a cold, miserable night. From the bottom of my heart, I am grateful."

"Well, aren't we courteous." A smirk developed along her lips. "And here I never would have guessed I would be joined by a war hero during a skirmish. I, too, shall be honest; you appeared like wild animals when first you arrived, yet I see what a difference good food can make."

Her eyes narrowed as she took another sip from her glass, savoring the spices. "Do tell me, what is your purpose for being so close to Candala? You say you are pursuing fugitives, correct? Last I heard, you were sent to the invasion front at Divnarost."

"Well," she said, her stomach twisting with uncertainty, "the siege at Miracor was a steady effort from my men and I. That's not mentioning how long it took us to advance."

"I'm assuming it was many months?"

"A year-and-a-half to be precise," she replied. "Once we breached the gates, we were routed by an offensive we had hardly expected. Somehow, the Islirians allied with a horde of star wraiths. Those of us who survived were forced to retreat." She remembered her desperation at the end—the humiliation, the unimaginable distress that came from the star wraiths stealing her vitality—the knowledge she would be condemned regardless of what had transpired.

"That is terrible! Did you not have reinforcements?"

"At first, aye. We hired mercenaries to weather our enemies' defenses, but it proved futile. As a solution, my appointed sciomancer suggested we summon an army of demons. And, well, considering the danger of the star wraiths…"

Helvia chortled. "That sounds like a foolish idea if ever I've heard one. I'm shocked you took him up on such an offer, knowing how unpredictable demons can be."

She bit her tongue. After what she had been through, Captain Helvia's words stung like venom.

"I still don't understand," she continued. "What does this have to do with your being here? Why did you not make the journey to Ilgrathié and receive punishment?"

The Falconer took a draught from her wine glass. "If only it were that simple," she said. "I discovered two young boys were behind most of it. They had somehow aligned themselves with the star wraiths and wrested control of the demons. We are but a small fraction of our original number. I know they are hidden somewhere near Candala, if not inside the city."

"Is that so?" Helvia stifled a giggle. "Your defeat is all because of two boys? Forgive my impudence, General, but your plans are shockingly incompetent. Gods, perhaps I would make a better Falconer than you."

General Caerst flushed with anger. "They are *not* just two boys! One of them is a powerful lightning sorcerer! The other fought through scores of my soldiers with little more than a spear and dagger!"

Silence lingered between them. Captain Helvia gave a knowing smile. "So this is why Ilgrathié's Falconer hasn't arrived home yet. To subdue a couple of adolescents out of wounded pride." Her laughter cut like a dirk. "I do apologize—it must be the wine. It's just all of this, you, it's so pathetic."

The Falconer drew her blade, leaping onto the long table as she attacked. Helvia's expression didn't change in the slightest. She had nearly struck until a wave of spasms halted her advance. General Caerst gasped, falling as glasses were shattered, plates overturned.

"Such a mess," replied Helvia. "Did you really expect to overpower me, Falconer? In my own home, no less?"

General Caerst's limbs bucked against the invisible force, but each attempt worsened her torment. The aches coursed through her body, wringing out a tortured cry.

Helvia delivered a firm kick to her stomach, enough to bring the Falconer to coughing and retching up a portion of her food. "What an ignorant slut. I would have expected better from one of your status—a Falconer known throughout Alcaron. Unlike yourself, I had a backup plan." Her smile widened. "Little did you know I've been aware of your exploits since the beginning. One might say you're the talk of the realm, what with your defeat at the hands of the Islirians."

She kneeled and reached out. The Falconer winced, her blood boiling as Helvia caressed her face.

"How does it feel, General Caerst, to be made a laughingstock by your inferiors? Would you like to know how I did this to you?"

Helvia's grip around her jaw tightened, fingers squeezing painfully. General Caerst struggled to bring her body back under command. It was futile. "What… What did you do to me?"

"I didn't do anything, my dear Falconer," she chuckled. "Consider it a stroke of luck, but the very second I began my search for these Moon Cups, rumors spread of an astromancer entering my city. An astromancer who had a lot to say about you."

She pursed her lips. "As is the case for an accepting host such as myself, I naturally showed him my care and hospitality. He told me the nature of his quest, and hence I learned of your defeat and disobedience."

Caerst noticed the drapes parting, leading to one of the adjoining hallways. Through it emerged a dark figure swathed in robes, with ebon hair and sad complexion. Aedas paced to where she knelt. To her surprise, the astromancer held a glowing stone, a gem pulsating with opalescent energy.

"Truly, it's amazing what wizards can accomplish with Dreamstone," she said, laughing haughtily. "A special augmentation to one's magic and Creation bows to your whim."

"How do you know of this magic?" Caerst hissed between her teeth.

Helvia smiled. "When one deals with the Order of the Sacred Twins, proper precautions must be taken. It just so happens Dreamstone can nullify such magic. Truly, it is a most wondrous material. Wouldn't you agree, Aedas?"

The astromancer stood motionless as a thin layer of perspiration lined his brow. He remained silent.

"Alas! Not everyone can wield such a stone. It takes time and mental discipline, as well as an interest in magic. Perhaps it is fortunate my friend here meets these requirements. With a simple command, I could have you burst into flames." Her hands tightened around her throat. "Or would you prefer I rearrange that pretty little figure of yours and have you become misshapen? How would you enjoy it, Falconer—O chosen one of Ilgrathié? Mayhaps there was a time when you held esteem among your rank, but now you are mine!"

"I… I will never bow to the likes of you!"

Another agonizing surge. Her muscles screamed as if over a roaring fire.

"What is it you want from me?" she asked desperately. Captain Helvia commanded Aedas to halt, enough for the Falconer to speak fully. "I can give you anything you desire. My body and mind—they are yours. Just tell me what you want."

"For a Falconer, you think in such simple terms," she said. "For the record, I am already content with my harem. How can the mere caresses of one such as you compare?"

"I'll kill you, you wretched-" General Caerst's words were cut off. She groaned, muscles clenching and contracting.

"I've heard enough," said Helvia, releasing her. "On the morrow, you will be taken to Mirungel. There you shall receive due punishment from Ilgrathié."

"No! Wait!" The captain halted, seeing that General Caerst fought her invisible bonds. "I can track the cult. I know there is a bond between the humans and nightmare-kin we fought. If you would let me help…"

Captain Helvia waved for the astromancer to cease. General Caerst lay on her side, nerves, muscles, and bones aching horribly. "And how would you help?"

She stammered. "I… I would give my sword to you. I have experience in tracking those I wish to kill, and I know you've struggled with exposing these cultists. Perhaps I could help you. Would not Ilgrathié reward you for subduing this cult?"

Captain Helvia paused, considering her words.

Aedas interjected, "The Falconer cannot be trusted. We must stick to our original agreement; I take her back to Mirungel and in turn you will be com-"

"You will have your Falconer, astromancer," said Helvia. "But first, I would hear what she has to say."

She knelt once more. "I must admit your fighting was impressive. And your conviction for killing these boys, it borders on obsession. Perhaps we can use it to our advantage."

"Captain Helvia, you must reconsider-"

She held up her hand. "Perhaps you make a good point, General. As you mentioned, there is merit in the two of us working together. Who knows? If you prove to be a good girl, we can search for the humans you talk about so much."

General Caerst blinked in shock.

"You have my gratitude."

"You can thank me later." Helvia rose to her feet. "Astromancer, make sure she receives a proper night's rest. Come morning, we begin our search for the Order of the Sacred Twins."

She faced the Falconer. "I trust you will stick to our agreement, General. If I notice any dissent from you—anything whatsoever—then your flesh is mine to ruin. I will bring you back to your goddess in pieces if I must, but rest assured, you *will* be alive."

Thus the Falconer was left alone, save for Aedas who stood close by. The captain's footsteps echoed along the empty chamber, vanishing into naught.

V

Golden Shadows

The drunken ramblings of the locals filtered through the tavern. The raucous laughter echoed out windows, hatches, and doors as it dispersed among the nighted streets, the permeating mist an ever-constant presence. From large kegs poured flagons of frothing mead served by innkeeper Galvos. This further incensed those who drank, sang, danced, and cajoled.

Away from the den of thieves, whores, and brigands, the brothers sat at a small table. Stormbright thought of Aurora, the girl they rescued the previous evening, who rested within their rented room. She had awoken twice in a state of delirium—the first during their time on the road, and the second once they reached the walls of Beggar's Respite, Candala's easternmost district. Judging by her slow breathing, she must have been exhausted. Since then, both she and the brothers had remained discreet.

Perhaps it was for the best, as it seemed a matter of time before General Caerst would arrive and the guards began their search. They surmised the tavern's inhabitants wished to forget the world and its many woes, as if the key to Paradise lay at the bottom of one's tankard.

Steel and Stormbright distanced themselves from the crowd as they drank, regretting their decision of arriving at Candala. Stormbright's intuition with "Golden Leaf" proved surprisingly accurate. He had a hunch she was referring to an inn, and perhaps his empathic side as a sorcerer granted him an edge in this regard. The Golden Leaf Inn was crowded more so than other taverns, judging by the wanton crowds milling about densely-packed thresholds. Steel's deft fingers were put to good use; he produced two silver coins, sylphs, from a pouch he had stolen earlier. The dozens of heads were overwhelming at first, until he recognized how ideal it was for stealing. Though a newcomer, he soon clutched the rewards of his thievery.

At their sides walked a bevy of unsavory figures—information brokers and harlots—who proffered their services through various means.

"I've got a bad feeling," murmured Steel.

"So do I," replied Stormbright.

The thief stared into his drink, then to the rowdy denizens. "I'm not talking about them," he frowned.

"What do you mean?" said Stormbright, taking a sip from his flagon.

"I mean that woman we saved. I'm not sure if you've noticed, Brother, but she isn't telling us the entire story. Something is going on. I want to be sure we have nothing to do with it." He took a swig from his drink, wiping his chin. "As for us, finding Aedas is our top priority."

"You do have a point." The sorcerer bowed his head. "The issue is we have no idea where Aedas could be hiding."

"Right. He told us to meet him in Candala, but that was from a dream."

"It wasn't a dream," said Stormbright.

"And how do you know?"

"I just… know."

Steel shrugged. "Either way, we're not left with much to go on. We should probably try to search around and ask the locals."

"Around these kinds of people?" Stormbright caught glares from a few unruly citizens. He lowered his pitch. "What I'm trying to say, Brother, is Aurora might be our best shot at learning what's in town. We're both new here. Maybe she could help us as a guide."

"Oh, sure," Steel smirked. "Obviously, we need her as a guide and it's not for other reasons."

"What do you mean 'other reasons'?"

The thief rolled his eyes, giving his brother an appraising grin. He cupped his hands over his chest, and Stormbright went bright red.

"You're disgusting," he said.

"That's not what I'm seeing," Steel laughed.

"Fine. If that's what you think, I will be turning in for the night." He shot Steel a glare as he rose, still blushing while taking his mead with him. "First, I'm going to check if she is all right. And no, it's not because of her breasts."

Steel mimed the gesture a second time, grinning as Stormbright headed upstairs.

He chortled while taking another quaff from his flagon. The frothing elixir was much stouter than he was accustomed, although it wasn't unpleasant.

Leaning back in his seat, he sighted a wrinkled palm in the corner of his vision. It strove for his coin purse. Steel caught the wrist as the shady figure stood rigid.

"Find another table to steal from," he said.

The man didn't falter as his words were a whisper.

"You are a man of many talents, I reckon. If'n you want, I can part with some facts for a few parcels. I am a Listener; secrets are my trade."

"Shove off."

The hooded figure didn't move. "I can tell you're a newcomer. The strangeness of your garb, the fact you have all your teef. Yes, I can tell you're an outsider—green as grass, it seems." He gave a low, raspy chuckle. "I can talk about the girl you've with ye."

Steel's curiosity got the better of him. He kicked out the chair to his side and gestured for the man to sit.

The figure did so without comment. And though he was hooded, Steel caught glimpses of a diminutive, wretched frame; a wrinkled face and bulging eyes; a mouth which bore a handful of "teef" as it grinned at him. On the surface, this Listener struck him as a pitiable miser, but the young thief sensed more to him. "I saw ye arrive with the initiate. I'm betting yer doubting whether she's with ye or not." Steel's silence was answer enough. Thus the man proceeded, "Judging by her robes, she is a cultist without a doubt. And not the harmless kind, I can assure ye."

"Oh really?" Steel watched him curiously. "Just what kind of cultist is she?"

The Listener rubbed his thumb and forefinger together. Steel responded by tossing a sylph, not as substantial as a drakon, as it was one-tenth the value, but it was no less appreciated.

"Does she wear a signet of two crescent moons joined together?" The Listener murmured.

Steel ruminated as he drank from his flagon. Now that the man mentioned it, he remembered spotting a dainty necklace of the sort around her neck. He nodded.

"She's like to be a child of the Sacred Twins. A most dangerous cult they are—one of the worst, if'n ye want my two parcels."

"Sacred Twins?" Steel didn't try to hide his ignorance.

"Taldriath and Bruann—ye know, the moons circling above us. They be a cult formed from those who once reigned over the city. That was long ago. The Ilgrathians rule presently, yet there be rumors of strange rites— orgies with commonly folk howling like beasts, ceremonies where sacrifices are made to their nightly lords."

The man licked his lips. "I cannot tell ye where they are exactly, but I'm sure they're out of sight. They're waiting, ye see, waiting for the day the Ilgrathians will be driven away, so their gods might reign supreme with the new age." He leaned forward, with naught but two dark orbs visible from his cowl. "Have ye not noticed it at night? The two moons peering from above. Deciding what they want to do with us." He grinned as Steel shook his head. "These are uncertain times. But who knows, perhaps there is merit in fighting the Ilgrathians. Even if it's cultists who do the job."

Steel sat deep in contemplation. The words of this Listener boded none too well for their prospects. No, he wasn't fond of this at all.

He tossed the man another sylph. "Take it," said Steel. "For the trouble."

The man chuckled. "If'n ye ever need talk of the town, we Listeners are the ones to speak to. Unearthing knowledge is this one's specialty."

The words barely registered as Steel considered their quest and its possible dangers. It was difficult to tell how much of the man's words were truth or fiction, but nevertheless, his doubt sat like a rock in his stomach.

Stormbright closed the door behind him. He saw Aurora was asleep. The young magician placed the flagon at a small table. His attention shifted to a wooden bucket at his feet. He removed the lid, where a thick cloud of steam wafted up.

Stormbright produced a damp towel, the fabric radiating with heat. He took the utmost care in placing it on her forehead, gently, so he wouldn't disturb the girl's rest.

Nevertheless, she stirred.

"How are you holding up?" asked Stormbright timidly.

"Well enough," she replied. "You didn't have to protect me as long as you did."

"It's nothing. We're here, just as you requested. You should consider yourself lucky, as nightmare-kin are dangerous in groups. My brother and I have encountered them during our travels. Only," he paused, "they were much bigger."

"I cannot begin to thank you." She stretched along her bed with an almost feline grace, slightly adjusting the many pillows Innkeeper Galvos had granted her. She hummed, eyelashes closing dreamily. Her behavior was a stark contrast to what Stormbright had witnessed the previous night.

"Please, drink this." Stormbright grabbed the flagon of mead. "You will feel better."

"Thank you." A joyful smile curled along her black lips. "I must admit, you're really nice." She lifted the container and drank.

"So you said your name is Aurora?" asked Stormbright, retrieving the half-empty flagon.

"Yes, that's right. Why is it you ask?"

"Well… I thought it was a pretty name."

He saw warmth in her face. She smirked slightly. Whether it was his words or the mead, he wasn't quite sure.

"I hope you don't say that to every woman you save."

"Not all of them." Stormbright chuckled nervously, turning his head. He caught glimpses of Aurora's brooding countenance, soft curves, and supple lips, all of which made his skin feel on fire. He tried his best to ignore the finer details, but merely half-succeeded. "You were in quite the bad spot when we found you."

"Oh? Was I?"

"Aye. Can I ask you a question?" She nodded, and thus Stormbright asked, "Were you at Driftwind when the village was attacked?"

She gave him a taciturn glance.

"I'm sorry. If I-"

"Yes, I was," she said.

"And you said these Ilgrathians were after two Moon Cups?"

"They were. Now they have at least one of the relics."

"How did you survive?"

He noticed her anguish, the struggle to recount such horrific details. "I hid," she whispered. "I was in the tavern when they arrived, killing and torching and… doing horrible things. It all happened so quickly. I'm not sure how I avoided them. I hid with Vana, my dearest friend, in a cellar underneath." Her eyes softened. "We heard the sounds coming from the surface, and I knew the Ilgrathians had stolen our relic. The night passed, but we did not rest. Over time the shouts ceased and the footsteps grew quiet. We wandered through the devastation. It was… It was horrible."

Stormbright laid a hand on her shoulder. Despite his gentle touch, she flinched and shut her eyes. Tears started to flow.

"We had to know if it was stolen," she said. "Vana and I rushed to the standing stones, the holy shrine where we commune with the moons and the Moon Cup draws its power." She wiped the tears from her face. "It was over. Everyone was dead, the Moon Cup taken. Then came those abominations."

"And then we arrived," said Stormbright.

She pursed her black lips. "It was the Sacred Twins who protected us."

"Who protected you?" Stormbright's voice was low, his expression quizzical.

"Taldriath and Bruann. The holy moons sent you to protect us—to protect me." Her smile was warm. "It means you are someone special."

"Honestly, I know little about such things." Stormbright laughed. "What of these Moon Cups? You mentioned there was a way we could use them to drive out the Ilgrathians?"

A shadow crossed her features. "Yes, but it's impossible to retrieve the relic. It was the city guard who took it. They are the ones who've been murdering us this entire time, led by that dreadful Captain Helvia. She has the Moon Cup, I can feel it. I know of a secret entrance inside the manor, but it's too dangerous."

She sobbed in front of him, though she tried to hide it. "The holy day commences in a week and I've failed. Gods, I've failed!" She sniffled. "There's nothing I can do."

"That's just it." Stormbright took her hands. "You don't realize who you're talking to. My brother and I have thwarted Ilgrathians on multiple occasions. Perhaps we can help."

"You think so?" Her eyes reflected the dim candlelight.

"Surely, we can help. But first," he paused briefly, remembering Steel's warning on how she might be dangerous, "you should tell me of your order if we're to help. What's so significant about this Great Equilibrium? How will it repel the Ilgrathians?"

"My order? Very well," she straightened, drying her tears. "I'm an initiate in the Order of the Sacred Twins. Twice a year we give our thanks to the moons, and so we are judged and given blessings for the next half of the cycle. It's a tradition going back hundreds of years."

She turned away. "But the Ilgrathians took everything from us. We're forced to live underground, terrified and persecuted. Always, we're trying to free ourselves—to liberate humans—so that Ilgrathié's children are driven beyond their borders. For years we've prayed... and now, the moons have shown us the answer."

"And what answer is that?"

"Mothers Ava and Ida have read the signs. They speak of a Great Equilibrium, a conjunction of realms unseen. They say the event will

herald a time of change. A shifting in the cosmos. Then will come the dawn of a new era—an age of freedom."

"A time where we'll be free?"

She nodded, beaming with hope.

"That's an honorable thing to wish for," said Stormbright. "Indeed, I couldn't picture a better cause."

She watched him curiously. "And what do you wish for, Stormbright?"

He tried not to stare at those sensuous eyes, nor her stark lips or full breasts. The necklace of two crescent moons dangled between them, reminding him of their time in Driftwind. Steel's earlier jabs resurfaced, and he was at a loss for words.

"I," he swallowed, "I want to find Father. It has been many years since we've been together. I'm not even sure if he's alive."

"If it means anything," said Aurora, "our priestesses have the gift of foresight. It is said they peer through great expanses. Perhaps they can seek him by communing with the Sacred Twins."

"You mean they're astromancers?" Stormbright was in disbelief. "Astromancers can peer into the past, present, and future; but it can be hazy. I know since I was trained by one."

"Oh, Stormbright." Her hand settled over his. "That is but one magic they can conjure. Ida can *see*, and Ava can *create* as is her wont."

"So… astromancy as well as oneiromancy?"

"Aye. Just so."

"That's wonderful!" he said. "I can assist with retrieving the Moon Cups, and you could help us with Father."

"Of course," she smiled.

"You have no idea what this means for us. I must speak with Steel."

He pulled the door open before turning. Aurora was beaming with joy. Stormbright did the same as he closed the portal behind.

Before he grasped his surroundings, the sorcerer was running to meet his brother. An abrupt collision and Stormbright barreled over. Steel was underneath him.

"Ow, watch it!" said Steel.

"I'm sorry, Brother. I was running back to find you."

"Well, you didn't have to be so reckless."

"I was meaning to talk with you about-"

"About the initiate," Steel said as the young sorcerer climbed back to his feet. He did so as well. "Yeah, I know, Zolan."

Stormbright halted, trepidation stealing over him.

"What do you mean you know?"

"Follow me."

Stormbright obeyed without question. They rounded a corner as Steel halted in his tracks. The sorcerer had nearly bumped into him again, but thankfully he stopped before it could happen.

"I know who she is, as well as what she's a part of. This woman—Aurora—she's bad news, Zolan."

"What do you mean?" Confusion swirled inside the young sorcerer. "Her order is trying to push back against the Ilgrathians."

"Yeah, and I've heard they act like animals and perform blood sacrifices to the moons."

"What? Surely, you can't be serious!"

"I heard what I heard."

"And *who* did you hear this from?"

"Just one of the Listeners in town."

"You mean the hooded men who are always prowling about?" Stormbright shook his head. "And you call me naive, Brother. Ever since we got here, I've had a strange impression of them. It may not be obvious to you, Serithas, but they've swindled honest people."

"And how do you know that?"

"I overheard one of them talking," he said. "And just so you know, Brother, sorcerers aren't the offspring of demons and androgynes. They're proffering lies to fill their own pockets."

"All right, all right, you've made your point. Look," Steel held his brother by the shoulders, "I'm just trying to care for you. You never know what kind of dangers are lurking in this city."

"I understand your hesitation, Brother, and I can't say I'm not a little suspicious myself. But what she told me could change everything. Her leaders are capable sorcerers who can locate Aedas and Father."

"Are you sure these are the people you want knowing about them?"

Stormbright shrugged. "What better choice do we have?"

"Fine." Steel relinquished his hold, stretched so his hands pressed into the small of his back. "If we're going to help, we need to keep a look out for anything suspicious. Do you follow me?"

"I follow," Stormbright smiled.

"Good." They arrived back at their room. Opening the door, they saw Aurora sipping from her flagon of mead. She set it on the neighboring side table.

"I'm assuming everything is okay?" she asked.

"Well enough," said Steel. He stood solemnly, his glare saying more than spoken words.

Her eyes darted between them. "I know this isn't exactly normal. If you help us, we will-"

"*If* we help you," interjected Steel, "it will be on our terms. In exchange for retrieving each Moon Cup, your master will find two men we're hunting for."

Her voice wavered as she spoke. "On behalf of priestesses Ava and Ida, and the Sacred Twins above, I accept."

Steel gave an approving nod as he bade her continue.

Aurora closed her eyes. "We will have to be quick. The time of the Great Equilibrium draws near. We have a week until the ceremony begins. There is also the matter of the other Moon Cup, which lies to the west."

"I can tell this is going to be fun."

"It may be necessary for us to split up," said Stormbright. He redirected his gaze to Aurora. "Don't worry. My brother and I have dealt with far worse than this."

She returned with a questioning glance. "I had meant to ask, but what are your names?"

"My name is Stormbright." He smiled. "My brother you may call Steel."

Her black lips widened in a grin. "Perhaps it is Fate we should meet. Two boys for two moons. It is a good omen."

VI
Bird in the Cage

"Honestly, I'm concerned for you, General."

General Caerst ignored Neto's comment. The occasional servant passed them in the opulent hallway, and a familiar personage stalked from behind. Otherwise, they were alone.

"There's nothing for it," she said. "We have Captain Helvia's orders to follow. Either way, we will be traveling to Mirungel soon." She saw the doubt and confusion in her subordinate. "This is what must be done, Neto. If I do my duty well enough, we'll be given aid in tracking Steel and Stormbright."

"Perhaps so," he said. "After our time on the road, I assumed you would have been less accepting of help."

"Things have changed, Lieutenant."

Neto cast a sidelong look as they walked, noting the Falconer's somber expression. Something was amiss. The Ilgrathian lieutenant had traveled closely with General Caerst for the last month or so, acting as mediator when her ambition and fury had reached their peak. He knew well of her fiery determination, the incensed passion as she ordered her men with utmost confidence, tirelessly pursuing the brothers who had ruined her military career.

What had happened between her and the captain of the city guard? Judging from their interaction, Captain Helvia had seemed like warm and inviting company. Or was that just a façade?

Judging from how the hooded astromancer strode behind them, he imagined the latter was possible.

"What should I tell your men?" he asked.

"Tell them to rest while they can. These many weeks have been trying for us. See to it they get their fill of eating, drinking, and whoring. They're going to need their strength."

"Quite so," Neto replied. "You should get some rest as well."

"I'm fine," she said.

Neto glanced in Aedas' direction. He was certain she was being kept on some sort of leash, although the lieutenant knew little concerning sorcery. Caerst turned to leave, but he caught her by the shoulder and brought her close. His words were hardly a whisper. "If you require my help, you need but give me the signal. I shall check here at least once a day."

The Falconer frowned as the lieutenant made his departure. The clattering sound of footsteps echoed along the corridor. Only she and the astromancer were left.

She felt him studying her. Her blood boiled in her veins.

"Would you *please* allow me some privacy?" Caerst's words were more accusation than question.

Aedas grumbled. "My orders are to keep watch until it's time to track the cultists. It is futile to try and escape. No matter what you try, you *will* answer to Captain Helvia."

With a swift motion, Caerst raised her arm and grabbed the man by his throat. Fingers squeezed into his windpipe with frightening intensity, until scalding, virulent energy coursed through her nerves, causing her to cry out.

The Falconer curled in a fetal position. The astromancer kept the Dreamstone in his palm, his concentration stolid as the magic held her in its grip.

Eventually, she was permitted to speak.

"You… slimy…" She coughed, groaning, gasping with each breath.

"You expected to control me?" A smirk curled along the edge of his lip. "If you are to survive, you will do exactly what is expected of you. Do you understand, Falconer?"

One second, two. No answer. The astromancer channeled his vitality into the spell. He gave a low hiss.

Three seconds, four. A cry rang from the Falconer.

Five seconds, six. She reluctantly nodded.

The magic was dispelled. General Caerst writhed where she lay, each breath a monumental effort. "I concur with your friend," said Aedas, "you should get some rest. Your room is the third door to the right. Take some time as we plan our next move."

A curse muttered between her lips, the Falconer limped to her feet and glared at Aedas. The astromancer studied her without emotion. Thus she stormed down the hallway, closing the door behind and leaning her head against it.

She allowed herself to relax while inspecting her living quarters. A bed lay well-tended along the far side. Surrounding it was an immaculate set of furniture: chairs, a pair of end tables, candles, a lone mirror, and an arrayment of draperies hanging over the ceiling. Yet what drew her attention the most was an open window which granted a perfect view. Zirvonia's twin moons lingered high above the countless streets and buildings, the latter gleaming with torches and street-lamps as if they were fireflies.

The serenity wasn't lost on her.

There on the bed lay a small nightgown, a thin piece of crimson silk with a comb laying atop it. "A well-groomed prisoner," she murmured. Having lived through the disrespect and cruelty shown to her tonight, the Falconer ached to be in something more comfortable.

Changing into her new clothes, she stroked at her blonde hair while gazing at the long mirror. Her reflection showed a strange melancholy. She reminisced on her younger years, recalling the name of Wildflower her closest friends had given her. The moniker, as she learned, was made because of her ambitious spirit, not to mention her natural beauty as a firstborn.

As was the case for Falconers, her allure was enhanced when she was granted a drop of her goddess' blood. To say minstrels celebrated her fairness was an understatement. However, the utility of such an attraction was limited, save for those who served Ilgrathié directly. Beauty was no longer a quality to be cherished, but rather a weapon used to prove one's mettle. And to Ilgrathié's pleasure, she had proved it time and again.

Her fingers roamed over lively cheeks and lips. The nightgown accentuated her lust-inspiring figure, the same that had lured and disarmed so many men to her unequivocal gain. Yes, she was still the same Wildflower; but what about her had changed? Why was she so scared—so powerless?

With a sigh, she relaxed her shoulders and climbed onto the bed. To her surprise, the window leading to the outside wasn't barred or protected in the least.

No. Deep down, she knew the astromancer was keeping a close watch. She imagined the courtyards below were bristling with patrolling guards, figures who were waiting for her to make a single step out of line.

"So Helvia is toying with me," she murmured. Her eyes roamed the densely-packed streets, towards the moons which yet shone clearly. Taldriath and Bruann answered as their auburn and yellowish hues reminded her of danger. She was incapable of explaining it, but the celestial bodies tugged at her emotions. A tinge of excitement fluttered in her chest, like she was being appraised by some unseen force for an unknowable purpose.

A knock at the door. Caerst snapped out of her trance, bidding her guest enter.

With a twist of the knob, a dainty woman entered the chamber. Her stature was shorter than average, and she was evidently on the younger side. Regardless, her appearance was remarkable as far as humans went, with flowing auburn curls, somber countenance, and shapely curves that displayed themselves clearly.

Her posture was rigid; fearful yet composed.

"What is it you want?" asked the Falconer.

"Captain Helvia has sent me here," she said, upholding a carafe on a silver tray. "She wished to inquire if you would enjoy some wine or a woman's caress."

"Are there no men you keep with you?"

"If it be your desire, I shall inform her of it."

"That won't be needed," she replied. "I am in the mood for wine." The Falconer indicated the tiny table beside her bed. The servant obeyed without question, placing the tray before filling a chalice with scarlet liquid.

General Caerst held the cup to her lips. The spice teased wonderfully with her sense of smell, but she did not drink.

"You try it first," she said, handing it to the girl.

The servant frowned. "Captain Helvia was worried you would think the wine poisoned or drugged." She took a draught before refilling the cup. "In my time serving, she has never used poison, not even when housing those she considers her enemies."

The Falconer merely shrugged her shoulders, smiling. Apparently, the cold slut was capable of some kind of honor.

"What is your name?" asked Caerst.

"Mikka."

"A pretty name for a pretty girl. Come closer." Caerst held out her hand, and the servant acquiesced in having her face held. "How long have you been a slave of Helvia's?"

"Captain Helvia prefers not to use the term," she replied, eyes drifting to some unknown corner of the room. "I've been here for three months. My job is to tend to her every pleasure, both myself and the rest of her harem."

"Is that so?" The Falconer grimaced. "Tell me, Mikka, what else does Helvia have you do?"

"My other duties? They are nothing of import. I am but a servant; I tend to her whims and see her guests are well-cared for."

The servant hesitated as General Caerst grew serious.

"You're a terrible liar."

General Caerst tightened her grip. The serving girl showed discomfort but made no sound.

"You are hiding something from me. Yes, I can tell."

The girl stifled a groan. "Captain Helvia doesn't take kindly to her servants being mistreated."

The Falconer frowned in response. Her fingers loosened as Mikka stood. "Very well. I would still urge you to answer my question."

Mikka swiveled back in her direction. "I help my master as an informant, instructing her on what I learned on the streets."

"And what have you told her, exactly?"

"I inform her of the cultists. As a serving wench, I've always heard of the order and what's happened among them. Captain Helvia instructed me to teach her their history, customs, and doctrine…"

Mikka trailed away. To Caerst, it was obvious she was hiding the truth.

"What else?" General Caerst's tone was laced with anger, but that didn't stop the girl from standing stolid against her beration.

Mikka replied, "She instructed me to help teach her the basics of oneiromancy. Although she doesn't have a Dreamstone, she wishes to harness its power."

The Falconer raised an eyebrow. "Why would she have you teach her something so abhorrent?"

"It is necessary, or at least that is what she told me. Only a select few are capable of using magic, but with time and discipline, many can learn how to use Dreamstone. It is a great equalizer."

General Caerst stifled a laugh. "So you are a magician."

She kept silent while pacing around the room.

"I learned it many years ago," she said, "from a guest who bought me for the night. He was a routine drunkard, but also intelligent." Her gait was slow, steady, and ponderous. "Little had I known of such a stone until that evening, as we lay in bed and he began talking, boasting of how he stole it from some ruin. He told me everything—how one might use it without becoming a sorcerer."

"So you learned this power from him?"

"Not precisely. I was curious so I had to learn more. Black markets, bazaars, soothsayers—it's surprising what one can learn in this city. Captain Helvia and the guards took notice of my talents, and so I landed here."

"And why is she demanding you teach her this sorcery?"

Mikka regarded the mirror and her silvery reflection. "Captain Helvia says there is no other way to defeat the cultists. They are powerful oneiromancers, ones who can bend reality and poison minds. The Dreamstone is a way to counteract it."

General Caerst pondered the implications of what was said. "She is clever, I'll give her that." She waved to the servant. "You may leave now."

The maidservant obeyed, and with the door shut General Caerst was alone. Despair gnawed at her insides. To think an Ilgrathian such as Helvia would be toying with the mystic arts. The Falconer had had her fill of such sorceries during their siege at Miracor, where her sciomancer, Dimorn, conjured hordes of demoniac fiends at her behest. Perhaps Helvia would experience an outcome just as disastrous? It was a pleasant notion, considering what she had been through.

Either way, it would have to wait for the morrow. Laying her head on the fine linens, General Caerst dozed. The silvery glimmer of the moons shone through the window sill, cooling her bronze skin until she drifted off into sleep.

Bird in the Cage

She lay in a vast, moonlit field, and she was making love to a man she did not know.

The scent of moonflowers was poignant as cold rays illumined their entangled bodies. The Falconer caught glimpses of the man's face. Her fingers became talons that clawed pale ivory skin and thick muscle. There was no hair to speak of, only a bald head that was stretched back, indicating he wasn't human.

It mattered so little. The night was alive! Within her, a profound sense of longing overcame her better judgment. Their kisses were manifold—loving, tender—and it was with great relish that her resolve bled away.

Was she becoming weaker? No, she was giving it all, willingly, to him.

I will be waiting for you, said the man, with a gentle voice like flowing water. *When the time is right, look above and They shall guide you. My dearest Wildflower.*

General Caerst awakened from her slumber, her face drenched in cold sweat. Her breath came in gasps as fingers ran over her scalp.

How vivid her dream was! It was so alive, so real…

Almost out of instinct, she rose to the window. *When the time is right, look above and They shall guide you.* That's what her lover—no, the figment of her imagination—had told her. Worse still, she could have sworn the moons were mocking her from above, teasing her with a love she hadn't known in ages, if ever.

Wildflower—the name lingered in the back of her mind.

No, it was simply a fabrication of her subconscious. There was no way the dream held any significance.

Even so, the desire for sleep had left her. Dawn couldn't arrive swiftly enough.

VII

The Heist of Helvia Manor

The light of the twin moons vanished, leaving the city streets in total darkness. Steel's footsteps were quiet and methodical, his shadowy form flitting past every manner of thief imaginable: cutthroats, con artists, prostitutes, and brigands. Dregs of the earth laughed, danced, gambled, and whored while he kept his hood over him.

The low fog hovered along the street corners, dampening the cobblestone path with a putrescent moisture. The stench was mold and decay.

The thief covered his nose as he walked to the end of the street and rounded a corner. A vague irritation gnawed at him, a doubt emerging from their plan to split up. He passed through the gate into Ancient's Hold, Candala's centermost district. He wasn't being followed, at least not to his knowledge. That was good.

A light flickered up ahead. Soon his destination loomed in front of him, the large building towering several stories above as it was protected by a high-reaching wall. Lights beamed from the opaque windows, casting an eerie glow on the decrepit city.

The nearby guards were enough to confirm his suspicion. Aurora hadn't led him astray in her directions. Indeed, how many residences were so heavily guarded?

Adjusting his cloak, he stepped away from the manor. His gait gained a light tempo until he sighted the emboldened letters in the sign above, *The Silver Hearth Inn.*

Steel circled around the tavern, hearing the vague murmurs coming from inside. With it came the heady odors of strong wine and various liqueurs. Up ahead, a manhole lay situated among the flagstones.

From the folds of his cloak, Steel produced a metal rod which he used to pry open the cover. A noxious cloud of steam wafted into his nostrils, threatening to turn his stomach. He persevered while pushing the manhole to one side, climbing down, and closing the lid up above. The ladder proved anything but stable as his hands alternated in tandem. What was worse, a slime coated the metal rungs. If he wasn't careful, grave injury would follow.

After minutes of careful descent, his feet found solid purchase at the bottom. The slow *drip-drip* of water resounded in full. Steel's sleeve did little to filter the putrescence; his stomach knotted in disgust as he tasted bile in the back of his throat.

Ahead, the sewer stretched in either direction. The floors were caked with the same ichor that clung to his hands and boots. Rubbing his clothes proved a futile effort to clear the strange slime. What remained was a profound, chilling stillness. To his vague curiosity, patches of black moss were strewn about. If nothing else, it was a notable contrast to the goings on above.

He trudged forward, producing a torch and tinderbox from his cloak. Clicking stones preceded a tongue of flame.

The torchlight stretched a short distance—beyond was total darkness. Steel's heart caught in his throat as he maneuvered along the slippery cobblestones. Cold sweat ran down his face. The thief detected skittering from the shadows. Not insects or vermin, but something bigger.

At that moment, he spotted something ahead. They were prints of some sort.

Steel tripped to the ground, suddenly aware of the crack in the stones. His torch rolled as it neared the walkway's edge.

Moving to retrieve his source of light, Steel glimpsed beneath him, spying shapes that swam with frightful speed. He rose back to a standing position. From where he stood, the waters had an odd murky quality to them. That wasn't normal, he said to himself.

He felt along the wall to his right, noting the tracks were marked with five long toes.

There were likely hundreds, if not thousands of rats.

Of course it was rodents. When he and his brother had spent their time in the Slave Pits, starving and fighting to survive, he remembered the many pests who roamed and gorged on the flesh of slaves. Steel and Stormbright always made a point never to eat those who feasted on their fellow man, even if it meant they would perish. He remembered the swarms of furry bodies, wagging worm-like tails, abominable squeaks, and beady orbs. One would have given him pause, but a group was enough to send goosebumps along his skin, robbing him of common sense.

The thief wiped his brow as he tried calming himself. He recalled their plan as he walked.

"For the first Moon Cup," said Aurora, "it's best that one of you go alone. It will undoubtedly be kept in Helvia Manor."

Steel remembered grumbling at the suggestion, and worse, how it also made the most sense.

"I understand your trepidation, Steel, but I know of a way that will take you past most of the guards. It shall lead you deep into the cellar. From there, I'm certain you will find the Moon Cup's whereabouts."

"You know what you're asking of me is suicide? To rob the most well-guarded manor in Candala?"

"That is true, unless you know the right path to take. The secret entrance will bring you most of the way. I do not doubt Captain Helvia will be keeping the relic in her private quarters or some vault. I'm not certain as to where it might be, however. You will be on your own in that respect."

"You seem to know an awful lot about the place."

"It's because I lived there once, as a servant." He sensed her despondency. Evidently, her past dealings had left their scars. "Trust me, I know Helvia Manor well. While Stormbright and I search for the other chalice, I will leave you these instructions: arrive at The Silver Hearth Inn and take the path under the grate and into the sewers. Be careful, for the old ruins of Candala are buried close." Such a phenomenon fascinated him. Indeed, the city's past was like a mystery unto itself. She continued, "Once there, follow the wall to your right until you meet a set of stairs. That is where your duties begin, sir thief."

Her words lingered as darkness loomed around him. In truth, he hated the idea of splitting into separate groups. Not only did they have a week to collect both Moon Cups, but the Ilgrathians were after them as well.

Time was not on their side.

He pondered this while turning right, his hand feeling along the wall until he arrived at a diminutive shack, one rotten at its foundations.

A house down here? It was difficult to imagine. That said, the ruined mass of timbers appeared to have housed many a thief in its time.

He remembered how Aurora had mentioned ruins.

The idea did not give him comfort.

Even worse still was the pair of skeletons splayed at his feet.

He searched around him. The thief knelt as he inspected the bones, curious to what the cause of death might have been. They were broken and gnawed in several places. Whoever these people were, they had been killed and eaten over time.

Hairs rose on his neck. A low skittering registered in his ears. Steel gasped in surprise once he raised his head, a large furry body pinning him to the ground. A pair of yellow teeth chittered as two black orbs sought his flesh.

The creature squealed as warmth ran between Steel's fingers. He plunged his dagger into the rodent's chest, kicking its carcass into the sewer canal.

Rising and stumbling, he beheld the giant rat floating in a pool of crimson. The waters bubbled around it, and ere he moved a muscle, the remains disappeared under a mass of scaly bodies and needle-like teeth—biting, gnawing, and tearing—until naught was left.

Steel shuddered, being glad he hadn't strayed too close to the water. As for whatever the things were, they didn't seem friendly. He instinctively took a step back, his breath dry and ragged. Continuing his walk, he arrived at a low staircase spanning along his right.

Suspiciously enough, the top led nowhere.

Inspecting the surface, Steel carefully maneuvered his fingers. He felt a slight breeze. The thief pursued this sensation, tracing the outline of a doorway.

It was just as Aurora had described. With an effort he threw his entire weight against the entrance.

Nothing.

Steel pondered how he might gain entry. His mind weighed the possibilities as he searched, growing weary and frustrated.

His fingers crept along a slight outcropping.

His curiosity piqued, he closely inspected the cobble. At first glance, it appeared quite normal compared to its surroundings, but instinct made him halt. He carefully pressed his palm. The hidden door parted in front of him—likely some hidden spring mechanism. He pushed until a pitch black corridor encompassed his vision, his torch doing little to stave off the gloom.

The warm light of his brand filled the narrow hallway. With it the skittering sounds returned, and this time they were coming closer. Peering below, Steel saw hundreds of black eyes staring back, and an issuance of squeaks which set his nerves on edge. The abominable scratching, gnawing, and small padded feet must have numbered in the thousands.

The thief barely held his composure. With a concentrated effort, he lowered his brand to the floor, causing most of the rats to disperse.

Steel knew that from here on darkness would be his ally. He prayed to whatever god who would listen for the rats to stay far, far away.

He laid the torch along the floor; the light sputtered but didn't go out. A short distance onward, he uncovered a similar cobble. Pressing the switch, the portal in front of him groaned open.

This time he pulled the hidden doorway towards him, enough for him to get a bearing on his surroundings. He was inside a temple of sorts. If Aurora was to be believed, this was, in fact, the cellar area for Helvia Manor.

The thief's skin crawled as he snuck carefully, each footfall as light as a feather. The grand chamber had apparently sunken into the earth. Large pillars were spaced at regular intervals along either side. He detected the faint scent of wood while passing stacks of wine barrels. An eerie breeze blew past, causing him to shiver.

The ghost winds howled among the ancient halls. Steel crept from one lonely room to the next, discerning its new purpose as a cellar. Certain rooms contained various kegs of wine, foodstuff, and preserved goods. Others, by contrast, were quite empty, save for a horrible musty stench.

A shadow flitted out of sight. By the time his eyes adjusted, however, the apparition was gone. His skin crawled, causing him to shudder involuntarily. The thief inspected his surroundings, heeding any signs that what he saw wasn't his imagination.

Fresh cold sweat beaded along his brow. He waited, listening for any sort of sound. Apart from the wind, there was little of note.

Perhaps it really *was* his imagination? At the least he was in the largest section of this cellar, which in ages past had acted as an audience chamber. The floor sank in a shallow pit, where a stony altar sat at the far edge. To the right a passageway led beyond and up, presumably into Helvia Manor proper. As for the altar, Steel found the top section was hollowed into a basin. Inside were old stains made of various shades of crimson, along with an idol of two crescent moons overlapping, meeting as one.

He furrowed his brow in concern; it was the same symbol Aurora had had around her neck.

His heart sank. The Listener was right, he mused; the Order of the Sacred Twins was indeed a cult, and this was the result.

A stirring came from behind. Steel turned in a flash, but whatever he heard was gone. Apprehension welled up inside him. It was time to move, he concluded, ere this thing had its way with him—whatever it was.

Steel kept silent as he stole down the corridor, rounding a bend and up a series of steps. A glossy pair of eyes spied the thief from the shadows. They studied and observed, before fading into obscurity.

Reaching the top of the staircase, the thief presumed he was on the first floor. Gilded furnishings lay in chambers to his left and right, and a series of decorative tapestries evoked a comforting atmosphere. Steel, by contrast, was anything but relaxed. His stomach was hard as a rock. Lit torches lined the walls, reducing his hiding options.

He heard echoes of laughter and conversation, and they were growing louder. Steel snuck into the room on his left, though neither of them had doors. Steel hugged his back as the voices came closer.

"And what do you say about our new guest?" said a voice with a high tenor. "Captain Helvia seems far too pleased to welcome a stranger among our ranks. Is it me, or is this perhaps foolish on her part?"

"Clearly she knows that, you idiot," another guard responded in a gruff baritone. "Little do you realize our captain has everything under control. This is General Caerst we are talking about—General Caerst, the esteemed Falconer and war hero! Despite abandoning her post, the woman is highly skilled. Do you not think Helvia would use it to her advantage? Let us not forget the sagacity of these cultists."

Steel winced. The bronze bitch had followed them here, and now she was closer than ever before.

The guard's voice grew louder. "Oh, I bet she's highly skilled if you catch my meaning."

"Get your thoughts out of the refuse pile, Brevus. Even if she is a traitor, she's still our superior."

"For the moment," the guard replied. "Regardless, I can't help but think our captain is playing with fire. If you ask my opinion, I think it's best that we send her to Ilgrathié and be done with it. We can handle the Order of the Sacred Twins ourselves."

"Your buffoonery aside, I must concur. Why, just this last week…"

The conversation grew indistinct. Steel walked out from the shadows, the adrenaline rushing through his veins. General Caerst was here. Of all places, she was here!

He gave a low sigh. This was going to be more difficult than he hoped.

With carefully situated steps, he realized the left passage led to a library. He poked his head in and beheld the two guards walking ahead.

Steel quietly dashed through the corridor at his right. Although completely empty, the massive dining hall spanned nearly three stories in height, with frescoes, mosaics, and a plethora of decorations lining the walls and ceiling. It was so unlike Steel's previous foray into the unknown—the city of the star wraiths, the manse of King Telinor, and the great palace at the metropolis' center. By contrast, there were no ghostly beings to speak of, no accomplices to lend him aid should he be caught.

Steel was awestruck. Either way, he was making little progress in discovering the Moon Cup. His doubts resurfaced as he considered what the Moon Cups would be used for. Was Stormbright safe with Aurora? Moreover, would the Order hold true to its side of the deal?

He thought of the relic. He could well guess the cup was located higher up, most likely in a secluded room. That said, his knowledge on the manor and the object's whereabouts were lacking.

His eyes rested on a corridor. Moving closer, he found a door with a note attached to it. It was times like this where Steel wished he had learned how to read. If nothing else, he recognized the falcon's symbol stamped on the stationery.

He produced a crude set of lockpicks from his bag, ones he had bought with the little amount of coin he possessed. The thief went to work, hoping and praying he would go unnoticed.

The tumblers clicked and the door opened. In the darkness beyond, Steel dug through papers, books, letters, adjuncts, and miscellanea. The study was small, yet he was certain to find a clue!

He poured through each desk and shelf with alacrity. Steel took care to stay as quiet as possible and put everything back the way he found it. That was when he happened upon a locked drawer. He produced his lockpicks once again. Another issuance of clicks as the lock resisted, until it gave way to his skill.

The thief lit up as he sighted the large key and folded note. He opened the page, and though he didn't understand its contents, being illiterate himself, Steel harbored no doubts this was in fact the key to some special door.

With his curiosity satisfied, Steel exited the study. Now came the challenge of locating this mysterious door, he thought. His sole clues were a page he could not read, as well as a key with the falcon symbol emblazoned on its bow. He imagined the hiding place, if it wasn't in the same room, would be on some nebulous floor above.

His feet shuffled across the floor. The discordant sound of guards echoed. He rounded a corner, pressing his back against the wall as they walked, muttering and cajoling.

To the surprise of his fellow sentry, one of the guards halted.

"Is something wrong?" asked the Ilgrathian.

Steel peeked around the corner, enough to spy the man's scowl. The thief held his breath. "It's nothing," said the guard. "Probably a draft."

The footsteps grew distant. Steel considered the direction opposite the patrol, scaling a wide spiral staircase. A long hallway stretched before him. Instinct told him the Moon Cup was close.

 *"The discordant sound of guards echoed."* 

At his sides were statues of Ilgrathian heroes, figures who were celebrated in all corners of the realm: Tiliana, Dekaro, Shalatar, Mideus; them and many others.

Steel regarded each with a healthy amount of reproach, checking the branching halls along either side. At first he tried one path, then tested another. He realized both led to large rooms where commotion was heard. Taking special care to stay quiet, he crept along a passage to his left, away from those voices.

His hopes were dashed when he learned it was a dead end.

There in front of him was a blank wall, littered with decorations and miscellany. He nearly turned when a peculiar glint caught his attention. It was the falcon's crest. Steel held the key in his palm, remembering how it bore the same symbol.

He had almost missed a small metal cover. Twisting it to the side, a keyhole presented itself. Steel inserted the key, twisting it counterclockwise.

A loud click sounded. The illusory wall faded, manifold decorations disappearing into naught, revealing the large vault door behind it. With a great heave, Steel tugged it open.

He beheld countless bags, stacks of glittering gold coins, jewelry, fine pieces of artwork, et cetera. Thousands and thousands in worth of drakons, sylphs, parcels, and gems piled around him. In the center of this tiny room stood a lone marble pedestal holding a thin ivory cup. The archaic silver engravings were unmistakable; this was indeed the Moon Cup.

He pocketed whatever riches he could—taking gold, gems, and priceless relics—before snatching the chalice. The dazzling silver reflected the low light at the vault's entrance, its wide base and arabesque patterns granting it an unfathomable beauty. The metal was warm to the touch. Power rushed through his fingers, running up his arms and dispersing among his extremities.

Perhaps it was some form of magic emanating from the cup? Pocketing the relic, the sensation quickly faded. He imagined his intuition wasn't far from the truth.

Thus closing the vault door behind, he was shocked to find three spears trained at his throat. He had become so engrossed with riches, little had he realized the guards preparing an ambush.

"We've got him!" shouted an armored figure.

"Very good," a tall woman responded, her dark hair flowing as she stepped forward. "You have my thanks for alerting me when you did. I always like to get a look at those who would dare steal from me." The thief noted how she was older for an Ilgrathian, considering how their race outlived humans by a number of decades. Gods knew how many years of war and debauchery she had witnessed!

The mere notion made his blood quicken with rage.

"Any intrusion on our vault is a crime of the highest order. And the punishment," she smirked, "is equally severe."

"Aye, I knew something reeked of the sewers," said a guard to the boy's left, the same man he recognized prior to ascending the stairs. "Either there was a humongous rat scurrying around, or someone had found their way in."

"In either case, this intrusion shall warrant investigation. Bring the Falconer," she said. "If he discovered a way in from below, I would wish to learn the details."

"Aye, Captain Helvia."

Steel's heart caught in his throat. Captain Helvia regarded him with a cool stare. She hummed softly. "If I didn't know any better, I would say you recognize the title."

He said nothing in reply, instead responding with a scowl.

She chuckled as a figure emerged, the face obscured by Captain Helvia who stood directly in front.

Helvia turned. "Ah, you are just in time, Falconer. I caught a rat trying to steal from our store room. Come! See who's here!"

Around her was the same woman whom Steel had hoped to avoid. His heart pounded in his chest, a cold layer of perspiration seeping into his clothes.

"Well, well," General Caerst smiled, "you're already holding to your side of the bargain, Captain Helvia. I must say, I'm impressed."

"It was child's play for my men and I," the woman said with a slight upturning of her lips. "Indeed, I had not the faintest clue this was one of the brothers you were hunting."

At this the Falconer showed genuine irritation.

"Whatever the cause," Helvia said, "he has information that's vitally important. I trust you will aid me in this endeavor."

The Falconer sauntered forward, her fingers clutching his throat. "Oh, believe me," she said, "I relish the thought!"

VIII

The Mystery of Moonhaven

"Are you sure we're on the right track?" asked Stormbright.

"As positive as I'll ever be," said Aurora, goading her bay past him.

Stormbright grimaced, keeping pace atop the mounts he and his brother had tamed. The fields west of Candala reminded him distinctly of home. He wondered how Steel was faring in Candala. The memory of its putrid stink loomed behind them. To his relief, the smog and pollution, the nameless cutthroats and thieves, faded with each league they rode. In its stead were the earthy sweet acacia trees and blue asters, a pleasant contrast to say the least.

He would have kept it that way, to stay here in the wilds where he belonged. Cities were never his place of choice, not especially after his experience with Mirungel. If it wasn't for his desire to meet with Aedas, he wouldn't have wished to be near Candala whatsoever.

That said, he would have to go back, if for no reason than Serithas and the Moon Cup.

His attention returned to the present. The grass swayed coolly with jaden hues, and whatever clouds crossing the sunlit skies were light and pleasant.

If only he could go back to his village of Harskul, to the sweet fresh-cooked venison, medicinal herbs, and aromatic smokes. He remembered the faces of so many he had cherished—so many he missed. He almost heard the bleating of livestock from where his horse trotted. Then came the screams, the all-consuming flames. Everything changed since his home was reduced to ashes. The boy recognized this as an immutable fact, happening as it had two years ago.

"Stormbright? Are you all right?"

He snapped out of his trance, noting Aurora's concern. He hadn't realized his bay stopping in its tracks. Had he become so distant from dwelling on the past?

"It's nothing." He tried laughing it off, although it was clear Aurora wasn't fooled. He goaded his beast forward. "I guess it's just nostalgia."

"You mean you've been through here?"

"Not exactly. My brother and I have traveled much these last several months. Here I'm reminded most of home."

She moved her bay beside him. "I wish I could run away. The Ilgrathians took everything from us, everything from me." She swallowed, a mixture of fright and anger showing in her expression.

Stormbright bowed his head. He knew where this conversation was headed, and the idea made him sick. Aurora perceived this as well, as the words lingered between them, going unanswered.

"How close are we to this Moonhaven?" he asked, trying his best to change topics. "We shouldn't be far from what you told me."

"I don't think it's too far." She blinked with heavy eyelashes. Their horses crested another hill. Their hopes were dashed as they beheld what lay in the valley below.

"It's..." His words caught in his throat.

"No." Aurora spurred her mount down the hillside, into the lifeless town. Stormbright wondered how beautiful this lonesome village might have once been, what with its picturesque surroundings and small road leading through the middle. The little huts and still-burning fires—all were empty, but not destroyed.

It was desolate.

"Hey, wait up!" Stormbright goaded his horse along, the memory of Driftwind fading. The sorcerer maneuvered the bay along the abandoned streets. The cold wind whistled with an almost human inflection. The uncanny silence wormed its way into his bones, causing him to shudder.

Aurora kept pace up front. Stormbright followed her example as he caught up. They stopped, dismounted, and searched for signs of life. Stormbright scanned for relics as he progressed from one structure to the next. He returned empty-handed. Aurora was just as unlucky. As was the case with Driftwind, there were no bodies to be found. It was like they had vanished overnight.

Aurora spoke aloud, her voice quavering: "There is nothing. The Ilgrathians passed through here as well. Not this… Not again."

Stormbright recognized her misery as he remounted. He would have liked to share in her sorrow, but something about this didn't feel right to him.

"It's over. Everything we bled and died for, all of it was for naught!"

"I'm not certain these are from Ilgrathians," said Stormbright. "I can see no signs of battle, no burn marks."

Stormbright looked down and winced. The large slug tracks confirmed his suspicion: this was likely the work of nightmare-kin. An ill omen, indeed.

Aurora's eyes searched for his. "But what could that mean?"

"It's a hunch. Come! We shall find out for ourselves."

Their two horses galloped swiftly along the narrow path and into fields of swaying grass. They arrived at a group of standing stones, being similar in make and size to what lay outside of Driftwind. Aurora maneuvered her bay to the center of the landmark and dismounted.

"Of course," she said, "the Moon Cup is gone. They've taken it!"

"Are you sure there's no sign of it?"

Her face flushed with emotion. "I don't know what it is you're searching for, Stormbright, but it's not here." She caught herself, taking a deep breath. "I'm sorry."

"I understand, Aurora," Stormbright said as he dismounted, giving her a warm smile. This shrine, like the rest of Moonhaven, was completely devoid of life. No signs of villagers or relics lay anywhere. He paused; there were more tracks, as he suspected. The paths converged along a myriad of angles, as if the things had flanked the humans here in one gigantic horde. The lush flora decayed rapidly, becoming dried and wilted. Similarly, a squat altar lingered along the edge of where they stood. It, too, was barren.

His fingers felt over the tracks. He tried getting a sense for their direction, forming a path out of the chaotic, criss-crossing trails around them. "Follow me," he said. Stormbright heard Aurora behind as he took the lead. The sorcerer allowed his mind to drift in a light trance. The traces of magic were faint, but they were present nonetheless.

The sorcerer kept close to the ground. Though he was nowhere near as experienced at tracking as his brother, he guessed there was a first time for everything. And besides, the scent of magic granted him a distinct edge in this instance.

"If I'm to guess," he said, "those things might have the Moon Cup."

"Are you talking about the nightmare-kin?"

"Aye."

"And how do you know it isn't destroyed?" The emotion crept back into her voice.

"I don't. But one can hope for the best." His attention shifted back to her, the magic fading from his pupils. "We should at least see this through. If for some reason the cup is destroyed, well... we'll cross that bridge when we get there."

Her anger faded as she rode beside him. A little longer and she behaved as normal. The two of them followed the decayed tracks. From behind, Aurora stole a glance towards the ruined village, the human settlement that had been massacred so quickly. Stormbright saw her soften a little. She cast him a cheerful look as he kept calm.

They turned southwest. The tracks conjoined in a path of remarkable width.

The echoing clatter of stones and rushing water met their ears as the grotto was revealed. A large waterfall sluiced atop the overhanging rocks, the sunlight forming a gamut of shimmering colors. Foliage, roots, and ivy split the stones.

"It's beautiful," said Aurora.

Stormbright made no comment. Shimmering mists refracted the light around them, granting their surroundings an almost ethereal glow. The colors faintly danced on their skin, and he experienced a more tender impulse. Evidently the idea had planted itself within her as well, as a slight blush registered.

"Stormbright?"

"Yes?" he asked.

She stared at him with an appraising demeanor. Whereas minutes ago there was an outburst of melancholy, he witnessed a fondness that was almost deliberate. "We… should probably go," she said.

"Right," was his response as he brought his nerves under control. He marched past the stunning scenery which deafened their hearing, off to where the grotto narrowed, changing into a low, winding tunnel. The tracks and black oblivion lay onward.

Aurora stepped alongside him, enough to make him blush in response. With a hint of reluctance, he steeled himself. They passed carefully into the gloom, leaving behind the wondrous sights and sounds of the falls.

Darkness permeated his vision. Aurora was close behind, her breathing unsteady along his neck. Stormbright withdrew a torch from his pack, and following several strikes with his flint and steel, the cave around them lit up with the flames.

At their left the cave howled as it descended. To the right, they found a narrow pathway. Choosing the latter, a violent shiver came as they recognized the corpses along their feet.

Aurora held him tightly. Stormbright advanced, noting how the remains were carefully arranged and mummified. That was an oddity considering the dampness of their surroundings. A few urns lay about as well, some of them intact while others had had their dusty contents smashed along the stony floor.

"I can't say I've seen anything like this," pondered Stormbright. "What do you think, Aurora?"

"I've heard of such places," said Aurora. "I recognize it from tales I was told as a child. It's a Gillaski tomb."

"Gillaski?"

"Men who revere the mountains," she replied. "They are skilled oneiromancers, or at least that's what my Ma always told me. The dead were wrapped in gauze and protected with spells. 'As one in the earth, so too are we undone.' That's what they used to say."

"Are they like Islirians?" He recalled the star wraiths, those haunting miasmatic figures. Stormbright shivered.

"How so?"

"Are they dead? Or worse?"

"No, they are alive. They lock themselves deep in the mountains. 'Guided by primordial beings,' so say the Listeners."

"An interesting custom," said Stormbright, remaining steady. "I wonder why these weren't disturbed by the nightmare-kin."

Sweat collected along his brow, and with a nervous swipe of his sleeve, he steeled himself and knelt. With his arm outstretched, he pressed one of the corpses with the butt end of his torch. The effect was immediate; the bodies secreted a foul, noxious odor. The torch cracked at its base, the wood drying and crumbling as it aged rapidly. Stormbright shouted in dismay as the brand was instantly consumed, the burning embers falling through his fingers. He yelped once the flames touched his skin.

Only a burn mark served as any indication of their light source.

"What in the…" Stormbright cared for his wound as the heat danced along his nerves. He swore. "What kind of hex was that?"

Aurora stood, just as perplexed. "I imagine it's how they preserve their dead."

"So it seems," Stormbright replied as he produced another torch, lighting it at a safe distance from the grisly bodies. Rounding the corner they entered, Stormbright listened intently while venturing down the remaining path. The cave grew narrower. They walked in rhythm, going deeper. Stormbright wasn't sure if minutes passed or an hour. Time was hazy as the air grew stuffy. All was quiet save for the air sucking between their teeth and the cadence of their footsteps.

It was some time later—how long, exactly, neither of them knew— that Stormbright's second torch ran out. He cursed under his breath. Before he could prepare his third and final brand, however, Aurora clutched his chest.

"Don't," she whispered.

"Why not? We need to-"

She lifted a hand to his lips. Her expression told him everything.

They were not alone.

Aurora crept forward. Stepping beside her, Stormbright honed his wizardly *inner sense*. The same magic was here, but something was amiss. A grimy corruption lingered in its aura, a sensation that frightened as the sorcery beckoned him onward.

A natural light spilled from the opening beyond. How was that possible? They were close to the Dreaming Mountains, and judging by the fact they were deep underground, Stormbright doubted the sun would be visible this far down. Even so, the natural chamber permeated with silver rays. Zirvonia's moons loomed in a sky of deep azure—an impossibility in its own right. Were they underneath the earth, or had they entered some archaic realm? Surely, it was an illusion of some sort. There was no other explanation for it.

The tall grass tickled at their legs. Chills traveled along Stormbright's skin, causing the hairs on his neck to stand. The air here was cool, pure, and refreshing, rife with honeysuckle and spring grass. This was a mighty contradiction, considering autumn had just started. The plant life around them swayed. The result was strangely soothing, calm.

Perhaps this *was* real. But if that was the case, where exactly were they? This couldn't have been the outside world. When they walked through the grotto, broad daylight had warmed the skies above.

Surely, their journey hadn't taken so long.

"What is this on the leaves?" asked Aurora, her eyes glimmering as she indicated a black ichor covering the brush. Stormbright speculated as to whether this was a sign of nightmare-kin, though the tracks had faded. The grasslands were boundless, neverending, save for a narrow, rocky pass where they had supposedly entered.

"I don't know," was his reply. "But I get a bad feeling from this."

They wandered further, hands clasped so they wouldn't be separated, where they crept until arriving at a small pond. A stream trickled and seeped into the pool. Aside from the bubbling rill, the main body of water was exceedingly calm, almost like reflective glass, as it mirrored the moons high above. Crickets chirped; an unseen owl hooted from its perch; the familiar sounds of night increased in profundity.

From his side, Stormbright heard Aurora gasp.

"What's wrong?" he asked.

The girl pointed toward a shadowy figure. The two of them crouched and took a single step, beholding the alien creature near the waters. The figure walked on two legs, yet its features resembled a man. From split hooves to thick tufts of fur, to stag-like horns and a gaunt complexion, the thing roamed in unsettling strides. It swayed and listened. *Woosh. Woosh.* They heard its breath. Stormbright scented the distinct odor of boars, reminding him how Serithas and Father had once hunted them. There was also a vague resemblance to the Brugmar, that horrid beast he fought in the Slave Pits.

Aurora had nearly spoken until Stormbright covered her mouth. He shook his head. The beast was clutching an object. What it was, neither of them could tell.

"What is that thing?" Stormbright whispered.

"A Faunus," she replied, her voice barely audible. "They're revered by my order as guardians of the Sacred Moons."

"Then why are we staying hidden?" He wasn't sure why, but he deemed it a sore mistake to consider such beings friendly.

Aurora could hardly speak. "I don't know. I don't know…"

Cubit by cubit, Stormbright snuck closer. Sure enough, the Faunus returned, placing the object it held on a bank overlooking the pool. Their intuition proved to be correct; it was indeed the Moon Cup they were searching for.

He heard a peculiar sound coming from the beast's lips, a low chant with a rhythmic cadence. *Ooh-mah-dah-niss. Ooh-mah-dah-niss.*

A crack of a twig from afar and it fled. The creature was likely distracted, perhaps by the promise of food. What was it the Faunus was saying? He caught the intonations of its words, but not enough to comprehend what it meant.

He circled around the pond, snatching up the Moon Cup in his palm. The ivory and silver-engraved surface sparkled in the soft light. He was about to move when he slipped along the banks, stumbling onto his side. The Faunus thundered back in his direction. Its gaze foretold black infinity; its veins were also black, lips muttering that abhorrent incantation.

Ooh-mah-dah-niss. Ooh-mah-dah-niss.

The air shifted around them. The quiet, peaceful night was gone. Eldritch beings slithered out of sight. The beast's chant rose—faster, faster, higher, higher.

Old Man Darkness, Old Man Darkness.

An inhuman bellow escaped its throat. Its bones snapped while flesh morphed. Stormbright experienced a wave of nausea. He heard the sound of boiling liquid as appendages sprouted from its form—first an arm, then a leg, then a disembodied mouth.

The groans morphed into terrible shrieks. What followed was a plethora of strange slopping noises. Countless nightmare-kin swarmed in around them, their gibbering moans making Stormbright's skin crawl. Blue energy leapt between his fingers. Aurora joined at his side, gripping a steel poniard. The monstrosities loomed closer. The sky was pitch black, save for the two moons converging high above—Taldriath and Bruann— forming overlapping spheres of reddish hues.

The skies became red. The land was blood.

Still, the Faunus chanted its abominable words.

Old Man Darkness, Old Man Darkness.

With an effort, Stormbright snapped into focus. Aurora flinched beside him. The sorcerer, unfazed, released swathes of lightning. The burning, putrid flesh wafted in the air as their adversaries perished en masse.

The young sorcerer turned as Aurora slashed with her blade. She stared at the Faunus, where its arms and tendrils were upraised in a gesture of supplication. One shot forth and tore the Moon Cup from Stormbright's grasp.

"No!"

"Kill it!" shouted Aurora, the terror dripping from her lips. "That thing is what controls them!"

The sorcerer obeyed. Having sustained a few wounds himself, the acidic swipes of the nightmare-kin burning deep, he slashed helter-skelter with his blade, hacking a wide circle around them. At that moment, Stormbright sheathed his weapon. Along his hands and fingers, blue lightning crackled and pulsated. The Faunus took the full brunt of the blast as its body was blackened and burned. The sickly stench nearly overpowered him.

"Old Man Darkness, Old Man Darkness."

The Faunus' legs buckled as it fell into the serene waters. The ivory relic tumbled along with it.

Stormbright cursed as the fiends pressed forward. "Please, Aurora! You must fetch it."

"What if it's not dead?!"

"I can assure you, Aurora, it *is* dead!"

The young woman stood rooted to the ground as the nightmare-kin swarmed around her. Stormbright fired off lightning bolts to his left and right.

Mustering her courage, she dashed into the shallow waters.

The entire world grew still. Even Stormbright's sorceries went unheard; all faded save the sloshing that befell each stride. A knotting anxiety bubbled up inside. Inhaling deeply, she submerged her hands.

She sensed something brushing along her fingers. Her grip tightened. She held up the Moon Cup, her eyes glistening in wonder.

"I found it, Stormbright! I found-"

A hand shot up. Black fingers covered her mouth, and she reacted with a muffled scream. They held her with surprising strength as a devilish head emerged. Evidently the damage Stormbright dealt to the Faunus had been most grievous, for not a spot on its hide was unburned. Flesh melted and sloughed, exposing muscle and bones. Knotted muscles tensed along its arms. Vital organs were visible from its torso, pulsating lumps of meat and black serpents for intestines.

The demon edged closer to her. Even now, it muttered those horrible words.

Old Man Darkness. Old...

The thing gurgled as a shortsword hacked through its skull, a swing which released torrents of ichorous fluid. Aurora stood motionless as Stormbright pulled her up by one arm. She was vaguely aware of the chaos, the fact she had perceived naught but dancing shadows, yet survival concerned her most.

The grasslands faded. The blood moons, skies, and stars vanished as soon as they had arrived. What surrounded them was a diminutive cavern, lined to the brim with nightmare-kin.

They raced for the exit—forward and onward, outward and upward. Aurora ran until her legs failed. She ran in her dreams until the next thing she remembered was being carried. She felt the magician's hot breath. He was running, with Aurora secured fast in his arms.

"Stormbright," she groaned. "You're bleeding."

The young sorcerer said nothing. Aurora spotted a thin rivulet of blood trailing down his arm. He was hurt.

"Stormbright…"

"Please keep quiet. We're almost clear of them."

A dull light shone ahead, coupled with the echo of rushing water. Stormbright realized it was the grotto from which they had entered. They were so close to being free!

Thunder roared. Water drenched them to the bone. Whether it was the torrential downpour or the falls themselves they did not know, nor did they care. Stormbright limped along until he reached the edge of the overhanging rocks. He laid her down gently.

Aurora sat up. She knew time was short as she tore off a piece of cloth and, with the utmost care, bound up Stormbright's wound. The bleeding had apparently stopped. Stormbright gave her a wan smile, his face showing a sickly white as he succumbed to exhaustion. Aurora fell seconds later.

The two of them lay still in the mud. For how long neither of them knew. Aurora was the first to awaken as thin streaks of lightning illumined her vision.

Stormbright lay at her side.

"Stormbright… Stormbright!" She listened to his heart. There was a pulse, but he was cold. Her vision blurred as she held the boy in her arms, doing her best to warm him.

Thunder crashed in her ears.

"Please… Stormbright."

Another flash streaked across the sky.

"Stormbright…"

She gasped. The boy in her arms stirred.

"Where am I?" he stammered. His eyes opened slightly.

There was no time for an answer. Aurora grinned as she quietly wept, leaning in and embracing him. Their lips met, the fear and worry pouring into a single fit of passion. The young sorcerer was surprised at the suddenness of this affection. He pondered at the unexpected advance, but his doubts soon bled away, his better judgment giving way to raw emotion. He smiled as he forced the questions to the back of his mind, pushed to some recess where it was easily overlooked.

Despite being drenched, he was no longer cold. Neither of them were as they held each other.

IX

The Palace of the Sacred Twins

Stormbright pushed onto his side, eyes boring deep into Aurora's. He was thoroughly shocked. "So that... I never thought that was how we would…"

Aurora regarded him tenderly as they shared another kiss. The moment wasn't without its lingering discomforts, particularly the wound he had sustained. By the time he came to his senses, he brushed his lips with a thumb. They were stained black with balm.

He smiled.

Stormbright beheld the ivory chalice. The relic glimmered with such beauty—a treasure among the thunderous downpour.

"We have the Moon Cup," he said, holding it up between them. "We should probably find Steel. Then we'll see about fulfilling our side of the bargain."

"Agreed. But first, we should look for shelter and get some rest. That wound of yours will require attention."

Stormbright studied the gash along his arm. "I'm with you there," he said. "I will be honest—I couldn't move far even if I wanted to."

So they limped until arriving at a narrow hovel—a place where the torrential rain had not invaded. Despite having no wood dry enough to burn, the two found sufficient warmth from each other. Perhaps they would have wanted more, if not for the grievous injuries and fatigue.

Still, the act of being close was far from unpleasant.

"How long have you lived in Candala?" Stormbright asked, his voice disrupting the grumbling storm.

"Me?" Aurora gazed at him warmly. "I guess you could say I've been here all my life. Once upon a time, I was one in a family of seven: Mother, Father, two brothers, and two sisters. I was the middle child."

"That sounds pleasant." A lump caught in Stormbright's throat as he asked, "What happened to them?"

"Alive. If you can believe it, my Pa sold me to pay his debts to the state. It's a common practice for many humans here; send off a child and receive two whole drakons to sustain you for the year. I hated him for it, for many years, but now I understand some sacrifices must be made to survive."

"I… I'm sorry."

Aurora smiled, kissing him a third time.

"No, I'm the one who should be sorry. You've been so good to me, Stormbright, and here I am being troublesome. Ask me another question. I promise I'll be cheerful this time."

"All right. Let's see… what's your favorite color?"

"Purple," she hummed a laugh.

"Do you have any hobbies?"

"Sometimes I leave the city and wander the fields. Once dusk settles and the glory of day is at its end, I love to hear the crickets and the hooting of owls. Even the wolf's howl holds an entrancing melody. In that solitude, I find myself singing; for the onset of night and the beauty neglected by the sun; for the many animals scurrying in the late hours. I've always cherished those times."

"I would much like to hear you sing."

"Really?" Aurora lit up with joy.

"Yes, of course!" Stormbright grinned.

She made no effort to reposition herself, though a pleasant hum rumbled from the back of her throat, passing her lips with subtle grace. The tune reminded Stormbright of a lullaby, one fashioned from sorrow and an admiration for the ethereal. It was an epithet to the dusk, the night, and the quieter moments in one's life. The cool whispers of trees, the chirping of insects, and the scents of flowers in the autumn breeze; these he felt in her song.

The melody was beautiful. *She* was beautiful.

"Stormbright," she said, her melody coming to a gentle halt, "I wish this could last forever."

"Yes. So do I..." he responded dreamily.

They fell asleep. The rain and lightning abated. Stormbright and Aurora awakened in the same intimate position they had fallen asleep. They checked their wounds, noting their cuts and bruises were less grievous than first imagined. The only exception was the gash Aurora noted earlier; that would require stitches. In this area the young initiate proved most helpful, for she returned with a handful of flaxen sprigs, as well as hemp fibers, which she fashioned into a long string. Stormbright realized one of the sprigs would act as a needle.

"I don't know about this."

She gave him a kiss, warm lips pressing firmly. This time he mirrored the gesture with eagerness. The result was nigh euphoric as Stormbright said little else. Holding a vial of bluish liquid, Aurora grinned seductively. "This is for the wound," she said.

Stormbright studied the potion, uncorked it, and drank its contents.

The process was slow, but by the time the sewing and cleaning were finished, the wound was closed.

"I don't know how to thank you," he said, exasperated.

She smirked, "Perhaps I know of something." She brought her face close to his. Stormbright blushed a vivid scarlet.

They shared a minute. Then she pulled herself away.

"Come back with me, Stormbright. I can show you many things once we're behind city walls."

"Right," he stammered. "But first… we should probably search for my brother. I need to know he's safe."

She was clearly disappointed, pursing her black lips. "Don't you think we'll find him where we're going? If he's not there, we can have the priestesses search for him." Her words grew low, sensual. "In exchange for the relic, we will give you information. Information and…" her fingers tickled along his neck. She giggled.

Stormbright realized the implication. His heartbeat quickened. His hands grasped for a proper embrace, but Aurora wandered out of reach.

"All right," he murmured, taking a deep breath. His base impulses aside, it made sense for them to learn as much as they could concerning Aedas and Kolthan. The sooner they discovered their whereabouts, the better.

Either way, Serithas would be there waiting for them. Surely their quest had taken longer, and he was anxious to see how his brother fared.

Standing, he followed her along the path they walked the previous day. They arrived at the lonesome village once known as Moonhaven. Neither spotted where their bays had galloped off to. Stormbright surmised that, in all likelihood, they were several leagues distant from where he and Aurora dismounted, assuming the horses had survived. He considered this possibility as they neared the far edge of town. To his surprise and shock, the bays were grazing among the tall grasses. Aside from trembling slightly, they were in good enough shape.

With a gentle stroke along the bay's neck, Aurora prepared to remount her beast. Stormbright was about to do the same, but the world around him swayed.

He had nearly fallen until Aurora caught him.

"You've lost a lot of blood," she said.

"I guess I have," was his response.

Stormbright struggled to his feet. Since the previous night, they had dined off rations they carried, so why did he feel so weak? Perhaps it was exhaustion and the toll of his wounds? Whatever it was, it would have to wait. He took the reins in hand as he climbed atop his bay. The unsteady clopping of hooves resounded underneath. As they ventured towards Candala, the clouds and thunder were completely absent. It was like nothing had transpired in the first place. The experience reminded him much of his time in that other storm. His memory of Calamtu was still fragmented, though the devastation lingered still.

Aurora eyed him as they rode. It was a momentary expression, yet it hinted at so much—affection, sensuality, and perhaps something greater.

Stormbright would have considered it longer if his vision hadn't blurred. Among his dizziness, he wondered if perhaps he had sustained a head wound during the fight. In his time at Harskul, he had seen the occasional adult treated for such injuries. A "concussion" was what Gulizar, their soothsayer, had called it.

He held up a hand to his temple. There was no soreness, blood, nor bruise.

Evidently, Aurora hadn't noticed his little episode. She simply trotted ahead, her jet hair and cloak granting her an otherworldly charm.

Stormbright said little for the rest of the journey. Before the sorcerer fully processed what happened, they were riding together underneath thick stone walls. The ruckus and clamor of city life returned. Their horses cantered until they arrived at The Golden Leaf Inn—the raucous, two-storied tavern with shanty decor to match—where they stabled their mounts.

Stormbright and Aurora looked at one another, then Stormbright at the scenery around them.

"Where's Steel?" he asked.

"Perhaps he's inside." Aurora shrugged.

Entering the tavern, Stormbright's unease heightened. Perhaps he shouldn't have expected Steel to be drinking at a table or resting in their rented abode. A quick check of either made him worry so much that he almost trembled. Aurora must have recognized his dilemma, as she held his hand in hers.

"Don't worry. I shall have Ava and Ida search for his whereabouts. They are skilled in prophecy and the art of divination."

Her grip was firm, and thus he walked beside her, the dizziness affecting his ability to question such a statement. They entered the main den. Stormbright pictured how uncanny they must have appeared, battered and wounded from their earlier excursion; yet what few people he spotted paid them no mind. The tavern was quiet, deserted.

They proceeded to the bar's counter. There they were greeted by Galvos, the Golden Leaf's innkeeper and owner. The bald, stocky man regarded them with a raised eyebrow. "You look as if you've had a brush with death."

"I wouldn't say you're far off from the mark," said Stormbright. The youth held up his head as faintness stole over him.

"Is he all right?" queried the innkeeper.

"He will be fine." Aurora cast a sidelong look toward the man. The quiet lingered long enough for Stormbright to notice. The innkeeper smiled.

"So you've brought an initiate with you?"

She nodded.

"Is he your first?"

She said nothing.

"I see," he replied. "Follow me."

Stormbright wanted to decline, yet his senses were too addled—too numbed—for him to do much more than keep close to Aurora. The innkeeper guided them down a long set of stairs.

The storeroom proved deceptively small. Galvos, meanwhile, knelt as his hand slid underneath one of the kegs. A dull *click* met their ears, a section of the wall parting open.

"By the way," interjected Stormbright, "have you seen my brother? He should have arrived not long ago."

"Your brother?" The innkeeper shook his head.

Terror held Stormbright in a vise. He was close to protesting when Aurora stared at him, following with a kiss. The angle granted him a favorable view of her bosom. She pulled him forward, her eyes promising him everything. "Don't worry, Stormbright. We can learn about him below. Put your faith in us."

Stormbright didn't immediately respond. He had never felt so alive, but that didn't stop the sinking in his chest, nor the paroxysm that had taken hold.

The hidden doorway shut behind them. They were left in total darkness.

The young sorcerer saw only black shapes as he touched the cold stone, inhaling the musty stench that permeated the hallway. It was like he never left the Faunus' lair. He wondered if this wasn't some purgatory akin to what he had explored months prior—only instead of a realm filled with swirling vortices and man-faced lions, he was in a maze underground.

Stormbright was vaguely aware of Aurora rounding a corner; carefully, dumbly, he followed. The corridor opened in a vast glade, one larger than was possible. He could spot no ceiling, though the cold rays of moonlight nipped at his skin. The sensation brought forth goosebumps as he knew it wasn't real. These were not the moons casting their light upon him, nor was the space above the night sky.

They were underground. They *had* to be underground.

A long and narrow bridge lay ahead. Upon crossing, Stormbright made the unfortunate mistake of looking down. The stony precipice dropped below them, terminating in a vast body of water. He staggered, swayed, and almost fell. Aurora kept him steady, however. As she held his attention, he was compelled to follow or perish. To Stormbright, she was like the very apex of sensuality, of precarious lusts.

She led him to the opposite side, and so they walked atop a wide platform jutting from the abyss. Not a platform, but a tower. The obelisk must have acted as a spring, for many streams rushed over its edges, granting the site an elegant sort of beauty.

A low archway bade them welcome. The path wound upstream, converging on a dais which led to a ringed series of arches, all draped in silk and permeated with mist, lined to the brim with pillars.

Silhouettes danced between them. They were obscured, yet Stormbright heard their playfulness; men and women; singing and dancing; engaging in acts of love. The incense tingled at his nostrils, hinting at untold delights. The laughs and moans ebbed in volume. Shadows emerged, figures dressed in scanty garments; their hair was long and flowing—both the men and women—and decorated with moonflowers. The men exuded a raw might as their muscles rippled with each stride. Conversely, the ladies were voluptuous and elegant. A few women giggled upon sighting him.

Embarrassment stole over him. The carnal side of his brain told him this was an earthly paradise. But why did it feel so strange? So… wrong?

A series of steps carried him and Aurora to another dais. This level was arranged much the same as the first, giving the hideout an almost otherworldly quality with its silken decor. Aurora halted in front of him. Ahead, a fountain gushed with clear waters as it sluiced into many streams. Beyond the watery cascade, two faces pressed into the light, scintillating drapes. He had assumed them as statues until they moved. Stormbright turned to his flank, realizing the persons he espied earlier were gathering around him. He wished Serithas were with him. Serithas always knew what to do, how to behave.

He beheld the two who peered into the depths of his soul. Their eyes were deep silver, hair white as ivory. The twin heads sat on the same pair of shoulders, sharing a single set of arms and legs, as their hands cradled a swollen belly. Stormbright had never witnessed such a phenomenon. Despite their inherent beauty, there was an aspect of this conjoining that profoundly disturbed him. He suspected they were aware of this instinctual response, yet their smiles did not acknowledge the fact.

In either case, they were with child; and judging by the stomach's size and roundness, the time of birth was soon.

"Stormbright, I would like you to meet Ava and Ida. They are my mentors," said Aurora.

Stormbright made an effort to speak, though he could say nothing. The conjoined twins gazed with solemn countenance. Their feet padded softly along the cold stone.

"I see Aurora has brought with her a friend," spoke the head to Stormbright's right. This, as Aurora elaborated, was Ida.

"A most intriguing twist of Fate," said the other, whom he learned was the priestess Ava. Unlike her twin—who seemed immovable, unbreakable as solid steel—she eyed him affectionately. "The moons have granted us an initiate in our time of tribulation. Aurora," she purred, "do you possess the relic?"

"Indeed, Mothers, we hold one of the Moon Cups. The rest of us were slain by Ilgrathians, and the survivors were ambushed by nightmare-kin. If it wasn't for Stormbright, I wouldn't have lived to tell the tale."

"A tragedy," said Ida, cold and viperous. "Ilgrathié and Her matriarchs will be punished for what they've done. We shall tear out their hearts and drink their life essence. So it is written."

"So it is written!" The others chanted her words.

The knot in Stormbright's stomach twisted further. His balance swayed, vision blurring. Somehow, he steadied himself.

"And how did you encounter this new initiate?" inquired Ida, seemingly oblivious to the sorcerer's plight.

"Stormbright saved me when Vana and I were attacked by nightmare-kin. Vana didn't..." She stammered, struggling to speak.

"Go on, child."

"Vana didn't make it." Her hand squeezed Stormbright's. "He has decided to help us, both he and his brother. Mothers, this is Stormbright.

His brother's name is Steel. If all goes as I've hoped, we will soon have both Moon Cups within our grasp."

Ava considered the youth. A smirk played along her features. "Is that so?" she murmured. "Then let us pray for his safe return. Woe be to the downtrodden, and retribution to the Ilgrathian monsters!"

"Woe and retribution!" the initiates echoed.

"Hearken, one and all! Let us uncover the whereabouts of this Steel. Fellow brothers and sisters, they are invaluable allies to our cause. Hush! Hush!"

The throng of cultists did so, bowing their heads in silence. An alien aura swam around them. The sorcery held the crowd in a trance. It was the reverence these people had for their leaders—the joy and fanaticism.

They opened their eyes.

"Something is wrong," Ida said. "We cannot find this boy, the one you call Steel."

"What do you mean you cannot find him?" said Stormbright, his heartbeat rising.

"It's like he is closed off from us. We are sorry, Stormbright; normally this would not happen. Come the morrow, we shall send scouts to retrieve him."

Stormbright was beside himself. "Please… let me go after him. He's my brother. I love him, I-"

The numbness returned, dulling his senses until he was certain he would faint. Though he kept his footing, his legs threatened to give way. Why was his body not listening to him?

Ida raised an eyebrow. "You are unwell, Stormbright. Perhaps you should leave this duty to us."

"Yes," purred Ava, "you have done much for us already. Let us take care of you, dear child." Their arms raised in a benevolent gesture, beckoning him closer. He acquiesced, hearing the vague incantation muttered between their lips. They gently touched his face. The resulting sensation was wondrous; warmth coursed through his veins as his wounds knitted.

"I can't believe it," he said. "You can use healing magic."

"It's a miracle granted us by the Sacred Twins," Ida replied. "Now, the Moon Cup."

Aurora took a step forward as she produced the chalice. Its wondrous ivory and silver engravings shimmered in the pale light, coming from some nebulous area above. A hint of reluctance gripped Stormbright as she relinquished the relic.

"At last!" said Ava, her tone brimming with delight as they situated the chalice upon a stone altar. "Is there aught you desire? Name it and it will be yours!"

Stormbright swallowed; the initiates were ogling him uncomfortably—some showing desire, others curiosity.

"Well, there was one thing I wanted to know. My brother and I are searching for an astromancer."

Ida spoke, "And what would this astromancer's name be, exactly?"

"Aedas," he replied. "His name is Aedas."

"And would you have anything on your person that's connected to him?"

"I'm afraid not."

Her brow furrowed as one twin eyed the other. "Very well," said Ava, "a name will suffice for our purposes. The spell requires a blessing. Steel is related to you by blood, so finding him was a simple matter in theory. However, we must concentrate, invoke the power of the Sacred Twins!"

Their voices raised and spoke in unison. "Fellow brothers and sisters, sons and daughters of the Sacred Moons, join us as we discern the location of Aedas. Show us your dedication! Grant us the strength to look through our enemy's eyes!"

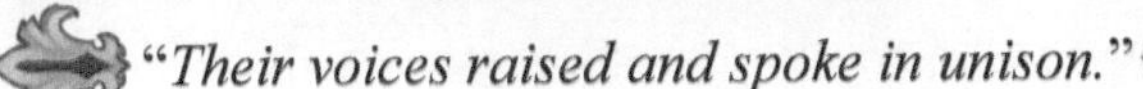

"Their voices raised and spoke in unison."

Around him, the cultists began to disrobe and embrace. Their lips met, breath increasing in tempo, bodies joining in a hundred acts of love. What started as warm moans became wild cries of ecstasy.

Stormbright held his head between his arms, trying to block out the sounds and smells and raw emotions. What sort of world had he stumbled into? Who could embrace such careless laughter, frolicking, and debauchery?

"Yes! We know you require blood!" exclaimed Ava. "Blood of the wretched and the impure! Blood will show us the path to its vessel, and brothers, and brothers' brothers! So it is written!"

"So it is written!" echoed Ida.

The throngs' lascivious moans intensified; Stormbright felt sick to his very core.

He stole a glance ahead. A fair, disheveled figure was taken before the conjoined sisters, wrists tied with hempen bonds. The Ilgrathian howled through his gag as he sweated profusely. His pleas went unheard as he was goaded towards the stone altar. Stormbright watched in terror as a serpentine dagger showed in the twins' hands. Ida gave a malicious smile. They held the weapon aloft in a gesture of supplication, an offering to the hidden Sacred Twins. The blade plunged downward. The Ilgrathian twisted woefully, blood streaming from his chest, his muffled voice echoing.

"Sacred Twins, we ask you accept this offering," said Ava. "We know you feed on the blood of those who've wronged us—killers, torturers, and defilers. Let this blood sustain you! Let it quicken your child who grows in our womb, so He might usher in a better world!"

It was in that frenzy, the blending of pleasure and sacrifice and pain, that the priestesses' irises turned white. Stormbright fell to his knees, almost retched. Was he in a nightmare? If not, then this was the threshold of some pleasure hell—a netherworld devised by mankind!

A hand grabbed him by the shoulder. With a flinch, Aurora brought him back to his feet. She hummed in a sensuous tone.

"What's wrong?" she asked seductively. "You seem tense, Stormbright."

"Please… I don't want-"

"I know exactly what you need," she said, giving a kiss and playfully biting at his lip. "Perhaps a moment alone would change your mind. You don't realize how much of a blessing you are to us. *We* need you. *I* need you."

Her hands interlocked with his, pulling him away from that scene of debauchery. The priestesses continued their chant as he and Aurora descended along a ramp curling around the tower, down into a lower corridor. The sounds of the ritual faded. He walked from one chamber to the next, too weak to protest.

They entered a room full of clouds of steam. Below them was a spring. Stormbright heard the running waters, felt the heat rising, threatening to calm his nerves. They were completely alone. What happened next was a blur; Aurora discarding her garments, revealing a voluptuous figure, flowing hair, and heaving breasts; Stormbright being undressed; and the warm rush of water as they entered. Perhaps it was the nature of the spring or the soothing effects of the water, but Stormbright did not feel quite as ill.

Still, he was on high alert. His experience in that other dimension, with the temptations from the manticore spirit, who had taken the guise of General Caerst to seduce him, flashed in his mind.

"What's wrong, Stormbright?" asked Aurora. She swam and held her naked form against his. Her breath was hot, arms wrapped around his neck so their foreheads touched. Her breasts pressed firmly as she spoke, "Is this not what you wanted? To *feel* my body against yours? To know what I can do to make you happy?" She kissed him intensely. Despite his better judgement, Stormbright reciprocated.

He eventually pushed her back, hands on her shoulders. "You did something to me," he stammered, "didn't you? I can't… I can't…"

"A minor narcotic," she said. "The potion I gave was a unique concoction made here in Candala. City prostitutes use it to loosen their clients' purse strings—make them agreeable. In your case," she reached down. He gasped lightly, "it was to calm you, prevent any altercations.

"You, Stormbright, you will be my first. Soon I will be an initiate no longer. I will be a true disciple of the moons for having known a man in Their name."

Her cheeks flushed warm as she kissed; hands caressing his arms. Her legs wrapped around him.

"You have no idea how much they mean to me. No idea how they cared for me when I was weak. Broken…" She breathed softly. "Stormbright."

"Aurora," he murmured. "Not like this."

"Stormbright…"

"No…"

A long pause went between them. She unfastened her grip. Water sloshed as she backed slightly. "I don't understand. I don't-"

He pushed her suddenly. "No!"

Aurora splashed into the waters, briefly submerging from the impact. She resurfaced; the glimmer of lust had left. What replaced it was genuine confusion.

No, it was fear.

"Not like this." He inhaled, his voice taking on an assertive inflection. "Not like this."

A scream resounded behind them. In the hallways, Stormbright heard some form of commotion. The sound was familiar—metal on metal. The echoes of crying cultists thrummed in his ears.

The Ilgrathians had arrived.

X

Captured

Steel saw little where he hung by his wrists. The cold metal chains kept him upright. The steady *drip drip* of water flowed in maddening repetition. This last fact was most aggregious, serving as a treacherous prelude for the real torture.

He would have to escape, no matter the cost.

Steel struggled to move himself. He wasn't sure how much time passed, for he caught not a glimpse of the sun or moon crossing the heavens, nor of Candala's wretched streets.

He grimaced. How he wished to reunite with Zolan! With any luck, his brother was staying safe.

Steel shifted underneath his manacles. His belongings had been confiscated, that much was clear, but perhaps he could discern some means of escape? He had lost his lockpicks among the chaos, so he would have to settle with an alternative. Maneuvering one hand with careful precision, he imagined it might slip through.

A door creaked open. Light spilled down a series of steps, illumining the stones at a far corner of the dungeon. A low *clack clack* reached his ears as three figures came to a halt. The first he realized was General Caerst, along with the one named Captain Helvia. The third silhouette grew clearer, forming a man with dark robes, ebon hair, and a rugged complexion.

His face lit up in surprise, a chuckle escaping his lips. It was Aedas! He had found Aedas!

Heat lanced up his stomach as the first punch landed. The city captain held up a hand, and the Falconer smirked.

"You are awake," said Captain Helvia. "And still you stink of the sewers. Tell me, Steel, how was it you managed to sneak your way into my estate?"

Steel did not answer.

She sighed. "I was afraid this would happen. Know that, for the moment, I will be kind, as this is my first question of many. But for your sake," she said, drawing a dagger, "it's in your best interest to comply."

She held the blade close to his cheek. Steel winced as the cold edge trailed along his skin, bringing a thin trickle of blood. His breath hitched in his throat.

"Oh? So this is what unnerves you?" She gave a devious smile. "I will be certain to remember. Interrogation is much like making love; with the proper amount of dedication, I can elicit the exact response I desire. You must understand time is something we cannot afford."

She took a single step back. "I shall give you two options. Either tell us what you know of your brother and these cultists, or subject yourself to unfathomable anguish. Our astromancer knows you have conspired with the Order of the Sacred Twins. Tell us their location, or you will suffer the consequences."

Steel lifted his head. A thousand emotions raged inside him— cooperation was not one of them.

"So it's going to be that way? Very well." She signaled the woman beside her, and General Caerst responded with another hit in the stomach. The force was incredible, enough to cause his body to shudder violently, vomit whatever food was left.

Helvia commanded her to stop.

"I'll ask again: *Where* is the cult?"

"Go fuck yourself," Steel replied.

So the torture went on. Caerst resumed at Helvia's discretion, as a rough series of bruises covered his chest. Each impact resounded deeply within. Every breath was made with horrible effort.

The Falconer ceased her pummeling.

"This is becoming tiresome," said Helvia. "Remember, Steel, that time is not on your side. We have a schedule to keep, and you are standing in our way." No response came. Evidently his resolve was true to his name, though it would mean little with time. With just the right application of heat and force, she mused, even the strongest steel could be broken.

Captain Helvia held up his left hand. She grabbed the middle finger for emphasis, and Steel experienced a rush of adrenaline once he sighted the small knife, holding its honed edge along his digit. He was breathing very fast. A sharp cry followed as the knife sliced along the skin, first in a gentle ring motion under the joint, then vertically up to the nail. The cuts were carefully practiced, made with nigh-surgical precision. Steel gritted his teeth. The worst came after she had sheathed her weapon, taking her fingers and prying underneath. The young thief writhed as Captain Helvia maintained complete control. It was like she had done this a thousand times in the past. The flesh parted. Torment and adrenaline pumped through his veins. Every second brought a tortured protest, until the skin was separated. He lifted his head in horror, his finger little more than blood-red muscle, bone, sinew, and a hint of a nail.

"Are you willing to tell us about the cult? Or should I let my friend join?"

Steel coughed and spit, shaking his head profusely.

"That was nothing," said General Caerst. "Allow me to deal with him."

With a hint of disappointment, Helvia retreated.

The anxiety returned as General Caerst drew closer. His rage ignited like a roaring flame. Holding the bloodied, mangled finger, her hot breath tingled along the unprotected flesh. His heartbeat quickened in terrible anticipation. The sensation was harrowing. She opened her mouth and bit down hard, warm blood rushing between her teeth, the bone crunching as it was severed.

A deafening scream resounded while she smiled, her teeth smattered with blood, as she spat the digit out to her side. His palm was stained red—so were her lips—yet he did not mutter a single word.

"How is that for getting him to talk?" said the Falconer.

"The execution is perhaps a little rough," Helvia noted Steel's torment, "but I think it's had some effect."

Helvia took charge by holding up his index finger, the panic filling him completely. The knife and flaying continued with excruciating slowness. A guttural wail emerged from the depths of his soul, echoing off the walls of the dungeon. Another series of questions followed, yet Steel doggedly refused to answer. General Caerst stepped forward a second time, biting off yet another finger. He thrashed and cursed.

Still, he would not relent.

Captain Helvia frowned.

"How intriguing," she said, gesturing for Caerst to halt what she was doing.

"Wait," said the Falconer. "He is nearly broken. With enough time, he will surely snap!"

"You underestimate his resolve, Falconer," said Captain Helvia, "and you forget time is short. The Order of the Sacred Twins is desperate; I can tell they are planning one final act against me. We cannot afford having him faint."

She gestured to Aedas. Feeling inside his pocket, he retrieved a stone that glowed with wondrous rainbow colors. Upon her insistence, the astromancer handed it over. The anger was apparent in the Falconer, whereas Aedas showed a degree of trepidation. Although Steel hardly saw it, as one eye had swelled up by this point, he could tell it was going to be bad.

"You heathen!" shouted General Caerst. "How dare you propose human magic!"

The city captain laughed. "Oh Caerst! How little you know of the world around you. Do not forget it was *you* who allowed demons to feast on your men. This is the perfect time to put hours of training to the test."

General Caerst glared at her, though she made no further attempt to challenge her comrade.

Captain Helvia brandished the gleaming stone. She saw a new terror manifesting within the prisoner, one not even General Caerst had provoked. It was obvious whatever tortures this Falconer might bring, he had witnessed it time and again.

The fear of sorcery, however, was a different matter.

She focused like the slave girl had taught her. Eventually, Steel was screaming, swinging back and forth as he struggled.

By the time his body convulsed she stopped. With muscles stretched far beyond their limits, he drew in ragged gasps.

Helvia sweated profusely, as utilizing the Dreamstone proved quite the strain. "Are you willing to talk?"

He coughed and heaved, but no more.

She grimaced. "Let us learn what happens when your bones are on fire."

Her words were not far from the truth. Excruciating flames spread along his nerves. The agony consumed his being. His vision swam, a sharp hum resounding in his ears.

He felt the Falconer grabbing him by the roots of his hair, holding his eyes up to hers.

"You will not pass out! Not here, thief! Not while you are under *my* control!"

He gave no response. Captain Helvia concentrated and thus his bones broke and mended. His anguish was palpable as she worked, bones writhing like jagged serpents in his body, enough so he was barely conscious.

Still, he refused to bend. Although his body withered under the assault, he held his tongue for his brother's sake.

"I have had enough of this!" said General Caerst. "Let me deal with him! I will make him talk!"

"No!" said Helvia. Beside her, she noted Aedas standing idly, his expression a mask of stone. "Perhaps, we could do with an astromancer."

Doubt stole over the man's complexion. Helvia studied him with suspicion. "Dredge up his memories, Aedas. Show him what we are capable of."

All eyes were on the astromancer. Steel sought the man in desperation, dreading what was to come.

Helvia's outstretched palm was reluctantly met by Aedas. Helvia shifted her gaze to General Caerst. "You as well, Falconer. You say you want the boy tortured, to exact your revenge? In that case, join hands with him and grasp the thief's head, and you will find your utmost wishes fulfilled."

General Caerst watched her and Steel. The thief's heart sank as a smile played along her lips.

"Please… no," he said.

"Oh, so now he speaks!" spoke Helvia. "Are you willing to tell us what we desire?"

Steel swallowed. He sweated profusely.

Helvia smirked, bidding her comrades proceed.

The astromancer's sorrow was evident as his pupils clouded a milky white. He clasped hands with the Falconer. She reached out and touched his forehead. Steel's vision went dark in an instant, any sense of his being in that dungeon a thing of the past. He was in a void. Kolthan, Zolan,

Kitala, those he loved, were in front of him. He witnessed their hopeless expressions, the emotional divide spanning between them. On some level he knew he had failed.

Steel cried as Kitala's head was crushed in front of him. Blood sprayed, brains scattering across the blank, featureless expanse in harsh streaks of red. The love of his life was gone in an instant. A bronze warhammer was lodged in her skull. A loud slopping came as the body fell, yet the weapon was suspended mid-air. Again Steel shouted, running toward the Islirian woman who had shown him so much affection. He held what was left of her in his arms, knowing she was truly dead. No star wraith would rise from her body, no chance at remembering herself.

General Caerst had taken that from him.

The others stared in horror. General Caerst's rage was a thing of monstrous proportion. Steel laid the dead thing that was Kitala to the ground. Tears blurred his vision as he drew his dagger. Somehow, the distance between them grew. Kolthan was next as the bronze hammer swung out and forward, landing directly in his chest. Bones broke, organs burst, as the giant coughed up blood and fell to the ground. The Falconer did not stop. She raised the hammer, each swing causing his father to appear less human.

"Brother, help! Our father is… is…" Zolan choked as he wept. The distance between them was so far. Steel fell to his knees, panting, his eyes bloodshot, mind overcome with feverish madness.

"Hang on, Zolan! Just hang on! Please… Calamtu, let him live. Let him live!"

General Caerst's footsteps rang loud and clear. Not this, he thought. Anything but this! Steel's one purpose—the boy he would do anything to care for, his twin half—clamored for his life. Serithas heard his innocent cries, his whimpering drawn into screams. He couldn't bear to look; the sound of it was horrible enough. All he heard was the gasping, choking, and silence.

It was over. His love, family, and life—it was all over.

He sobbed as the metallic boots came closer. He uncovered his face. General Caerst held his brother's mangled head, fingers gripping the long hairs so it dangled in sickening display. She smiled. "That was just the beginning," she said.

She tossed the head away. Serithas felt his own head being lifted.

"Give them back," he said.

"On the contrary, I have so much more to take from you."

She shoved him onto his back. Tossing the weapon aside, her hands squeezed along his throat. He could only struggle as his adversary choked the life out of him. Steel was powerless against her. The torture commenced as he roamed the edges of oblivion. The demoniac eyes pierced his soul, feeling along every scar, every past experience with its sickening presence.

Something inside of him snapped as he laughed and wheezed, spending the last of his defiance with a strained effort. So this was reality! This was unavoidable! His body no longer thrashed against his constraints. He was Madness itself! He was the object of chaos—revenge—conquest.

He was nothing.

Above the hellish din came a voice, loud and clear and feminine. "Submit," it said. "All you need to say is one simple thing, and it will be over."

Golden.

He laughed, he wept. Of course, none of it mattered. What was it he was hiding? It was such a small thing, he mused. So insignificant.

Golden Leaf.

The torment, the screams of his loved ones, his looming demise, they were gone at once. He was suspended by chains, his one hand a bloody mess. Before him stood Captain Helvia and General Caerst, a wide smirk spread across the latter. Aedas, by contrast, appeared shaken to his very core.

"Say it." Captain Helvia faced him.

"They're… They're at the Golden Leaf Inn," he said.

"Very good!" exclaimed Captain Helvia. "That is where we will begin our search. And how were you able to sneak into my manor?"

"There was a secret entrance," he panted. "One leading in through the sewers."

Captain Helvia frowned. "Very well. I will have to instruct my guard to search for where he entered. That is a later discussion." She stepped up the stairs. Aedas cast one final glance at Steel before following, regarding the young boy he had helped to break.

However, General Caerst remained close.

"I will be back for you later," she said, grabbing the area between his thighs. She squeezed hard, enough for it to hurt. "Take care, Steel, and remember what I've done for you. What I will do to you in time."

She released her hold and pummeled him twice—once across the cheek and another in the stomach.

"Falconer! Enough with the prisoner!"

Showing her reluctance, she stepped away while Steel spat out a tooth.

White hot flames coursed through his stomach, welling up in his chest and throat. Steel sobbed and hung his head, realizing what he had done to his brother, how he betrayed him.

"Stormbright—I'm sorry. I'm so sorry…"

Darkness enveloped him as the door shut.

XI

Raiders in the Dark

By the time Stormbright rose to his feet, the battlecries were too much to ignore. They were still naked. His head reeled from the poison, and though he stood upright, he was terribly nauseous.

"We have to get out of here!" Aurora slipped into her old clothes as she spoke. "I don't know how, but the Ilgrathians found us. Please, Stormbright..." She held his attention while helping him dress.

"What about Serithas?" he asked absently.

"There is no time," she said, handing him a small vial. "The poison was bound to wear off in a few hours. This should dilute its effects."

Stormbright hesitated as he held the vial and its mysterious contents. He eyed her with utmost suspicion. "Are you sure this won't do anything to me?"

Aurora nodded sincerely, or so he thought amidst his drugged haze.

He still didn't trust her; that had gone to the wayside after what he experienced. With a glower he tossed the vial, allowing it to splash in the waters.

"I don't believe you," he said, ignoring Aurora's cries of protest. His head grew marginally clearer. He donned his shirt and trousers, buckled his sword up by the hip.

Aurora followed him, much to his chagrin. As for preparedness, he was right on time. Down the hallway ran two Ilgrathian guards, armored from head to toe. Stormbright was quick to attack, despite his weariness. He channeled magic into his fingers. Lightning streaked, causing them to smolder inside their armor. The sorcerer dropped to the floor in a stupor.

Steel's absence flickered in the back of his mind. Stormbright shivered at the possible link between these two events. What had they done to his brother to extract their location?

Stormbright tried not to dwell on it. If he managed to survive this, he would have to investigate further—to find his brother.

He prayed Steel wasn't dead—or worse.

"Are you all right?" Aurora knelt beside him.

Stormbright was tempted to answer this question with one of his own, such as why was she helping him? How was she so tolerant of the Order of the Sacred Twins, who reveled in such degeneracy and sacrifice?

His hatred brought him to stand, the knowledge of what she tried and failed to accomplish fueling his resolve.

"Stay away from me," he said.

"I'm sorry, Stormbright, for getting you into this mess. You may resent me for it, but we need to work together if we hope to survive."

Stormbright glared at her intensely. As much as he wanted to flee from her and this abhorrent den, he couldn't deny the truth in her words.

The roars of battle echoed. Feeling more in control, Stormbright wearily ventured through winding halls, back to the entrance along the tower's side. Both sorcerer and initiate began their ascent. Ahead, an Ilgrathian was subduing a pair of cultists. Stormbright drew his blade, clumsily stabbing at the guard. The man gurgled and bled, perishing as the sword plunged through the neck.

A dozen battles had broken out from the initial assault. Guards and cultists were obscured by draping silks. Shadows slew one another as Stormbright and Aurora ran by. Shrouded blades rose and fell, blood splashed, and voices howled and choked. Traces of copper wafted in the air. Countless corpses must have surrounded them. Among the pandemonium, Stormbright was certain of one thing—those who hadn't died were fleeing, and the Ilgrathians made swift pursuit.

Ahead, Stormbright and Aurora beheld the conjoined twins lying near the blood-stained altar, with a few wounds for good measure. They cradled the sacred Moon Cup. A dozen cultist and Ilgrathian corpses surrounded them, as well as the one captive they had sacrificed earlier.

From behind charged a pair of attackers, thirsting for blood. The two Ilgrathians froze when lightning enveloped their forms, causing their skin to crackle and break as they fell. Stormbright collected himself, his body weak from the poison and his use of magic.

"You should have left us, child," said Ida.

"Don't worry, mothers. You're safe." Aurora helped the priestesses to their feet. "We need to escape from these devils."

"Then we must head towards the docks."

To Stormbright's surprise, they were perfectly calm and collected.

Heedless of this fact, Aurora stepped alongside them. She grabbed Stormbright's hand, leading him back to the ramp. The massacre was all-encompassing. Among the corpses stood an armor-clad figure, one who had dogged the brothers' every move from the start.

It was the Falconer, General Caerst.

As if out of instinct, she turned squarely in his direction. Her bloodlust was evident. One of the zealots thrust at her with a poniard. The Falconer retaliated with ease, batting aside the blade and piercing through with her rapier. Her opponent went limp in her arms. She discarded the corpse as blood pooled underneath. As she raced towards him, murder pulsing in her veins, Stormbright raised his hands. Lightning arced as General Caerst shuddered. She stood rigid, her head thrown back in torment.

As the magic abated, he fell to his knees. Ragged air tore through his lungs. He cursed with what little breath he could spare. Although she was wounded from his onslaught, somehow she was conscious.

Aurora pulled him into a hall off the main level. The path's downward angle was steep. The twins gained distance ahead of them, the Moon Cup held tight.

"Go!" said Aurora. "We will catch up with you shortly." The underground docks loomed below. Worshippers were gathered along a dozen-or-so rowing vessels, each made to fit around four people. Candala's vast subterranean expanse loomed around them, though its oppressive nature was forgotten; the chaos of battle was too fervent. Over half their number escaped by the time Ava and Ida arrived, being ushered into a boat as it swiftly departed.

Very few were moored when Stormbright and Aurora caught up. Footsteps echoed behind until two soldiers faced them directly. The Ilgrathians brandished steel claymores, with the blades reaching much further than the usual shortsword.

Stormbright channeled for the fourth time, the magic connecting with one of the blades. Flesh seared and blackened in an instant. By the time the sorcerer took another breath, his enemy was on the ground. A horrible odor made him cough and shudder. He realized that his magic had dispatched but one of his foes. An incredible force collided with his temple. In an instant he fell, his vision going dark.

Aurora witnessed the guard striking with the pommel of his blade—a desperate maneuver in its own right, as movement was limited. The Ilgrathian smiled wickedly. Raising his claymore in a swinging arc, a blade interrupted the killing blow. The retaliating initiate was jet-haired, strong, and athletic, showing a grim countenance as he parried. He knocked the guard off-balance. Before the assailant could recover, however, his disembodied head rolled along the dock.

Aurora, Stormbright, and the initiate were alone.

"We must go," said the man, his words registering in a deep, guttural tone. He indicated the Ilgrathians who were swiftly approaching.

The man carried Stormbright onto one of the boats. The vessel rocked and swayed; they heard the waters sloshing underneath. Aurora held a dagger and cut the rope. The stream swiftly took them in its current, drawing them from that lonesome tower.

The din of battle vanished. Aurora mourned for their lost home, the reclaimed tower which belonged to them no longer—the one sanctuary in the dark days of her life. A lone figure, hazy and too far to make out, proceeded to the dock's edge. A sharp roar thundered in the air. If anyone was capable of such rage, Aurora conjectured, it was the woman she espied earlier, the same who sought them with such anger and wanton bloodshed. She did not know her name, but Aurora was certain the Ilgrathian loathed them.

Perhaps she was hunting Stormbright?

The idea lingered. Aurora and the initiate, whom she knew as Berrin, peered across the waters. She kept a lookout whilst the latter took control of the oar, steering their course.

"There's no sign of the others," she said.

"Nor can I hear anything coming from up ahead." Berrin squinted his eyes. "This doesn't bode well for us, Initiate."

Aurora peered down, seeing that Stormbright had sustained a nasty bruise along his head. She knelt and lightly rubbed his temple.

"I'm sorry," she muttered softly. "I didn't want it to end like this. I'm-"

A splash erupted in front of them. Aurora gawked in confusion. She saw little as the shadows made her skin crawl. Other splashes followed. Out across the waters, shrouded in darkness, she heard the screams of her fellow cultists.

"Sacred Twins! What is happening?"

"I'm not sure," said Berrin.

The noise came again. Aurora spotted a globule of mud slithering beside them. No, it was something else.

"Nightmare-kin!"

The amorphous body slid up the side of their vessel. A blade hissed as Berrin slashed with his sword. The monstrosity went limp, drifting further downstream. Terror held her in a vise. More of the things emerged. Aurora shook Stormbright as he stirred slightly.

"Get up! Get up!"

"What's happening?" he mumbled.

Suddenly, one of the hideous things latched onto her side. Acid spread as the monstrosity sought to devour.

Her screams stopped, however, as Stormbright reacted, clumsily unsheathing his blade and stabbing upward. There came a sharp squeal and a torrent of black blood. The thing sloughed, and so she kicked it into the canal.

"Are you okay?" he asked weakly.

"I'm all right."

Around them the nightmare-kin swarmed in greater numbers, their viscous bodies floating among the foul waters. The youth panted heavily as he swung his shortsword. The results were more sluggish than he hoped. Even if he had the energy to deliver a bolt of lightning, he knew the risk was high. Beside him Aurora struck with her blade. Often the aberrations would reform, devouring their dead in an effort to grow in size, but a second or third strike put an end to it.

A shout grabbed their attention. From behind, Aurora saw Berrin, the initiate who saved them, was swarmed by a dozen nightmare-kin. The amorphous bodies swelled and pulsated. One had already covered his head, stifling his cries.

Stormbright hacked at the things. The monsters fell away as Aurora gasped. The young sorcerer grimaced. What was left of the cultist was indeed a grisly sight.

"Where do we get off?" he asked, frowning as he pushed the man's remains into the waters. He had barely done so when a pair of nightmare-kin swarmed over the corpse, dragging it into the depths. Stormbright hadn't known the man, yet he felt sorrow for one to perish in such fashion.

"There should be a dock around here somewhere. I've heard it leads outside Candala." She winced, glancing around their vessel. The realization hit her. "The oar! It must have sunk when we were attacked!"

"Surely we can use something else to steer," said Stormbright.

His heart sank once the peals of crashing water reached his ears. Turning, they realized the canal led into a great fall. How such a drop was possible this far down was beyond him. He suspected if there was a dock, they had well missed it by this point.

He chuckled at their situation and its cruel irony. All that struggle and desperation, just for it to end this way.

Amidst their dire situation, Aurora kept a short distance between them, perhaps as a token of respect. "I'm sorry, Stormbright."

They said little else before falling into the abyss.

"No! They will not escape me!"

General Caerst felt along her side, her palm caked in red. She grimaced, unwilling to give up. The enemy was so close!

She stabbed through an initiate who blocked her path, and so the Falconer limped to the docks. The boats were gone. There was only the faint outline of two cultists and… Stormbright! She stopped at the edge, giving an enraged, guttural cry.

General Caerst wavered as the pain grew, her legs buckling.

"No…"

By the time General Caerst recovered, seating herself along the tower's cool stone wall, Captain Helvia and the astromancer emerged into view.

"It appears the den of heathens has been cleared," she said. "However, our mission is not over. Those slut priestesses have eluded us."

The Falconer rose, head swimming from her injuries. "We will make haste," she said. "We must pursue them at once!"

Helvia raised an eyebrow. "We are far ahead of you."

Their men carried half-a-dozen boats, enough to ferry most of them down the waterway. Each ship was supported by six men to a vessel, each working as if possessed.

The Falconer was about to follow when Helvia raised up her hand.

"Do not worry," she said. "I shall pursue them while you get some rest. Those wounds look like they could kill a man."

"They are nothing," she replied. "Please, let me fight!"

"I see what our scholars mean when they talk of Falconers and their unusual resilience. Nonetheless, you will need to dress your wounds and regroup with your men. Aedas will stay behind and help you."

"But they are getting away. We nearly have them!"

"So it may seem, but you are not aware of how cunning they can be." She gestured to Aedas, who pulled the Dreamstone from his pocket. The material glittered in the darkness. "Picture, if you would, what this magic is capable of; how dangerous it can be in the wrong hands. What's worse, imagine they are skilled in the art of oneiromancy. It's a process that takes years, perhaps decades, before one can change reality on a whim. *They* do not require such trinkets as Dreamstone. All they need is to channel, and wondrous things happen."

General Caerst was about to respond, but she stopped. Despite her efforts to soldier on and fight, to resist this woman who held her by an invisible leash, she couldn't deny Helvia's words made sense.

"I know what you think of my methods," Captain Helvia continued. "Perhaps this is heathen magic, yet if we are to catch our foes, we must understand it. With our combined numbers and cunning we can flank them, make certain this never happens again."

General Caerst remained silent.

"I know you want to pursue them," Helvia smiled. "Do not worry—your time for revenge will come soon enough."

She gazed toward the docks. The boats were situated.

"My men and I shall make haste and pursue them. In the meantime," Captain Helvia glared at her, "you will stay here. Is that understood?"

The Falconer gritted her teeth, her jaw setting, as her temples pounded and ached.

Blood boiled in her veins.

She said nothing.

"You and Aedas will meet me at The Silver Hearth Inn in three days. Time is running out, but perhaps we can rally our forces and destroy them."

The captain of the city guard gestured to her subordinates, black hair flowing as she boarded the boats with her two-dozen guards.

General Caerst and Aedas watched her departure. Her fury faded. What took its place was intense resignation, that her strength was spent and still she failed.

A hand gripped her by the shoulder. She knew it was the astromancer.

"Do not touch me." She shrugged him away, knowing it was his duty to keep watch.

"If it means anything," said the astromancer, "there is a bathhouse where you may treat your wounds."

Aedas indicated her to follow, and she showed little in the way of resisting. Pacing along the circling walkway and underneath a low entrance, they happened upon a room that was warm and inviting, almost enchanting.

"Get some rest," he said. "I shall inform your soldiers."

The Falconer placed her armor at the pillar's base. Her burns were less grievous than she feared, the reddened patches streaking above her right arm. The fabric was tattered and stained in red, though she stripped with no less gracefulness.

Indeed, one had to observe closely to realize she was wounded.

That changed, however, when she descended into the warm waters. General Caerst hissed, giving a long exhale as her wounds were submerged.

"You have done much today," said Aedas. General Caerst held up her hand, bidding him to silence.

The astromancer produced a suture kit from his cloak, placing it at the pool's edge.

Gently, she stretched out her fingers.

"What am I to do, Aedas?"

"The answer is simple," he replied. "It is your duty to follow orders."

She chuckled. "So that's what this is about. I should obey like a good soldier, even when my life is forfeit and my career is ruined."

No answer.

She waved. "Leave me. My men are likely drinking and whoring as we speak. Someone needs to put them to good use."

The astromancer faltered. Evidently, he noticed her frown.

"Are you sure this is the path you want to take? Do you truly wish revenge against two young boys?"

"Yes," she replied coolly. "I am as good as dead either way. They took everything from me. Ere the end, they will know what it means to cross a Falconer."

"Perhaps," he murmured, turning quietly as she relaxed, the mists of the chamber obscuring the distance between them.

XII
Old Ghosts

Steel awoke to the sound of dripping water—a low ponderous echo filling the dungeon with its sorrowful song. His hand burned with the two fingers missing; a peculiar itching developed over the last few hours, as well as a slight fever. The bruises across his chest and stomach were so severe that it hurt for him to move. However, his misery no longer mattered. What replaced it was hollowness, a notion he was falling deeper into the abyss.

It was like he had never left the Slave Pits.

Steel hardly felt his limbs, but even if he had, was there any purpose in using them? He had betrayed his brother and allowed Stormbright to be targeted for the exact same treatment—this hellish existence.

No, there was no point to it. Not anymore.

"Please, God—Calamtu—whoever will listen—just let me die. Let me die."

A door opened. His heart pounded as light spilled over the stairs. Two pairs of feet wandered down. One figure was swathed in a dark robe, a grim countenance surrounding it. He saw Kitala, his love, standing beside this foreboding presence. The light danced along her grayish skin, lighting her blackened hair like a smoldering ebony fire. It was strange she appeared as such, no longer being a star wraith.

To his surprise, she held a bucket full of water. Setting it before him, she soaked a dainty wash cloth. The wet fabric soothed his bruised flesh. It was cool to the touch.

He was about to open his mouth, to ask how Kitala was alive and why she was treating him in such a peculiar manner. The shadowy figure slouched. Kitala stepped back. With it, her form shifted; in lieu of his beloved, she became a girl with auburn curls. She was light-skinned, with a dainty robe covering her body from head to toe. There was that same spark in her eyes, yet it shone as a dull azure.

The thief lashed at his torturer.

The man did not flinch, however, as he knelt, uncorking a vial.

"Kill me," said Steel, his speech broken. "Get it over with."

The girl stared at him. To his astonishment, her aspect wasn't fearful or worrying, but instead a blank mask. It meant nothing, he reassured himself.

"Kill me," he sobbed.

"Very well," replied the larger figure in a deep, melodic voice.

A potion was held to his lips and he drank. So this was it. This was how his life would end. The numbness followed and, as his eyes shut closed, he caught a brief glimpse of wondrous colors, of a small stone being held by the embodiment of death.

Then he was in a formless, yawning abyss. The Great Beyond, he thought absently. Perhaps by some miracle he would happen upon the heavenly realms with their marble structures, crystalline skies, and boundless valleys full of fruits and life and joy. Most likely, however, he would find himself in the lower hells, a suitable punishment for betraying his lifeblood and kin. He had broken at that pivotal moment, and now his soul would pay the eternal price.

The dream faded as he awoke. Steel realized he was lying on his back, and that Aedas stood over him. His body was wrapped in bandages. The young thief raised his left hand, seeing it had been treated as well. To his shock, both his middle and index fingers were present. Had that also been a cruel dream?

A ghostly pain lingered whilst he stretched them, a sensation that the fingers he possessed were not his own.

He lifted his head, and Aedas regarded him with melancholy. Kitala, or at least the apparition of her, was no longer there.

"Have I gone insane?" Steel asked.

"Not exactly," replied the astromancer. "I used the Dreamstone to heal most of your wounds, including your fingers. If we had the time, I could have mended you completely." He cocked an eyebrow. "How do you feel?"

"You lied to me."

"You were delirious," said the astromancer. "Hallucinating as well, from what I witnessed."

"And the woman… Was she someone I imagined?"

The astromancer shook his head. "She is one of Helvia's servants. Once I had arrived, I was offered her help by the other serving maids. Evidently she is well-renowned for tending to Helvia's prisoners."

"Why would she tend to me? I'm the enemy. Captain Helvia wishes me ruined."

"She is… unique."

Steel pushed himself up with his arms; however, they buckled under their own weight. Aedas supported him, bringing the thief to a sitting position.

"Drink this." The astromancer held a cup of clear water. "Take small sips."

He did so, the cool water filtering between cracked lips. Though the water was stale, to him it tasted like ambrosia.

"I'm sorry for having done this to you," said Aedas. "None of it was meant to happen. It was my fault you had no means of finding me. Perhaps

I harbored doubts that the two of you would survive and cross to the enemy side. Possibly, after years of scheming, I had misjudged my allies."

"But you were a part of it. You did this to me."

Aedas breathed in. "I was given little choice. But you are right—this *is* my fault. I cannot mend things as they are, but know that I have Kolthan with me. He is unharmed."

"Father? He is with you?!"

Aedas waved a hand dismissively. "Not here. He is north of the city, in a village called Shadevale. He's in disguise, though he is safe."

Steel lowered his head, relief rushing over him. After what he had been through, he hadn't expected Aedas to bring their father along with him. He thought it impossible, though somehow the astromancer had found a way.

"I can't believe it," he said.

"And that is why you must escape," Aedas said. "I'm recalling as many of the guards as I can. Captain Helvia and General Caerst are amassing their forces to hunt down the Order of the Sacred Twins. They will strike soon. I know this for certain."

The thief was dismayed. "And my brother?"

"Gone, I'm afraid. I presume he's escaped with the other cultists. It's not a perfect solution, and there is no guarantee he isn't still in danger, but at least he is outside of the Ilgrathians' control."

Steel was relieved until remembering what he had done. He grimaced, drew in air between his teeth.

"There was nothing you could have done." Aedas gripped him by the shoulder.

"You're wrong," he replied.

The astromancer raised his eyebrows. "In either case, you must leave. Do you understand?"

Steel nodded.

"It is early in the morning. Although your peril is great, there are yet good omens for you. You must come to The Silver Hearth Inn by dusk three days from now. I will tell you what I know once there. You must stay hidden—do not meet me directly. I can promise you will find a means to save your brother, and your father. This I know."

Aedas handed him two vials. They were filled with a liquid not unlike the water he had drunk, yet he suspected a hidden medicinal quality. "Drink one to numb your injuries. Traveling through the sewers will prove difficult."

"But the Moon Cup..."

"Forget the Moon Cup. The cultists have your brother, and I fear he has been taken hostage. If my knowledge is anything to go by, these people have a habit of ensnaring young men. Some are sacrificed while others are seduced into joining their order. If Stormbright is with them, I imagine something of the sort must have happened."

"You don't get it," said Steel. "If we can't rescue my brother, we may need an alternative. A stratagem will give us leverage."

"You would be unwise to do such a foolish thing." Aedas leaned forward. "Focus on escape and leave the risks to me. I am capable of that much, at least."

Aedas turned to leave. The door narrowed until it shut. Steel was left alone, holding the vials of medicine in his palm.

"I'm sorry, Zolan," he said. "If you're alive, just hang on. I'll be there for you soon. You as well, Father."

He shifted to his feet, the hours of sustained torture aching through his body. Moving his arms and legs proved a significant effort. He considered the medicine he held, shrugged, and downed the elixir in a few gulps. As the minutes passed, his senses numbed. He was a little stiff, though he could at least limp forward.

Pocketing the other vial, he carefully crept up the stairs into a low-lit hall. As Aedas told him, this floor seemed empty enough. In fact, the area was much like the temple he had found. He imagined it was a straight enough shot to make it to the underground sanctuary, the hidden passageway, and finally the sewers.

He drifted to the shadows, staying careful so he wouldn't be spotted. A dark corner; the underbelly of a staircase; behind tables and low-standing shelves—these he utilized as he skulked. Only after spotting a few drunken guards did he quicken his pace.

Steel knew what was likely to happen if he was recaptured by Helvia's guards, and the idea of what he might divulge, about Aedas and Father, made him shudder. He dearly wished to be free of this place, whatever the cost.

At once he detected a pair of guards closing in from behind, their voices rounding a nearby corner. He heard another group walking in from the same direction as the cellar.

The remaining option was a stair spiraling ahead. Ignoring his better judgment, he circled up and around, arriving at the same floor he had explored previously—the same as the vault. Several doors lay situated along either side. To his dismay, he heard the clatter of footsteps coming up from the staircase behind him. Steel cursed, slipping through the closest door. He held his breath, locking every muscle in frightful anticipation. The seconds trickled by until the noise grew distant.

He relaxed, half-leaning on the doors. Lit braziers illuminated the area in warm incandescence. He spotted dozens of bodies around him, lounging as if they were asleep. They were decked in naught but jewels, women and men who dozed without a care in the world. It was obvious Steel had happened upon Captain Helvia's pleasure chamber, and what was worse, they were human. The implication filled him with nausea and anger.

He was about to leave until a girl lifted her head. Surprisingly enough, she was the same who had dressed his wounds earlier; the one he imagined, amidst his tortured hallucinations, was Kitala. His eyes widened. She did not seem afraid but, rather, curious. Her movements were lithe and graceful, much like a feline. Long auburn locks flowed akin to ribbons. The thief heard nothing.

"You should not be here," she whispered.

Steel spoke at a similar volume. "Trust me, I was just leaving."

"I knew there was something about you." She took a careful step forward. "I can tell you're a thief." She gave a wide smirk.

"No no. I'm only here to…"

"You're here to escape," she said. "I heard Captain Helvia speaking of you earlier." Her voice took on a lower pitch as she spoke cautiously. "You were the one who tried raiding the vault. Weren't you?"

"Well… I-"

She held up a finger to his lips, indicating the sleeping concubines. Her tone was aloof. "I know where Captain Helvia keeps the key. If I show you, would you help me escape?"

Steel paused, the fear of being caught ever-present. It made sense to retrieve the Moon Cup while he was up here. Judging by how she acted around him, this girl didn't seem the type to align herself with Helvia. He sensed a strangeness in her tone, though she did not sound malicious, nor did he think her as disingenuous.

"All right," he said. "You have a deal."

"Follow me," she replied, moving before he had time to react.

"But, what about the-"

"The guards? Don't worry, it will be fine. I've wandered these halls many a night without being sighted. Helvia's men don't come up here in too great a number." She flitted past him, opening the door and checking if anyone else was close. "Captain Helvia's chambers are nearby. I've been inside many times, so I know it like the back of my hand."

The halls were barren. The thief stood vigilant as the girl strode casually, rounding two corners, and stopping along a door to their left. Steel realized it was locked.

The slave girl showed little sign of worry. Pressing her palm against the lock, a low click resounded. The door opened wide.

"What in the…" Steel remarked, utterly bewildered.

"I'm an oneiromancer," she said, noting Steel's surprise, "although I'm not a very good one. Simple locks are a trifle for me to break. I'm not quite so confident with the more complex ones, however."

"Which means you can't break the vault."

"That is true," she said. "The key is in here, though."

"Why are you helping me?" he asked. The room was an assortment of chests and containers, with a desk and chair situated at one end of the chamber. A large bed sat along the opposite side.

"Why? I'm not sure of the why, or when, or how—I merely wish to leave. I was sold and bought by Captain Helvia, and once she learned of my talents, I taught her the fundamentals of what I know. But as for why I want to leave the manor? You could say I hate living as a concubine, despise being a means for satiating one's knowledge and lust. That is what most women would say. As for me, truthfully?" She shrugged. "Perhaps I am simply bored."

"You really are strange," said Steel.

"To survive in a place like this," she ran her fingers along the shelves of books and scrolls, "I suppose I have to be. The name is Mikka, in case you were wondering."

"Steel," he replied, as he joined in searching the room.

"That's a peculiar name."

"That's because I chose it." He stopped at a rather large storage chest. Opening it, he found an assortment of clothes, books, and scrolls. Alas, his armor and belongings were not among its contents, nor anywhere else in the room. He cursed.

Taking one set of clothes, he changed as quickly as he could. The garments weren't a perfect fit, being a simple pair of trousers and a fine linen shirt, but any disguise would have to do. He realized Mikka was preoccupied along the one shelf. By the time he finished, her finger pointed five rows from the bottom. She pulled out a large tome and began leafing through. She stopped, holding up a key.

"*The Natural and Unnatural Properties of Dreamstone.*" She smirked. "Captain Helvia, you are awfully predictable."

Soon afterward, they arrived at the doorway. Steel held up his hand.

"What's wrong?" Mikka asked.

"Stay here until I'm back. The last time I snuck through this way, guards were swarming the halls."

"Don't worry, I'm a familiar face to them."

"Are you sure they won't be suspicious of you loitering around the vault? Besides, it will be much quieter if I'm sneaking around."

"I disagree. You're in no condition to be risking your life. On the other hand, I have lived here for some time. Allow me to fetch it."

Steel eyed her reluctantly.

Mikka moved towards the edge of the doorway, redirecting her attention. "Do not worry. I'll be back soon."

The door shut in front of him. Steel turned the lock, pressing against it for good measure. Inspecting his surroundings, he seized a lone candelabrum, should worse come to worst. Steel grabbed the object, holding it to his chest as he waited. There was no telling how long his mind raced with the possibilities, all the worst-case scenarios appearing as matter of fact.

A knock sounded. Steel warily peered through the keyhole, seeing it was only Mikka. To his amazement, she held the silver Moon Cup, along with a few pouches bulging with gold and gems.

He slowly undid the lock, keeping the candelabrum close should he need it. He opened the door and looked to either side.

"Were you followed?" he asked.

Mikka shook her head. "At this time, guards are usually in their barracks or on the first floor."

"I see you helped yourself to some valuables."

Mikka gave a playful smile. "Consider it as payment for me helping you."

"All right then," said Steel. "We make our way to the cellar. Is that understood?"

"It is," she said, glancing at his improvised weapon.

"It was just a precaution. I didn't know if I could trust you."

She shrugged. Steel might have questioned her response if he wasn't so intent on leaving. He strode carefully, his muscles protesting with each step.

Steel halted, raising his blunt weapon almost instinctively. He wasn't sure why, as he saw and heard nothing. He turned to Mikka.

"What is it?" she asked, confused.

"Didn't you feel something? It was like a shadow passed us."

She remained motionless. A hint of uneasiness colored her cheeks.

He considered their options, but determined there was nothing for it. The thief crept with Mikka close behind. It was subtle, but the oppression of Helvia Manor eroded their resolve. Passing each corridor, they expected a pair of eyes. For every stair they descended, they braced themselves for a group of guards.

It was difficult to tell how long they trudged on, paranoid as to whom or what was watching them. The only constant was growing terror, a burning desire to flee this wretched manse.

At long last, they descended along a stairway which, Steel knew, led into the cellar. The guards had thankfully cleared the area after Steel's close call. His grip was firm, guiding her carefully to ensure they were hidden. Mikka tugged at his arm until they slowed.

"What's wrong?" asked Steel.

Mikka shrugged in reply. "I just have an awful feeling."

"So do I," he admitted. "Don't worry. So long as we take special care to avoid the guards, we-"

"It's not the guards," she interjected, her voice lowering to a whisper. She spoke carefully. "There's a legend of a spirit who haunts these parts. No one's truly seen it, but we've heard sounds at night coming from around the cellar. Captain Helvia believes it is merely superstition, yet we servants know better."

"And what is this 'spirit'?"

Mikka swallowed, her words low and quivering. "Once, a priest beseeched the Sacred Moons when Candala was invaded, almost fifty years ago. In desperation, the holy man begged and pleaded that the conquering Ilgrathians be cursed. They say since, he skulks and haunts the living at night." She shivered where she stood.

"Have you seen anything?"

"No, but servants have gone missing." She kept close to him, at which Steel politely pushed her back.

"I know you're scared, but there's nothing to fear. You and I are fairly capable, so let's focus on getting ourselves out of here."

Mikka nodded. She appeared to suppress some emotion, although she did not speak of it. Steel trudged on as she remained at his side. He could almost hear the rapid beating of her heart.

She halted. Her insistence was enough to take Steel off-guard.

"Come on, we're almost out," he said. "Just a little farther."

"Do we have to go through there?"

"If we want to escape. Why? What's wrong?"

"It's just an impression I've had for some time. It's as if we're being watched."

"It's all right," he said, "you have me with you. We should leave before anyone catches us."

The darkness loomed like an omnipresent force. They moved on; on through the large sacrificial chamber; on past winding corridors that

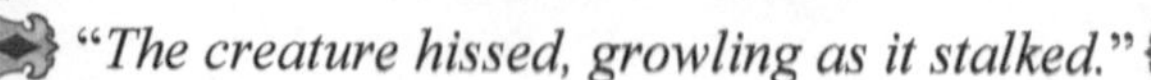

"The creature hissed, growling as it stalked."

pressed on their sides, reminding them of stories concerning the mighty boa constrictor and how it crushed the human body; on until the secret passage lay to their right. The female statue stared solemnly. Steel pushed against it, but it did not give. He pressed once more, shoving with his entire weight.

Steel felt another tug at his arm. Mikka trembled. With a shaking hand, she pointed to where they had come from.

Hairs raised on his neck. From the gloom, rheumy eyes peered through the shadows. Neither Steel nor Mikka had to guess the manner of its prey. The thing shambled as Steel guided Mikka behind a rack of wine bottles. He peeked around the corner, spying a vaguely human face with pointed teeth. Its body was tall and covered in fur. The creature hissed, growling as it stalked. He heard the monster sniffing, trying to divine where they might be lurking.

Mikka gave a horrified gasp. Steel pulled her to his chest, keeping her silent as the thing crept closer. What surprised him most was how quiet it had been. Mikka's breath was hot against his palm, slight but rapid, muffled as it was. Steel grabbed a pebble at his feet. Soon enough the Ghost of Helvia Manor would catch them, tear them apart with monstrous teeth and nightmarish claws.

He would have to be quick about it. Among the darkness, the thief spotted a rack of wine bottles. The stratagem had its risks, yet he could think of no better alternative.

With a careful aim, the pebble flew and collided with the solid wood, emitting a *thok* with the impact. The monstrous thing responded immediately, lumbering with noiseless gait towards the disturbance.

Steel saw the creature was out of view. He released Mikka from his grasp and gently guided her toward the statue. He detected the faint sounds of footsteps. Peering close, he glimpsed a small latch underneath the idol's arm. He pulled the handle, and the secret entrance propped open. They covered their noses, stifling their urge to cough.

Steel heard a low growl coming from behind. He had just perceived the lumbering figure as it closed in on them. Guiding Mikka along with him, they stumbled through the opening.

They caught their breath while pushing the stony entrance shut. Safety was mere cubits away when the door halted. A horrid screech erupted from the fiend. Its large bulk was pressed on the opposite side, a clawed hand stretching around, searching for them. Their feet dug into the earth as their bodies tensed and strained. Steel grit his teeth until the arm was gone and the entrance clicked into place. A resounding thud slammed against the stone, the vibration penetrating their souls. To their vast relief, the monstrosity's growls were muffled, almost like a distant memory.

By the time their hearts slowed, Steel's legs buckled underneath. His entire body quivered with panic. He rose, falling mere seconds later. The thief realized he was on his back. The aches swiftly returned.

"Mikka," he whispered.

The girl's hands were gentle as they pressed along several points. Each practiced touch was accompanied with a groaning protest.

"Your muscles are strained to their limits," she murmured. "You will need some rest and a healer. You are fortunate, as I know a thing or two of it, myself."

"Just leave me," he protested. "I will be fine."

"You saved my life. Now it's time I saved yours."

Steel groaned as she massaged his bruises. He was sore, and his mind swam with dizziness.

"Here, in one of my pockets," he said. "There's an elixir that will help. I can manage until we get out."

She quickly located the vial. Mikka uncorked it and held it up to his lips. He drank heartily.

"All right," he said, coughing, taking her hand as he was lifted up, his arm around her shoulder. Limping along the corridor, Steel's thoughts drifted back to Zolan and how his brother was faring. Worry overtook him, though at least he was one step closer to saving Stormbright.

He smiled. They opened the portal farthest from them, and Steel took in the fetid air.

The sewers had never smelled so good.

XIII
The Pool of Desire

The Falconer relaxed as she dozed in the heat. By the time she settled, General Caerst perceived the guards who marched in at Aedas' discretion. They stood vigilant and motionless, ready to respond should she act against them.

Her eyes shut as she ignored the sentries. She felt the warm waters—the sting of her cuts. Those, too, faded.

She realized the twin moons yawned overhead, Taldriath and Bruann. Moving up to a sitting position, she found herself in a familiar grassland. White flowers grew in patches around her, their silvery incandescent petals reflecting the moons themselves. An entrancing scent drifted along the wind. With it, her mind wandered to recent memories, recalling that this was where she and her bizarre lover had mingled.

Strange—she had almost forgotten. To her surprise, she shivered at the notion of his arrival. Yes, this must have been a dream.

I have been waiting for you, Falconer.

She turned swiftly. Never before had the Falconer minded her nakedness, but for some reason she was cognizant of the fact. She felt exposed, more so than past excursions; there she had flaunted her assets with abandon, but something was different.

I am close, said the voice.

She looked around, unable to tell where the voice was emanating. It was like the presence shifted through thin air—a shapeless ghost. What was this man to whom she had shown her affection? She quietly ascended the crest of the hill, peering in either direction. The natural world resumed its calming tempo. The wind swept at her hair as crickets chirped softly.

Fireflies twinkled in the night.

"Where are you?" she asked.

I am with you. For this night and the last, you have never left my sight.

She looked above and beheld the twin moons in their glimmering majesty. The vista evoked such beauty that she shivered.

"Don't tell me you are…" The words clung to the roof of her mouth.

I am neither of the moons, quoth the voice. *Rather, I am their progeny. One might call me a champion.*

"What nonsense is this? Show yourself!" She instinctively moved to retrieve her blade, only realizing it was no longer at her hip.

A dark shape flitted from above. The moonlight cast a shadow, solidifying in a form which resembled a human. The foggy substance was enshrouded with hues of moonlight, coalescing into the shapes of arms, legs, and an oval head. By the time it touched the ground, the mighty figure was gazing fondly at her.

She stepped back, a vague anxiety stealing over her. Was this a god?

Do not be afraid, it said. *My name is Amu'uth. I have come to deliver a message.*

She hesitated. "Then tell me your message and begone. I have no business with heathen gods."

As she said it, melancholy spread over the deity's expression. It couldn't have been that this thing cared for her. Could it?

He disappeared. Her surroundings, too, changed from a wide field into black oblivion. The despair encased her with its malevolence, constricting as black emotions bubbled to the surface—doubt, rage, hopelessness, and abandonment. She experienced a rush of wind as she plummeted deeper. There was no way of telling how far she had gone. As time elapsed without measure, so too did her insane musings cease. She walked along a barren flat plane. A bubble of light loomed in front of her as its growing brightness blinded her with its intensity.

Peering within, she espied a wondrous scene—it was the majestic halls of Ilgrathié. The holy luminescence caused the dream to shimmer with golden hues. She observed herself, weakened and in tattered rags for clothes, kneeling before her goddess—begging, pleading. Gnawing fear bubbled up from her stomach, her heart pounding in her chest. She witnessed her other self weeping as tears stained her cheeks. The mirror image of Caerst struggled among her captors, fought as the guards restrained her with inexorable certainty. Her ambition, training, and discipline, it would be for naught. The quest for vengeance had failed, and her goddess had deserted her.

Seek not the counsel of Ilgrathié, hummed the voice in her mind. Regardless of what she experienced, all she had lost in the name of her pride, the words were calm and gentle. *You will only find suffering. The one you cherish most will abandon you.*

She blinked. Once again, she was standing in front of the alien god, back in the field with the moons and cool grass. Her vision blurred. General Caerst felt along her face, realizing they were tears.

She will abandon you, He repeated. *Nay, She has* already *done so.*

"You lie," she spoke, her voice breaking in a discordant note. General Caerst sensed the truth in His statement, but the fact it was spoken aloud affected her greatly.

I offer the truth, He said. *You have strayed from your path, and I know how afraid you are to fail. You have lost everything, and so you risked your life for one final chance at vengeance. Is that not so?*

General Caerst brought a hand over her mouth, stifling a sob as she denied what this heathen told her. Surely, He was wrong!

She had never been so alone, so hopeless before her future. A cold wind blew past, causing her to shiver amidst her nakedness.

I implore you, said Amu'uth, *for I see the power you hold within—the potential that has gone unnoticed by many.* He stopped upon noticing her

"General Caerst sensed the truth in His statement..."

retreat. *You are an exemplar of your race, Falconer. You do not realize it, but your people shall fade into decadence, then will come the inevitable fall. This Paradise your deity proclaims is little more than falsehood. She doubts you. In fact, She has already lost faith in you.*

"You are wrong," she replied. "You seek to deceive me from my holy path." She regarded Him with a sneer, her voice lowering to a whisper. "Would that I had my rapier, I would slay you where you stand!"

The god was unfazed.

You already have your weapon, Caerst, He said. *You have always had it.*

She raised an eyebrow, seeing her sword was held securely in her palm. The weapon was cold, as if it harbored no desire to fight.

She winced. Never had she experienced such doubt.

"This is a dream," she murmured.

The deity pursed His lips. *This is as real as you wish it. You do not realize I have given you a chance at redemption. Soon you will understand how much your men have come to hate you, and you will be left with nothing, forsaken by your own people. What will be left but for you to turn in shame towards Ilgrathié, begging for a swift death as your reward? Little do you know it was She who set the path for your destruction.*

Can you not feel it? The sense your life is closing around you? Death is waiting, Falconer. It will come closer than you can fathom.

He took another step. This time she did not resist.

"I will not be some pawn in your game! Ilgrathié is the truth. She will bring us to Paradise!"

A false Paradise.

"So what if it is! It's the one chance this world has of bringing order! What other choice do we have? Do we live as equals and forget the past? Do we abandon all hope and go back to the dark ages? Nonsense! I would rather see the world honed to perfection. Pain is the ultimate motivator! Pleasure is our reward!"

The figure shook His head. *You have been deceived.*

"No… I am a Falconer! I am-"

He held up her chin. His eyes were shimmering silver discs. The cool scent reminded her of moonflowers—a sensation not unpleasant. *You are an enigma. Like a beautiful moonflower, you were not made to flourish under the sun. Night is your calling. Your path, darkness.*

Gently, their lips met. With it came a rush of ecstasy.

She tore herself away, facing the distant black line of forest. "This cannot be," she murmured, her voice having lost its previous edge. "Even if it means death, I will answer to Her. I swore an oath."

She heard the god walking closer from behind. *There is more to you than you think, Falconer. You are the budding flower of a new world. A Wildflower.* She felt His hands sliding over her shoulders. The underlying strength made her body shudder. She realized that instead of fear, she quivered with excitement.

She slipped from His grasp. Caerst faced Him, her eyes wet with tears. Sorrow and anger consumed her heart, yet she couldn't deny the comfort in what He said.

He gazed at her with a benevolent smile, a marble-white thumb passing along her cheeks, drying her tears. A laugh mingled with her sobs. His fondness bored into her soul, showing greater compassion than even Ilgrathié had given her. The cold discipline faded. In its place was earnest affection, a form of pain… and pleasure.

I am a light which will sustain you, He said while kissing her forehead. She did not resist. *Perhaps I am not the sun, but I am a light nonetheless.*

He drew back. In Him, she saw loving and tenderness. With a rapt motion, she kept a close distance between them. She returned with a soft kiss, the gesture uncharacteristic for a Falconer, as it was gentle and affectionate.

She kissed Him again, and this time He reciprocated, their arms wrapping in a loving embrace. She experienced the tension between them, the joy that came with their love. At this she lost all apprehension. Her limbs worked of their own accord as they lay among the grass. Their pace quickened; the silvery moonlight caressed their bodies with cold splendor. General Caerst's nails became talons, digging into His neck and back, clawing as she moaned softly.

She had never felt so safe—so secure.

So this was what it meant to be loved! Her heart thrummed with longing, the image of her old future dashing into pieces as this new dream assembled from the fragments. It was a new love, a new chance at life.

At first her fingers clawed along His back. Then they wrapped over the god's neck. Her grip tightened. She wasn't sure why she was strangling Him.

The god said nothing.

Why was she doing this? Why was she resisting this temptation for a better life? Why was she sobbing? Why did she not waver in the least?

"I cannot disobey." The words shocked her as she said them. "I will not."

She would not allow herself to be loved, not like this. Amu'uth had tricked her. He had bewitched her to fall for His wiles. Even if the goal was love, her path was formed by Ilgrathié long ago. She had sworn her life to bring Paradise to this land of Zirvonia, and Paradise she would achieve.

The god retaliated. Her anger was strong enough to restrain Him, however. To her surprise, He smiled while mouthing a series of words.

Old Man Darkness… Old Man Darkness…

"Stop it! Stop your wretched chanting!"

It is not a chant, but prophecy. You do not know what you are fighting for.

Her grip tightened. She knew not why, but she screamed.

You will know where to find me ere the end. When all hope seems lost, Taldriath and Bruann will guide you.

His body was fading, like sand through one's fingers, as it became one with the fog and mist around her. The Falconer stood, her body shaking as she wept. She had changed. The land changed, the moonlight dimming as a voluminous cloud hovered above.

Shadows lingered along the corners of her vision. Indistinct figures flanked her on all sides. Were these nightmare-kin? Either way, they were like grim facsimiles of her brothers-in-arms. Fury overtook reason as she held her blade. The illusions expressed confusion and terror. No, this was but a test made from that abominable god—the one who called Himself Amu'uth!

Although she was unarmored and her wounds hadn't yet healed, the Falconer delivered her sword swings with perfect precision. Her enemies resisted, crying in a stark mockery of her comrades.

It was blasphemy. She would not stand for it!

Black blood streaked across her face. She did not relent when her opponents appeared no different than Ilgrathians. She feinted between their attacks, reared her blade, and stabbed. Ere long, the wondrous fields and moonflowers were dampened with the blood of those she fought.

She would not be a slave to some god's whims. She would rather die than betray her calling. She was a Falconer—she was General Caerst!

By the time she stopped, she was sorely fatigued. Wiping the blood from her face, General Caerst observed the fruits of her deeds.

The land changed.

Around her, Ilgrathian guards lay in pools of crimson. Directly below her, another was floating atop the pool's surface. It was like she had drowned the man with her own hands.

The realization hit her as soldiers entered the chamber. The sounds of commotion and ringing steel had prepared them little for what transpired.

"This cannot be." Lieutenant Neto walked slowly, a shadow stealing over his features. His voice was quiet yet firm. "Seize her. The Falconer has gone mad!"

Guards ran with their swords drawn. Her weapon fell, clanging along the ancient stonework.

Excruciating fire coursed rapidly through her body. She did not resist. Her comrades' confusion betrayed the spears pointed at her neck.

"I could not have predicted this," said Aedas, stepping into view. "Bind her up. It seems we're leaving for Mirungel sooner than expected."

XIV
The City Depths

The roaring falls splashed and roiled as they rushed into great pools of murky black. Out from the depths, a lone figure broke the surface. Aurora swam with her arms and legs thrashing underneath, coughing up water from her lungs. Darkness surrounded her, although faint hues of illusory moonlight trickled down to the depths. Monolithic stone walls encased the impossibly large chamber, as it appeared cylindrical in nature, with the large body of water serving as its lowest point. She also spotted a series of alcoves, each twice the height of a regular man, leading to gods-know-where.

Aurora remembered the people she had once known as family, how they were all gone.

Every sound was overpowered by the thunderous torrents. It was enough that she didn't hear herself paddling, as if the waters encompassed the entire depths below Candala. It was so profound that she nearly forgot the nature of their descent, nor what happened to them.

"Stormbright," she whispered. She discovered the magician floating nearby.

She took swift hold and pulled him to shore.

"Please, don't be dead."

Aurora held his face to the side. A thin stream of water escaped before she breathed into him. The girl pressed firmly and in rapid succession. Such was the technique she learned, many years ago, when a wandering magician had tended to one of the local village boys—a geomancer he was called. She envisioned the technique he used when the lad had nearly drowned, the same he taught her village shortly afterward. Opening Stormbright's mouth, she blew in sweet air. Aurora felt his chest expanding, and so she repeated her rhythmic pressing.

Stormbright stirred. He turned, coughing up whatever liquid was left.

"Where am I?" he asked weakly.

"You're alive!" she exclaimed. "I don't know how we survived, but we are somewhere below Candala's sewers. How far, I'm not entirely certain."

Wherever they were, Stormbright determined it was far from civilization. He rose to a sitting position, remembering how she had tried to seduce him.

Aurora's smile faded as she offered a hand to pull him up. Warily, Stormbright took it. He swayed, ultimately steadying himself.

"Is there an easy way out?" he inquired.

Aurora spoke awkwardly, "I imagine we are in the city depths. If we take the right path, we should find an exit."

A sequence of tunnels branched out from where they stood. Stormbright and Aurora said little, studying which path was likeliest to lead them to safety.

"How deep does this city go?" asked Stormbright.

"No one really knows," Aurora replied.

He shrugged his shoulders. "I suppose we should get moving."

Stormbright started forward, slowly at first, as he was pale as a sheet. Aurora wished to help, but she was aware of his scrutiny. He hadn't gazed at her fully, though it was enough to give her pause.

She handed him a small flask.

"What's this?" he asked.

"Drink. You look terrible."

He regarded her warily. She seemed to be telling the truth, although her tone was no different. How *could* he trust her after that?

"You keep it," he said.

"Stormbright-"

"You heard what I said." He glared while pressing the vial to her chest. Aurora pursed her lips, eyes gleaming with confusion, guilt, and a myriad other emotions. "Where do we go from here?" he asked.

Aurora breathed deeply and shrugged her shoulders. "I've never been this far. I assume we pick a direction and go back if it's the wrong way."

"I guess you're right." He inspected the tunnels, identifying seven in total. He pointed to the third one from the left. "How about this one? It should lead us south, I think."

"Good enough. Let's go."

Although their vision had largely adjusted to the gloom, the passage was maliciously dark. Stormbright held up two fingers, utilizing his lightning so they observed at brief intervals. The flashes were blinding in intensity, and despite its sparse usage, the effect proved terribly disorienting. Ultimately, Stormbright gave up on this endeavor, content to roam with his hands and hearing to guide them. They caught glimpses of the narrow tunnel they traveled, constructed of smooth stone and growing with stalactites, not to mention a disorienting amount of forks in their path. Aurora made no protest. A ghost wind howled as the depths loomed around them. The roaring falls faded into obscurity; what remained was a distant echo of dripping water.

"I believe we're heading southwest," said Aurora.

"Are you sure?"

She shook her head as the gloom abated. He caught the outline of her face, tracing the glint of her eyes and shape of her lips. "I guess you could say it's a hunch."

Stormbright was taken aback.

"Why are you staring at me?"

"I wasn't," he replied.

"If you have something to say, you should speak it now." Anger crept into her voice. "If we're to survive, we need to protect each other."

"Aye. Perhaps you have a point." Seconds passed between them. He knew Aurora wanted an answer. "Why?"

"Why what?"

"Why did you save me? Why didn't you just leave me to die like the others?"

She scoffed. "I never intended on leaving you. What do you mean by that?"

"Your fellow initiates, they were each seduced for their initiation, correct?"

"Yes, but it doesn't mean we aren't caring. That's why it's called the art of love."

"That's not the kind of 'love' I mean," he said. "Did you really think you could prove yourself by seducing me?"

"No... I-"

He spat bitterly. "At the end of the day you were just using me. It didn't matter who you inebriated or sacrificed. It all goes back to those priestesses. You were fooling me—fooling yourself."

The initiate struck him. Tears spotted her face, though she made no sound.

"It isn't like that," she hissed. "Our goal is to bring an age of prosperity to the world. To give a new chance apart from the Ilgrathians."

"Do you really believe that?" he retorted. "When I was there, they sacrificed an Ilgrathian in the name of your cause."

"The Ilgrathians are monsters! What's wrong with taking their lives? They persecute us, bind us in chains and take everything we hold dear. This is a war, Stormbright!"

"Aye, a war where the same horrors are committed on both sides. You don't realize how similar you are to those you hate."

She shook her head. Was her denial a product of her belief in the Sacred Moons, her faith in Ava and Ida? No—there was something else.

"That's not true," she said, "It cannot be true."

Stormbright did not reply, peering off to some far corner of the tunnel.

"I'm guessing you are faithless?" asked Aurora. "Someone who chooses not to follow the gods or doesn't believe?"

"Not at all," he said firmly, shaking his head. They rounded a bend and crept through a connecting series of tunnels, their sight inferior to their other senses. She hovered close to his side.

"You have a funny way of showing your piety."

"It's because I only saw my god once. The result, as you can see." Lightning stretched between his fingers, lighting up their surroundings. They were nearly blinded as the magic cast wild shadows along the walls. The effect was harsh, though the point was made.

"So you are a chosen one," she said.

"Chosen one? Honestly, I'm not sure if I was chosen for anything. I was gifted this magic, true, but it was something that always resided within me. This I learned from my master, Shariz'lan."

"Very well," she said. "Who is this god then?"

"He is Calamtu—a master of storms and destruction." Stormbright vividly remembered his encounter with the deity in question, the same who thundered across the Fields of Man like a living giant. He spoke of the terror and the overwhelming awe he felt. "He is a dangerous god, and I would argue He's the one who put us on this path, bringing me to the Ilgrathian's attention and that of General Caerst. They destroyed our village and took us as slaves. But I don't hate Him."

"You were a slave?"

"Aye. Steel and I lost our home. So did Father. We learned how to stand, how to fight. Those years were most demanding, and we suffered each and every day. However, we endured."

"So," she stammered, "what am I to you? What does that make me?"

Stormbright pondered. "I believe there's more to you than you can imagine. I also think you are afraid. Afraid of the world—afraid of me."

She gave him a pensive stare.

He said nothing.

"You are right," she murmured. "So tell me about your god, this Calamtu. What was He like?"

"To be truthful, there's little I can tell."

Thus he described his experience from two years ago; he and his brother riding atop their mares across the Fields of Man; becoming separated in the midst of the storm; Stormbright resetting his dislocated shoulder. Then he spoke of that distant figure—the giant who was ten times his own height, made up of clouds and lightning and rain. He had Aurora's full attention. So he continued:

"It took me a while to figure out who I was, what I'm capable of. But when Steel and I were on the verge of being killed, that's when I learned how to use it—this lightning of mine."

"That's an intriguing way of learning."

He nodded. "When you're enslaved by Alcaron and forced to fight to survive, things like introspection and doubt fall to the wayside. Or at the least, they become dependent on your own survival."

"Perhaps so." She blushed slightly.

Stormbright did not reciprocate. "What about you? How did you end up with the priestesses?"

Again, he sensed her hesitation. "I don't want to talk about it."

His interest was piqued. "I understand what you went through must have been difficult."

"If only you knew." Her scorn was palpable. "You, never having to experience the way Ilgrathians lay their hands on a woman. How it feels when they prick and prod with their fingers, wandering to places that make you feel shame and the need for it to be over." She chuckled bitterly. "Or maybe it did happen to you. Maybe you're just too shy to admit it."

"No—it never happened to us. We saw it while we were chained and starving, though we could do nothing."

She glared at him. His intuition had been right. All this time she was afraid—a victim of society who, almost out of circumstance, had become that which she despised so much. He doubted the rape was the real cause for her behavior; it must have been Ava and Ida, her beloved priestesses, who exploited her desire for retribution. After experiencing the horrors Ilgrathians were capable of, how could one person not want a chance to wipe the slate clean, to usher in a better world?

That explained the seduction, the need for her to be in control.

Stormbright asked, "How was it you escaped?"

Her expression softened by slight degrees. She took a reluctant step back as she replied, "It was by the grace of the Sacred Moons. Somehow, I noticed the statue's hidden doorway as I worked in the cellar, fetching another bottle of wine for Captain Helvia… that atrocious woman. They never found me as I fled through the sewers, weak and hungry as I was. Ava and Ida took me in and nursed me back to health. It was never spoken between us, but they understood my plight. They prophesied a world without Ilgrathians, where humans weren't mistreated or enslaved."

She trailed away in that instant. Stormbright studied her expression, unsure of what to say to someone who had been wronged in such fashion. Perhaps there was justification in her wanting revenge?

The idea disturbed him profoundly. He averted his eyes, wanting to reunite with his brother most of all.

"The feelings I had for you were sincere," she said.

"Perhaps they were," Stormbright replied. He didn't protest as she walked alongside him. "But I'm not certain I can return them. I am sorry."

In between stretches of walking, they rested for minutes at a time. Both were exhausted, although they kept quiet. Stormbright imagined blue skies and how wonderful it would feel to be above ground. He sighed; the complete absence of light and sound made his skin crawl.

After some time, Stormbright held out his arm.

"What is it?" asked Aurora.

At first he couldn't quite place it. He had nearly forgotten to use his sorcerous *inner sense* as a means of detecting magic. He did so now, feeling the air was black with corruption—malice—hatred.

"Nightmare-kin," he said.

XV

Plegma

"Are you certain we shouldn't head back?"

Aurora lowered her voice. Neither of them knew why this was, but it simply felt right to do so. "We can try, though it would take us several hours to retrace our steps."

"It's still a better alternative to here," Stormbright hissed in reply.

It was around a dozen paces that they halted. Stormbright honed his *inner sense*. He knew not what the presence was, other than it being exceedingly powerful.

He swore; they would have to go on.

"Is something amiss?" asked Aurora.

Stormbright tugged her back along their original path. "Something horrible lurks back where we came. As much as I hate to say it, we will have to go forward."

A cold chill lingered between them. He sensed her hesitation. Warily, Stormbright and Aurora trudged, the air growing denser.

The corridor widened. Stormbright channeled his lightning in brief flashes. Around them were glimpses of barren stone, this time broken up by strange stalks and walls of meaty substance. A foul stink, resembling rotting carcasses, almost made them reel in disgust.

"What is this?" Stormbright asked fearfully.

Aurora's words were tinged with fright. "I remember hearing about it from Ava and Ida. Far below the city, one of the nightmare-kin was sealed by some form of ancient magic. We were always taught Candala was a stronghold built on top. No one remembers the spell that imprisoned it, nor do we have any way of knowing its true power. Those who know of the creature call it Plegma. It is most dangerous, or so I've heard."

"Was it your sacred order that did this?"

She shielded herself from the flashes. "Nay, it is older. An ancient race who vanished after the city's completion. Even among Candala and its scholars, little is known of them. All that's left are ruins."

They warily stepped forward; maintaining his magic, Stormbright spotted a number of appendages—arms, eyestalks, tentacles, and legs— writhing and contorting.

Aurora trembled with fright. The wet, sticky air was horrendous—like they were walking through a slain beast's digestive tract. The sickly-sweet rot clung to the back of their throats. The humid air hugged their skins and dampened their clothes.

Stormbright's heart beat at a rapid tempo, as if it hammered against his windpipe. They emerged in a vast, expansive chamber. The ceiling was only a faint suggestion above, and their path split off in two directions. The left circumvented a massive sculpted pit, arriving at an exit along the far side. The path to their right, however, spiraled along the edge, descending into whatever lay below.

The humidity was so thick that it hung like a putrid fog. Beyond what was revealed with Stormbright's magic—the pit, various limbs, and tendrils swaying some distance away—they were completely blind.

Stormbright stepped along the stony edge. The depth of such a precipice sent a shiver down his spine.

"Do you see the bottom?" asked Aurora.

"I'm not sure." Stormbright produced another flash. The light faded quickly amidst the looming expanse. "I guess there's one way to find out."

"No, please don't!"

"It'll be for a second," he replied. "Stay close, and we'll be fine."

"I'm not sure you realize, but we are in a very dangerous spot. What if Plegma is down there?"

Stormbright concentrated. "I can sense nothing, myself."

"What?!" Aurora shook her head in dismay.

The sorcerer began his descent along the rampway. Albeit with reluctance, Aurora crouched behind him. The fog wafted in thicker clouds, obscuring their vision almost entirely. The walls and flooring were of an old, decrepit stone, smoothed over by the ages.

All they heard was their own breathing. The rapid beating of their hearts was so loud that it thrummed in their ears. After an interminable amount of walking, they reached the bottom. Tendrils undulated in sporadic patterns, resembling both a rat tail and a serpent's tongue. Myriad eyestalks peered in their direction, yet Stormbright maintained his distance. "Stay here," he said to Aurora. At first she refused, but with insistence she held back.

Carefully emitting a steady spark, Stormbright spotted a gigantic shape looming ahead of him. It resembled a large door of sorts. Rubble lay strewn about as a massive breach formed at its center. He channeled his *inner sense*, detecting hardly any traces of magic in the air. The seal must have been broken for some time, he concluded.

Sneaking back to Aurora, he saw she was pale, her jaw clenched in morbid anticipation.

"Did you find anything?" she asked.

"Nothing."

"What do you mean 'nothing'?"

"I mean the seal is broken. There was little other than piles of rubble."

Aurora froze. "That can't be. If Plegma is free, then…"

"Let us keep forward," he said. "Perhaps with any luck we can escape."

It was clear that neither of them believed what Stormbright said. Ascending the ramp, they considered the path they had neglected earlier.

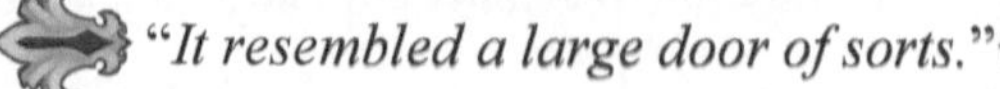

"It resembled a large door of sorts."

Plegma

A low slithering reached their ears. Glancing back whence they had come, Stormbright and Aurora spotted a shape, one so large it rivaled an oliphant.

Plegma.

Aurora stayed quiet. At least so far with this Plegma creature, their disgust was justified. It slid from where they had ventured, its shape almost resembling that of a slug. How was it possible this thing crept through spaces so narrow unless it could compress and reshape itself? The explanation was unlikely, yet it made the most sense.

They hardly saw the abomination, though they knew it was close. Stormbright grabbed Aurora's hand and tugged in the opposite direction. He prayed the left path wasn't a dead end. He kept quiet, as he believed Plegma hadn't yet noticed them. Nevertheless, it was only a matter of time before they were discovered.

Both panted as their misty environs grew more archaic. He used his *inner sense* to guide them, difficult though it was. Large slugs crawled along meaty walls; shadowy forms danced and played with their sense of reality. This was to say nothing of the tunnels themselves, which twisted, curved, and looped in illogical ways. Was this some design of Candala's architects, to deceive trespassers so they became lost? Surely it wasn't, but then what was it? Had these demons changed their environment? Was it possible that perhaps they were capable of sorcery?

Stormbright detected slithering from behind, as well as the faint gibbering of human speech. They were getting louder. He was certain Plegma had spotted them.

They broke into a sprint. Aurora trailed behind, Stormbright gripping her tightly.

A faint glimmer from beyond bled in shades of silver. The chamber was otherworldly, the idea of it being fashioned by humans a nigh impossibility to the sorcerer. A pungency lingered in the air. The architecture twisted in unnatural ways, with columns spiraling in helix shapes as a blend of stone and flesh. There was no ceiling to speak of, other than a sickly mist. It was like they were on the fringes of reality—a shockingly frequent occurrence of late. The one suggestion to the contrary was a solid wall at the far edge, where hung a portcullis and a turn-crank.

Dashing, Stormbright put his entire weight into operating the crank, though the gate hardly budged.

"Aurora, help me with this!"

A large shadow crossed his vision.

Amidst the chaos, he spotted Plegma. It was a gigantic mass, with arms, teeth, and appendages protruding from its form. Its shape changed constantly, forever dissatisfied of which aspect to take. Aurora kept perfectly still. Evidently, she peered into those eyes that swiveled wildly in their sockets, ones glaring with diabolical hunger.

The creature had no face, yet at its summit protruded a sharp beak. The sickly mouth opened and closed in horrible anticipation, eager to devour the humans in its path.

Instinctively, Stormbright stepped away from the crank. Lightning flashed between his fingers, dancing along his hands and arms. His hair raised with the sensation.

He released the lightning as it cascaded in swift streaks. Bluish energy tore through skin, bone, and sinew. Plegma screeched horribly.

The magic fizzled. Stormbright had given much into the blast, but it was not enough.

Plegma quaked violently, its horrid shrieks almost deafening as flesh rent along its form, chunks of meat separating along several places.

"What's it doing?" Aurora shouted, trying her best to operate the lever with little success.

Her answer came sooner than Stormbright could reply. Globular masses of meat tore themselves from the nightmare-kin's form, splitting into miniature variants of their mother. Plegma did not change position, as the process took its strain. The smaller nightmare-kin slid closer, mouths and angular teeth forming along their oozing bodies.

"Turn it if you can," said Stormbright. "This is going to get messy."

The nightmare-kin advanced. Stormbright raised his arms, lightning coursing through the monstrosities with frightening speed. The aberrations squirmed as they sank to the ground, melting into viscous pools of liquid.

Aurora grew pale. "Keep turning," Stormbright repeated. He detected a creaking sound. It was merely half-a-cubit, but the gate shifted upward.

Her triumph was short-lived. A tendril, unobserved, slithered around her ankle. She was only halfway through screaming when she found herself hoisted above Plegma's massive beak.

"Stormbright!" she screamed.

Below her, as she was suspended mid-air, the nightmare-kin rumbled. Its beak opened wide. Rows of dagger-like teeth circled the outer edges in alternating revolutions.

Despite what Aurora had done to him, Stormbright couldn't bear for someone to be devoured by such a monstrosity. Thus he drew his blade and aimed for a group of bulbous eyes near the front, knowing full well that his lightning would harm her should he use it now. His blade struck true as the creature shuddered. He gasped and stabbed again. Despite his lacking skill with a sword, the tentacle swayed, loosening its grip. Aurora fell shortly thereafter, tumbling down the monstrous mass of tissue. She was unharmed. He sheathed his sword as he dragged her, deftly avoiding its swinging appendages. Once they were at a suitable distance, Plegma quaking with wrath, he focused with his magic and released a final bolt of lightning. The streaks of energy caused it to squeal and writhe in anguish.

He doubted they could defeat it. Such was evident in how quickly it regenerated.

He pulled Aurora up to her feet. "We need to get out of here," he said.

"But we don't have time!"

"We can both operate the turn-crank. Plegma is distracted with healing. Come on—we have to try!"

She wanted to protest his decision, but sought the exit regardless. Aurora resumed her labors, and sheathing his sword, Stormbright joined in as well. At first it resisted—then a loud *creak*. The turn-crank groaned, though Plegma regained its composure.

The portcullis was high enough for one of them to crawl through.

"Go on!" shouted Stormbright, wedging his sword between the gears so it held. He waited until she passed through safely, keeping the blade in a secure and fastened spot.

The inhuman screeches grew louder. In the corner of his vision as he scrambled towards the exit, the gears struggled. He crouched on his hands and knees, crawling underneath and through. Plegma was slithering fast in his direction, its many arms seeking to pull him back.

Stormbright's heart dropped. The gate wasn't falling.

The massive nightmare-kin stretched underneath, its body elongating as it slid to where he lay, quick enough for two sickly hands to emerge and grab him. The sorcerer struggled. He sought Aurora, seizing her outstretched arms as he was caught. One arm clung to his right foot, another to his left. Plegma was too strong for them. He imagined how he would be absorbed. Agonizing death was certain to follow, and then he would be nothing.

No—he would become one with Plegma.

He heard a sharp, metallic rattle. With an effort he looked past the abomination, seeing the gears were jostling from where Plegma pressed along the gate. The sword fell from its hold. A moment of uncertainty followed, as if the portcullis would simply hang there, before it came crashing down. The iron bars narrowly missed his legs, instead piercing through the horror, as well as one of the arms holding him. The hand fell in an instant, and Aurora stabbed at the remaining arm with her dagger until scarcely few ligaments held it together. Stormbright yelped as he kicked back, scrambling away from the monstrosity.

He realized Plegma was stuck. It voiced its protests in a thousand distorted, human-like voices, struggling to tear through the opening.

"Let's get out of here," he said, panting and exhausted. "It will only hold for so long."

The gibbering faded with each stride. Limping along the dark tunnel, the light intensified. Stormbright felt instant relief. Although exhaustion gnawed at his resolve, at the very least they were clear from Plegma.

The room they entered was illumined, almost to the brim, with daylight. The stony walls reflected this hopeful atmosphere as Stormbright's legs buckled underneath.

"I'm sorry… I will have to rest here." He gave a harried breath, trying to steady his nerves. "That took more out of me than I realized."

Aurora sat directly beside him. Her smile was warm, yet Stormbright's despair was equally poignant. He had saved her life, yet she was still no different from the other initiates.

She knelt close with the intention to comfort. This time Stormbright pushed her with the slightest force.

"No," he said.

She paused before backing away. The irony of it was sickening, he thought. This beauty who had tried to sway him to her cause, to ensure he would side with her, was just as scared as he was. He saw it by how she distanced herself. It was true that a part of him still lusted for her, what they had together; but he did not love her, nor could he mend her scars.

At that moment, he detected a peculiar sound. Were those voices?

"Auroraaaaa."

They listened. Fear wormed its way back into Stormbright's heart. Aurora responded, "We're here!"

By the time Stormbright twisted his head, two figures stepped into view. As expected, they were indeed Aurora's fellow initiates.

"It's like Ava and Ida said," spoke one initiate. "We thought you were dead, but after the priestesses read the entrails of the stag, they proclaimed you would survive. We were told to search the south edge of the city, and here you are." He smiled. "Truly, Aurora, it is a miracle!"

Aurora shook her head in relief, grinning with newfound hope.

"Aurora," said the other initiate, "we have no sacrifices for the Great Equilibrium. The Ilgrathians are gone. Those who weren't killed have since escaped."

The tension between the initiates and Stormbright grew uncomfortable, the atmosphere intensified by the fact he could hardly move. "No," said Aurora, "we have one more we can use." She faced him, the hurt showing in her grim aspect. "The sacrifice must have known a great deal of pain in life, is that correct?"

"Aye. The more one has experienced, the better it should please the Sacred Twins."

Stormbright said nothing. In truth, he was paralyzed.

"This one has suffered," she said.

The two grinned joyfully. "Praise be!" exclaimed the other man. "The Sacred Twins will be pleased when our lord is born. Let us go! The priestesses await us as we speak."

The cultists grabbed hold of Stormbright and hefted him up. Although he wished dearly to resist, he knew deep down there wasn't any magic left for him to draw upon. He glared at Aurora, who showed a hint of doubt. Did she still believe that Ava and Ida would save them?

It was a dangerous sort of faith, and now he was the one who would perish for it.

XVI
An Improvised Plan

Steel grimaced as Mikka tended to his injuries. The aches along his neck, back, arms, and hands were very much alive. Masking this affliction, however, were the many elixirs and ointments he had drunk and administered. Regardless of his lightheadedness and the persistent aches, he appreciated her help.

He peered outside the window of their rented room. The Silken Dove lived up to its grandiose name, what with the amount of drakons and jewels they spent for the last several nights. Back then he had sent Mikka to scout the place, as Steel was in no condition to remain discreet. She returned without incident, reporting that the innkeeper was not only human, but was one who held no sympathy for Ilgrathians. This gave Steel some amount of relief, knowing that for their brief time in an upper-class lodging they might regain their strength and devise a plan.

High-Town was renowned for its luxuries.

Three days passed. The sun sank in the afternoon sky. Although from this vantage point the crowds of Candala seemed orderly, Steel knew it was a façade. Tonight there would come the bi-lunar eclipse, a phenomenon where the moons would cross at such an angle so they were one and the same. The rumor was that such occurrences were extremely rare.

However, Steel knew of the greater implication.

It was the Great Equilibrium, the time Aurora had spoken of several days prior.

His one hope was that he could save his brother before night's end.

"Please hold still," said Mikka, taking the last dab of ointment she had bought. In truth, Steel couldn't have been happier with freeing this girl from the manor. At the time she appeared so affluent and carefree, almost suspicious. Now she had proven herself. The former tavern wench had apparently learned much in her time among the streets. A portion of that knowledge came in the form of connections: knowing which apothecary held the best unguents, as well as a healthy understanding of their ingredients. She was the first to discover a black market fence who sold them daggers, arrows, and a specialty garb allowing one to blend in with the night.

Now he was in as good a shape as he could hope.

He prayed it would be enough.

"I'm nearly better," he said, standing at the window, shirtless as he surveyed the crowds below. He faced Mikka, noting the warmth in her features. He knew she was fascinated by him. He wasn't sure if it was romantic fondness or simple admiration. Bitterness welled up inside him. He recalled the dream where he lost everything—witnessing the death of his loved ones. Steel clenched his fists, honing his fear and torment into black, searing hatred. He despised the bronze whore, General Caerst, and what the Ilgrathians had done to them—what they had done to *him*.

"Steel, your hands are bleeding."

Mikka had said it so nonchalantly, that it was a shock when he sighted the blood welling between his fingers. He opened his palms, marvelling at the shallow cuts he himself had made.

"So I am," he said. "Look, Mikka, I know you've taken care of me these last several days. And I couldn't be more grateful you came along to help. That said, if you are seeking love, protection, or whatever it is you desire, I cannot give them to you."

Mikka regarded him curiously. "What has brought this all of a sudden?"

"I've been thinking about it. Why is it you've tended to me and not sent me to some chirurgeon? If I were you, I would have fled the city borders by this point, off to somewhere not so dark or perilous."

The girl shrugged her shoulders. "I see your point, but that is not the reason I joined." She paused, calmly peering out the window. "Is there another who cares for you—who loves you?"

He nodded.

"Is she close by?"

He shook his head.

"Is she deceased, perhaps?"

Kitala's death and rebirth as a star wraith grew vivid in his memory. He recalled the blank expression his lover had shown him, having little recollection of the days preceding her demise.

The memory ached like an old scar.

Mikka kept her distance, perhaps as a token of respect. "You would think me foolish; all I wanted was my freedom. You helped me achieve that, and I am in your debt." She observed the city and its myriad inhabitants, giving a warm smile. "Many have I known in the throes of wanton passion, but it compares little to the real thing. I do not know this woman you speak of, though I can see your resolve." She smirked. "I know better than to challenge it."

"So what is it you want, Mikka?"

The girl shrugged her shoulders. "I'm not quite sure yet. I've learned to trust my instinct, and I can tell there is something different about you. Perhaps it's my *inner sense*, as the magicians call it, but I feel as if it's my own intuition. It's like you were defiance incarnate. How could I not follow you?"

He was unsure as to her actual meaning. Mikka was indeed a strange one.

"I understand," he said, "but you have to realize I'll be heading into the heart of Captain Helvia's forces. My brother is trapped with those cultists, and whatever it takes, I'm bringing him back alive."

"I do not fear death or torture," she replied. "I'm not sure how, but you will need me for the trials ahead."

"Is that also your intuition speaking?"

He caught her smile.

Steel shrugged. "Very well, if that's what you want. There is also the matter of rescuing our father. But first," he said, "I'm heading out for some fresh air."

"Be careful. Your wounds haven't fully healed."

"They're as good as they can be," he said as he donned his garments, weapons, armor, and black cloak. He walked past her, grunting from the soreness that nearly left him immobilized. The aches were a shadow of what had been, but walking still proved an arduous proposition.

He really needed a drink.

Steel ignored the impulse, instead choosing to retire from *The Silken Dove*. He paced along the crowded streets, where above the sun sank lower. Panic threatened to overtake his better judgment.

Please let him be alive. Let them be alive…

He fingered the polished moonsteel daggers at his sides. They were a suitable replacement for the ones he had taken and lost within the manor. Feeling underneath his cloak, his fingers caressed the small crossbow he had bought. Although he would have preferred a regular bow, such contraptions proved surprisingly useful.

Moving along a back alley, he found he was alone. Of the places he had frequented during his time healing, this area caught his attention the most. He stared at the slight indentations in the brickwork. Steel had tested his climbing ability the day previous, and that almost ended with him falling squarely on his back. He had to hand it to Mikka—his recovery was quick. At first, placing his hands along the footholds was a struggle. His muscles strained, fingers aching from their remembered torture, as if they were fake and not his own. Stepping over the roof, he beheld the moons Taldriath and Bruann spying him from above—a familiar sight of when he and Kitala had mingled. The celestial bodies were somewhat faint, as dusk was beginning to settle.

How much, he wondered, was really true about this cult and their reverence for the twin moons? Surely they were mad. But perhaps the world was just as insane.

The vista only fueled his resolve. To his left, a large tower jutted well above the surrounding habitations. Its surface was climbable enough, though the footholds were smaller.

As he was midway up the side, his arms and legs working in tandem, the thief's mind raced with questions. Was Zolan still alive? What would he find at the cultist hideout? Could either of them save Kolthan at this point, considering their predicament? Especially with the Moon Cup in his grasp, he concluded it was the key to solving this problem. He gripped the ledge and hoisted himself over.

The view of the city was all encompassing. Steel sat perched for what must have been an hour. Truthfully, he did not know how long. All he cared for was the approaching dusk and Taldriath and Bruann overhead. He was no longer concerned with his own troubles, nor the dangers of this city; they were superfluous compared to his family and what Steel would do for them. Somehow the moons had robbed him of that joy—whether they were intelligent or not.

The hatred wormed its way into his heart. His fists clenched in anger.

This was not the end, he mused. Although silent, his heart cried for retribution. He was determined to keep his brother safe, and their father alive and well. Steel had learned how powerless he was, but by the gods above and below, he would save Stormbright. Then he would find Kolthan, together with his brother.

He would not give up. He would not back down.

"Not again," his lips worked soundlessly, miming the words. "Not ever, not again."

"He would not give up. He would not back down."

He beat his chest with a fist, offering a challenge to those moons who longed to be joined—who mocked with invisible grins. If their intent was to stop him, his father, or his brother, he would defy them as he had done with the Ilgrathians. The moons had witnessed his fighting among many foes; they observed him in the throes of passion with the woman he cherished most. Now they would bear witness to his revenge.

Minutes faded by slow degrees. Wind rushed as the heights spanned below.

He stirred from his perch and descended along the tower's side. Steel hovered close to the bottom before leaping to the southern wall. His body still ached from periodic cramps, though he would not allow it to best him. He avoided the few patrolling guards along the ramparts bordering Ancient's Hold. He leapt across the rooftops—a shadow in the twilit dusk. Steel's brow was caked in sweat but he felt good, ready for what was to come.

He was ready for The Silver Hearth Inn.

The thief surveyed the area below. Above the din of drinkers who swayed and laughed, whores offering their services, and cutpurses lurking in wait, his ears detected a low, familiar voice. Steel judged it must have been coming from his right. He crept along, spotting a large structure at three stories' height. Below he spied a hanging sign which read *The Silver Hearth Inn*.

Keeping his stance low along the rooftop, he spied the astromancer. The man was conversing with Captain Helvia, who stood adjacent to what must have been a hundred Ilgrathian soldiers. Upon sighting the captain, anxiety crept over the young thief. Where was General Caerst? The question put him on edge, heightening his fear almost to insanity. The Falconer had caught onto him and Stormbright from the very outset of their journey. If she discovered them, he doubted either of them would be able to escape.

Steel took a deep breath, focusing on the mission. His terror slowly subsided.

He saw the astromancer, city captain, and a fraction of their soldiers walking into the tavern. His view was partially obstructed by a caged wagon. That was different, he noted. He studied a little longer, giving a smile that bordered on sadistic. What lay there was a bronze-skinned beauty, reduced to a wretched thing. Golden hair trailed along her body, which was covered in a pitiful sack cloth garment. Normally Steel would have harbored pity, even for one such as General Caerst, but after all he had endured, he was perfectly content to let her rot in a prison. He was uncertain as to what had transpired, but no matter! Let her starve! Let the rats feast on her bones!

He jumped another two buildings, giving a final leap at the ledge bordering The Silver Hearth Inn. His hands clung to the precipice, though there was no purchase below. He swayed before lifting himself, slipping inside like a shadow.

The tavern echoed with uproarious cheers and laughter. Guests and clientele drank and rough-housed along the wooden floor. Thankfully, Steel climbed through the window as if it was the most casual thing he had done. For those on the same level as him—which was a deck overseeing the establishment from the second floor, with a wooden railing serving as a barrier—it seemed no one had noticed. The clamorous shouts ebbed as he located Captain Helvia and Aedas, as well as their many armored compatriots, who seated themselves at one of the tables. Their conversation was quiet. The thief sauntered along the upper landing, keeping his cowl overhead as he peered below. Straining his ears, he almost heard what they were saying.

"That is unfortunate with General Caerst," said Helvia, her voice faint though distinguishable. "Had I known she would go mad, I would have had her bound and taken to Ilgrathié much sooner."

"It is indeed regrettable," said Aedas, "but not unexpected. I am sorry to say anything resembling good sense has left her." The man beside him nodded—an Ilgrathian with tufted hair whom Steel did not recognize. "It was after rallying Neto and the rest of her men that I realized how unstable she had become.

"Please accept my humblest apologies. I shall bring her to Mirungel forthwith. There she will be tried for the crimes she has committed, not to mention the atrocities at Divnarost's border."

From where he stood, Steel saw the man who sat near them, presumably Neto, bore an uncomfortable look.

Captain Helvia broke the silence: "Is there a reason you aren't leaving with them?"

Aedas scoffed as he replied, "Isn't it obvious you have a problem with the cultists? If you would allow me tonight to lend my aid, I believe a Dreamstone wielder should be effective for your cause. Neto and three others will accompany the Falconer up north."

She stroked her chin in thought. "Very well, but only if I'm allowed to pick the soldiers."

"And why is that, Captain?"

"It's a precautionary measure. Without you and your Dreamstone, I would ensure we don't have a repeat of last time."

"A wise decision," Aedas said. "You would do well to trust in your subordinates, for tonight is filled with evil omens. Our Falconer has lost her mind, and what's more, I am unable to glimpse into the future as I normally would."

"Is the situation so desperate?" asked Captain Helvia.

"Regrettably so."

"And what about General Caerst? Are you certain she won't try and escape?"

"Dear Captain, you need but step outside to see the Falconer as she is. I can tell you her sanity is gone. She is hardly the same person. We have her tightly chained by manacles connecting at the boards. She will hardly be able to move, let alone escape."

"Very well," she said. "You have my blessing, as well as my dearest thanks. My scouts and I have followed the cultists' trail towards the Caprian Forest. I should've known they would have a base in such a cursed area…"

While Helvia spoke, the astromancer peered above, his eyes boring into the thief's. His gaze shifted back to Captain Helvia and the Ilgrathians, like nothing at all happened.

No, there was something the astromancer wanted him to see.

Once the instruction and planning was concluded, the group stirred from where they sat. Steel pursued with the utmost discretion, pacing down stairs while keeping his head covered. The caged wagon and the two horses remained stationary. General Caerst hadn't stirred one cubit.

Steel's heartbeat rose as he trembled. How he wished to slay the Falconer! How he yearned to show what it meant to maim and torture.

Cold sweat collected along his brow. It was then he steadied himself. If it meant she was out of the picture, even as the Ilgrathians' prisoner, perhaps it was for the better.

He spied the Ilgrathian lieutenant boarding with four soldiers. True to Captain Helvia's word, she picked them individually. The lieutenant climbed onto the carriage, gripped the reins, and goaded the beasts with a lash. The carriage jolted before rolling steadily.

Aedas and Captain Helvia, along with the rest of the Ilgrathian force, had stayed behind. A few words passed between them. As she turned to leave, the astromancer cast another glance in his direction. Aedas' intentions were unmistakable. He was about thirty cubits distant. As he started walking, Steel followed. The astromancer resumed his conversation with Captain Helvia.

Steel noticed a small pouch held in his left palm. Someone collided with the astromancer, causing it to drop right at his feet. Aedas responded with a brief apology, the hooded figure keeping quiet as their face was hidden. Captain Helvia frowned at this person who proved so careless as to stumble into them; yet before she uttered a word, Aedas redirected her attention to the horses ahead.

The figure picked up the pouch, the angle providing a brief glimpse of her face. Steel's heart twisted, as it was Mikka whom Aedas had bumped into. The Ilgrathians walked by at this point. He rushed forward.

"Mikka, what are you doing? I told you to stay inside."

"You were gone for some time," she began.

"Everything was under control. What is that thing, anyway?"

She loosened the draw strings and opened the bag. A faint glow illumined her cheeks. Steel realized what the astromancer had left for them. He pulled the purse strings closed, peering around them.

"This way," he said.

They stopped midway along an alley. Mikka opened the bag once more. The glow was brighter among the shadows. There was no mistaking it.

"Why do you think he left it?" asked Steel.

Mikka did not answer, holding the stone between her fingers. A flash and a frightened gasp, then came a faint brushing sound below. Along the walls, much of the brickwork was overgrown with wild flora, the flowers enchanting in their beauty.

"I'm sorry," said Mikka. "I pictured how nice it would be for us to be outside the city. Just to walk along gardens and flowers…"

Steel smiled. He even stifled a laugh.

"I understand," he said. "Mikka, I've got a plan to save my brother. If you wish it so, you can come along as well."

"Of course," she said in reply, lighting up like the flowers around them.

XVII
The Passion of Zealots

The carriage rattled along the cobblestone streets.

The Falconer stirred where she lay. She could hardly shift her position, as the shackles kept her rooted to the floorboards underneath. Guards hovered close at either side. Darkness loomed underneath the large city gate, where a vast series of plains spanned with swaying tall grass and large acacias.

A sharp gust of wind made her shiver. Goosebumps rose along her skin as she hugged the boards of her cage. Never had she been so humiliated. All she knew and strove for in life was gone—her life, career, and reputation. Perhaps she deserved it. She had abandoned her post after failing to besiege Miracor, and thus her ruin would follow.

Perhaps none of it mattered.

The stars winked at her from above, a series of endless specks illuminating the sky. The carriage bumped and jolted over the uneven road. Her wrists and ankles tightened as she repositioned herself. The Falconer replayed the same events in her head, those that cost her freedom and, soon enough, her life. What had transpired within that pool? How had she slain her comrades without comprehending it? Was the dream of her and the god even real?

The Falconer would have to believe it; it was the only explanation that made an inkling of sense. Either that or she had truly gone mad.

She peeked through the bars, beholding the moons in the sky. The two were closer than she had previously espied, save for the nights when Caerst gazed into the heavens as a child. Amidst her despair, she pleaded to the deity of her dreams; to whisk her away from this death which Fate had devised.

The answer wasn't immediate, though a cold radiance fell along her face and shoulders.

The sensation filled her with hope.

There is still something you must do, Wildflower, said a voice in her head.

The Falconer's eyes widened. It was the same presence from her dreams—the god who was yet to be born—Amu'uth.

"What is it you need from me?" she whispered.

You must hasten south to the Caprian Forest. There you will meet me in person. There you will find your hope.

Hope.

The mere notion filled her with purpose, spreading warmth where otherwise was cold.

"How can I serve you?" Without saying it or gesturing, she indicated the chains holding her.

Fret not, for my power is strong tonight. Although I am unborn, those who behold the Sacred Twins are powerless against my bidding. The men around you are weak in mind and wild-hearted; so I shall cause them to stir.

The Falconer watched and focused. She would not die here today. Shifting her hands, she found that, given a sufficient amount of time, she could likely slip one free. That left the problem of her ankle bindings, but at least it was a start.

She was halfway through one of the manacles when she stopped. The light of the moons appeared to intensify; one of the Ilgrathian soldiers fidgeted from where he walked. Was it so that the man's gaze swiveled toward his comrades? Did he hide a smile as he gripped the pommel of his blade?

The remaining guards did much the same. Nearly all of them twitched, a few laughing while others cursed.

One of them raised his voice. Neto, who idly guided them, turned as the Ilgrathian shouted: "Stop the carriage! The prisoner has a weapon!"

The lieutenant peered behind, seeing the Falconer had hardly budged. He murmured a curse. "I personally inspected her for weapons."

"You do not understand," said the guard. "She is hiding something. You should stop and check to be certain."

With a lurch, the carriage halted in its tracks. Neto stepped down from the driver's seat, eyeing the one guard as he mused his displeasure. "I will not tolerate your interruptions. You and I inspected her thoroughly before we left. We must hurry to-"

The guard drew his blade, swinging at a wild, reckless angle. The lieutenant fell to his back, genuinely afraid, as the other smiled his wicked smile. A soldier withdrew his weapon; Caerst realized it wasn't directed towards Neto.

"You vile fiends! Abominations!" The man spoke erratically, wildly, the rage apparent in his voice. The Ilgrathians raised their blades, the cold steel reflecting the light of the Sacred Twins above.

Metal clashed against metal. An issuance of screams came once sword point met flesh. Men gurgled as their throats were slit and hearts pierced. A struggle ensued between the two who survived, battered and bleeding as they were. The one guard locked hands over his enemy's throat, the other trying to gouge his attacker's eyes using his thumbs. They rolled around in the dirt, struggling to determine who would emerge victorious.

The strangled man slowed. His opponent reacted with a horrible, frenzied laugh. The Ilgrathian maintained his viselike grip, squeezing the life from his friend turned adversary, until the man went pale.

The Ilgrathian stood up, mist passing between his lips. He looked on towards the Falconer. General Caerst shot back with a stare, though in her heart she knew only fear. The guard moved to the cage, his gaze distant. He stalked toward his former companion, stooping low while retrieving a metallic object from the corpse.

The soldier stopped beside her, a key held in his open palm. Passing through the bars, the metal object clanked atop the boards. General Caerst flinched as this happened, her fingers clutching the key as if she had recovered a precious belonging.

The Ilgrathian gave a smile. Pacing away from her, he withdrew a long dirk from its sheath. The blade slid beneath his neck. He fell to the ground shortly thereafter.

Save for Neto, whom Caerst hadn't glimpsed since the beginning of the skirmish, she knew she was alone. The Falconer wasted little time, the key twisting as the bonds were removed. She inserted it into the cage's lock and, to her relief, heard a faint clicking sound as it swung open.

The moons bathed the grasslands in an almost ethereal glow. A short distance beyond the horses, Neto lay motionless.

General Caerst spotted no trail of blood. She felt along his neck and wrist for a pulse, and exhaled softly. He was unharmed. That was good, but how had he fainted with such quickness? Surely Neto was an Ilgrathian with nerves of steel.

I sensed the bond between you, murmured the voice in her mind. *So I have brought him to sleep on your behalf.*

She smiled with the revelation. How affectionate Amu'uth was to her, even when her time had run out.

"I am sorry you got involved in this, Neto."

Her hands worked quickly, unfastening each piece of armor with care. She removed the chainmail shirt and leather jacket underneath, first covering herself with the padding before strapping on the shirt, armor, and longsword.

It was a tight fit, yet it would have to do.

She dragged his limp form to a thick entanglement. That would do well enough until he awakened.

The Falconer turned to the two horses in front of the carriage. She unbuckled the reins, freeing the one on her left while saddling the mount to her right. Amidst her perusal of the supplies, she withdrew a simple bedroll and a few days worth of rations. These would last her long enough, she mused. She mounted and lashed forth. The roan galloped as Taldriath and Bruann loomed above. Deep down, the Falconer remembered the same comfort in her dream, the sensation she was finally coming home.

Home.

She goaded her horse along the path. Her beast dashed onward until it was time to circle Candala. She maneuvered it to the left, speeding past featureless hilltops and fields of tall grass. The moons shone white ivory above, hovering like lodestones about to collide, drawing her forward as if by some invisible force.

As if they were guiding her.

General Caerst refocused, temporarily ignoring her fascination with the celestial bodies. Now was the time to meet with her beloved! Amu'uth, who had shown her so much compassion, was waiting for her. Perhaps her vengeance was too short-sighted of a goal. She would still slay Steel and Stormbright—or any individual—who stood between her and this chance at a new life. Even so, it would mean little after tonight. She was certain of it! With this end, there would come a bright, new beginning!

The shadow of Candala loomed on her right flank, and continuing her roundabout at the metropolis' edge, she arrived at the southern gate. She remembered Captain Helvia and the astromancer speaking on heading this way, though it did not shake her resolve nor slacken her grip.

This was it—the path to her destiny.

A wave of revulsion hit her then. She instinctively brought her roan to a stop. The moons had commanded her to do so—an impulse born of pure clairvoyance—but why?

The roan whinnied, shifting several paces back, as she spotted a gigantic mound of flesh emerging from the base of the city wall, apparently from some alcove or opening. It slid with shocking speed. The trail behind it was one of corruption. The flora blackened and wilted in its immediate vicinity, drained of its vitality.

General Caerst could hardly believe it. The twin moons had ordered her to witness this abomination. This was her biggest threat! This was the type of devil that Ilgrathié, her comrades, and the world at large would have to subdue. The aberration was massive. She shuddered to consider what might happen if it grew any larger.

Follow. Conquer, said the voice.

It was like the deity stood next to her. Upon turning, however, she knew she was alone.

"My goddess, forgive me," she said.

General Caerst goaded her mount onward, following the black trail in her path to Amu'uth.

XVIII
Of Tricks and Traitors

"Where are we going?" asked Mikka.

"To Captain Helvia," Steel replied as his bay breathed heavily underneath them. "She knows where my brother is."

"Does she?"

Steel grunted his approval. Their ride through the starry night had been uneventful up to this point. No riders were present along the path; thus they spurred on their mount with greater urgency. The desire to rescue Stormbright drove Steel onward, as the knowledge of his brother filled him with guilt. He would not give up, not let Zolan be slain by those heretics.

He knew, deep down, they were getting closer.

Moonlight bathed the grassy fields in silvery luminescence, the blades swaying softly as the two rode atop their horse.

They kept pace before stopping along the line of trees.

Steel wasn't sure what to make of the Caprian Forest, considering he and Stormbright had traveled through here previously. He never liked these woods. The trees, the all-encompassing darkness—they always brought with them a measure of fright, like something was watching from deep within. Chills ran up his spine, and his palms grew sweaty.

"They are inside," said Mikka, her face turning pale as she clung to Steel's back. "I can sense magic coming from within. It is old and powerful."

Steel kept her arms around him so she stayed upright. Whatever this was, it was powerful enough to weaken her slightly. He felt her breath growing faster, her hold tightening.

"It'll be all right," he said.

"For both our sakes, I hope so. My mind is clouded in this place."

"Aye. Now that you mention it, I can feel it too."

As the bay trotted, Steel and Mikka kept careful watch of their surroundings. The shadows danced along the edges of their vision. A thick shroud of fog wafted and obscured the ground.

"We are very close," said Mikka.

Below him, the bay grew erratic. He slowed till it was safe to dismount, guiding the horse off the path to a copse of trees. "It might be best if we continue on foot. Discretion will be our greatest aid if we're to survive this."

Mikka grinned. "On foot, then."

They stepped silently along the forest floor. Massive trunks flanked them on all sides, yet there was at least comfort in knowing they wouldn't be spotted easily. The shadows and mist tangled around them with such intensity that Mikka had little trouble staying hidden, save for a clearing where the moons' light poked through the trees, their radiance dispelling the fog like it was a living, knowing presence. Steel was impressed. For an amateur, she glided soundlessly through the black forest. He felt his ebon tunic, tracing the outline of the Moon Cup he had tucked in a sack. The relic was almost hot to the touch.

Passing a half-dozen trees, a peculiar sensation washed over him. An orange light flickered from the hills ahead. Steel pulled Mikka to a crouching position as they kept quiet, cresting another mound. The fog thinned around them. Out at thirty-cubits' distance stood a throng of figures within a circle of marble slabs. An altar was erected at its center.

A faint burning incense lingered in the air. The men and women chanted as they danced in wild motions. Above them, the twin moons rose high in the heavens, the clearing so wide that Steel spotted the two celestial bodies coming together, almost meeting at the outermost edges.

Their dancing abated, however, as Captain Helvia and her squad of Ilgrathians marched into the clearing. It was almost too easy for Steel to have missed them, considering the odd magicks the cultists exuded.

"Cease this madness at once!" Captain Helvia declared, drawing her sword in a swift, graceful arc.

Some continued their swaying, though others of the two-score humans halted. A fraction stepped close to the altar. It was at this point the thief espied his brother laying upon the slab. Among those surrounding him, chiefmost was the dark-haired girl who had hired them—the traitor Aurora! A priestess stood beside her who, strangely enough, had two heads on the same pair of shoulders. Their faces radiated beauty as they gripped a serpentine dagger, regarding Helvia with contempt.

It was like they were waiting for something.

Again Steel felt the Moon Cup's twin inside his pocket. It was clear they expected him to arrive at some point, given the peculiar nature in which they behaved.

"What do we do?" Mikka whispered.

Steel grimaced. He wasn't sure how long they had invoked these powers, but he knew the ritual was near its completion.

He had to fight the compulsion to dash into the clearing and finish the wretched captain and cult members. To do so would have been foolish. Thus he remained crouched, hidden among the bushes and flora. In response, the conjoined priestesses took a dainty step. Even from this distance, it was hard to miss the smile playing along their lips.

"It's time your cult answered for its heresy." Captain Helvia strode forward, this time followed by her subordinates. "Your reign of terror has lasted long enough."

The priestesses sniggered in reply. Thus spoke Ida, whose head was situated at Steel's right: "You speak as if we were strangers to our own city. Little do you realize, invader, that it was we who claimed it first. You stole our homes and our families. You raped us. Starved us. Now the time has come for vengeance."

"My men and I outnumber you three-to-one," responded Helvia. "If you have any sense, you would surrender."

Once more the priestesses laughed, this time raising their arms high towards the heavens. "Either way, we march off to Old Man Darkness! It is you who should be afraid, Ilgrathians! Can you not see it? The moons wax high in the heavens tonight! It is time!"

At this, Steel glimpsed the moons crossing, intersecting. The skies turned a deep orange, intensifying until it was a stark, blood red.

"It is upon us!" said Ava. "The Great Equilibrium! The birthing of Amu'uth! The time is here!"

Steel and Mikka circled the ruins from behind. The far edge appeared much less guarded, although Aurora was adjacent to the altar.

A cold presence weighed on his shoulders. The cultists raised their heads skyward, chanting that abominable name: "Amu'uth! Amu'uth!"

Captain Helvia took a step back.

Was that fear he detected?

A cold wind whipped by, sending the bonfire into a sputtering frenzy. The cultists dropped their blades as hands spasmed and heads jerked back. A low growling emerged whilst their bodies expanded. Bloodshot pupils darted with a feverish rage.

Steel shuddered, the hairs on his neck rising. Now they appeared as a perverse crossing between human and animal. They resembled humans, but were nonetheless covered in layers of fur.

He suppressed his desire to flee, to forget the cult and their savage ways. Such was the effect these creatures had on him. His brother, however, brought him back to reality. He forced himself to behold the fiends who resembled the Ghost of Helvia Manor.

They roared, cackled, and tittered. The two sides clashed with an abundance of screams. Only one of the guards hit their mark, beheading a changed woman whose mouth foamed white. The others, however, were swiftly beset by the cultists—slashed, beheaded, and disemboweled. The disciples of the Sacred Moons fought on, with fingers like claws and teeth sharpened into horrific needles. Blood and sulfur suffused the air, sickening the guards who, with surprising courage, remained stalwart against these men turned monsters!

Steel crept to the sacrificial altar, with Mikka keeping a tight hold on the Dreamstone directly next to him. They were beside a pillar when a shadow darted from the corner of their vision. Steel was about to charge when a hand caught his arm.

It was Aurora.

He had forgotten her amidst the chaos.

"Let go of me, you wench!"

The girl said nothing whilst turning abruptly. Steel followed her gaze, seeing it was Mikka who glared at her. The Dreamstone was held in her upraised palm.

Aurora unsheathed her shortsword and pointed it towards Steel. An ounce of concentration from Mikka, however, and the girl froze.

"Ah, look!" said Ava. The tumultuous battle ceased as the priestesses glided to where Steel and Mikka stood. Among their enemies, only Captain Helvia and Aedas were alive. The battle had reached its grisly conclusion. "Our offering has come for his brother. We were beginning to worry, but our faith in the Sacred Twins remains true. They reveal everything to us—life, death, the world, and you."

"What do you mean 'offering'?" Steel swallowed. The priestesses gave a warm smile.

"You and Stormbright have the honor of spurring on a new glorious age," said Ida. "A new god is soon to be born—sacred Amu'uth, progeny of twin moons." They held their swollen belly as they grinned. "He is hungry. Stormbright—Zolan—shall be the sacrifice that brings him into this world. And you, Serithas, will be the one who grants him tenacity. You have endured much—we can feel it in your souls. Life has dealt you a harsh hand, as it has with the rest of us. We are victims—tortured by those who would rule us. Imagine using your lives for a greater purpose. Take pride, for such an opportunity comes once in a thousand lifetimes."

Steel was about to protest, but the cultists walked closer. Their progress halted, however, as a barrier came up in front of them; the magical fabric shimmered in almost intangible waves.

Ava and Ida raised their eyebrows, turning to Mikka who was close to Aurora, the latter unable to struggle. The former focused on the Dreamstone in spite of her fear.

"No," she said. "You will keep your distance if you know what's good for you."

The cultists eyed her with hatred. Ava and Ida expressed what might have been pity. The tension of dealing with pure, unfettered zealotry was palpable.

"I've got a different idea," said Steel, pushing Aurora so she fell harmlessly. It was true they possessed the Dreamstone; however, Mikka struggled to maintain her hold. He imagined their luck would soon run out. "My brother and I made a promise to you, but you failed to honor your end of the bargain. Give him back and let us leave unscathed. If not," he revealed his own chalice, "you leave me no choice but to destroy this."

He heard the priestesses' laughter. "My dear boy," Ava chortled, "you make a good point. But what would you propose we do without a sacrifice?"

The thief shrugged. "Why not choose someone like Aurora?" He saw she was pale along the ground. "It seems your people have known misery aplenty."

"You insolent fool!" shouted Ida.

Ava smirked as she spoke in place of her twin. "She is one of us. We would never offer one of our own as a sacrifice, we who have toiled for years, persecuted by Captain Helvia and the astromancer." Her eyes widened, as if a new thought occurred. They pointed towards the astromancer. "You may have Stormbright so long as you do not interfere. This one shall serve as a sacrifice."

Captain Helvia stood defiant as Aedas kept still. "We will not be used like some bargaining chip!"

"From where we are standing," said Ida, "you and your lackey hardly have a choice."

Steel frowned, noting Captain Helvia's ire and Aedas' despair. He considered what it would mean for the astromancer to be killed in such a manner. Although the man harbored good intentions, he remembered Aedas' complicity in his own torture, a decision that had brought him to the brink of madness. More importantly, he had learned where their father was hiding. Was Aedas' life worth protecting, compared to his brother?

An acute mixture of anger, dread, and confusion swirled inside him.

"So be it," he said.

"And you will leave the Moon Cup with us."

"Only after you bring me Stormbright."

The twins smiled. With Mikka at his side, the thief produced the relic within his palm. He studied the holy chalice, its gleaming surface reflecting the twin moons.

"No! Stop this madness!"

Steel noted Aedas' intense glare.

"You do not realize what you are doing. If you give them the Moon Cup, the fate of this world will be changed. It's an irrevocable shift which none of us can affect once set in motion."

The thief held up the item in his palm. He glanced towards the astromancer, then to the priestesses.

He couldn't betray Zolan again.

"I am sorry, Aedas."

"No…" His words were cut off as the shapechangers bared their claws.

"Halt!" announced Ava and Ida in unison. The cultists did so, allowing the two outsiders to approach the altar. Steel shook Stormbright awake. In the corner of his sight, he saw Aurora shifting in discomfort.

"Where am I?" asked Stormbright.

"Don't worry, you're safe. Let's get you out of here."

"But-"

Steel's glare was enough to silence him.

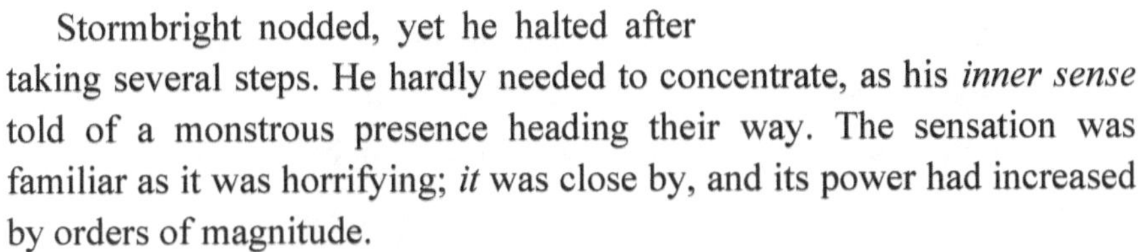

Wearily, Stormbright struggled to his feet. He noticed Aurora, her eyes pleading for him to stay.

"Can you walk?" asked Steel.

Stormbright nodded, yet he halted after taking several steps. He hardly needed to concentrate, as his *inner sense* told of a monstrous presence heading their way. The sensation was familiar as it was horrifying; *it* was close by, and its power had increased by orders of magnitude.

"Can you not feel it?" The astromancer's words were potent as if they would shatter through glass. "An abomination comes this way."

"What's he talking about?" asked Steel, the tension rising in his voice.

Stormbright cast his brother a fearful look. "It's something Aurora and I encountered underneath the city."

"*Underneath* the city?!"

Stormbright swallowed. "Do you remember the things we fought with Kitala and Aurora? The nightmare-kin?"

"Yeah?"

"This one is much bigger," he said.

"Do you mean the flying ones we saw? Like when we ventured with Kitala?"

"Not exactly. This one is different."

As the trees swayed violently, the moons' bloody hues deepened. Distorted voices grew louder. Sluggish bodies moved over untainted grasses, each one leaving behind a trail of destruction.

Mikka cried out. The nightmare-kin emitted a deafening series of screeches, appendages flailing.

Although they slid near, Aedas' Dreamstone magic proved sufficient in holding them at bay. Those that breached the barrier erupted into flames.

"You, girl! Come hither!" yelled the astromancer.

Her heart beating rapidly in her chest, Mikka joined Aedas and Captain Helvia. He gripped their hands tightly, the Dreamstone linking their thoughts as one collective force. They struggled as the magic took full effect. Helvia said nothing to the girl who was once her serving maid. All she gave was a piercing glare. The horde of monstrosities faltered as the trio held them at bay.

For the time being, the nightmare-kin were immobilized from the front.

Stormbright heard a shout coming from Aurora. He turned, seeing she was dealing with her own horde of nightmare-kin.

She dispatched with the first, delivering a lateral slash to its torso. Blue streaks coursed along Stormbright's fingers as he incinerated several more.

Aurora grimaced, acknowledging the sullen youth. Immediately she sensed the distrust buried beneath the cold exterior—the fear that came with her betrayal.

She knew Stormbright hated her—everything she believed was an affront to the idea of creating a better world. Yet she would at least help them to survive. That was why he saved her.

Feeling the magic's strain, Stormbright redirected his attention to Steel.

"I hope we can last long enough," said the thief.

Stormbright shook his head. "I'm sorry, Brother. The attack has only begun."

At that moment, the nightmare-kin were drowned out by a deep, booming tone; behind the growing horde emerged a gigantic mass, tentacles and appendages writhing as it slid forth with frightening speed. The brothers were paralyzed as Plegma emerged, crashing along the trees and the Dreamstone barrier. Mikka and Captain Helvia struggled as they barely held it off, their power united by Aedas.

"We can't hold much longer!" the astromancer bellowed.

Steel and Stormbright fought on as the nightmare-kin swarmed them. Disfigured arms, legs, mouths, and eyes strove with collective purpose. Indeed, Stormbright was almost petrified. He was so tired, so weak.

Steel gripped him tightly by the arm.

"Stay calm," he said. "We'll need our wits if we're to make it out alive."

"Right."

Stormbright steadied his breathing and channeled lightning into his fingers. Those close enough were finished by Steel, Aurora, and the cultists. Their swings were quick and desperate. Dozens of monsters perished from the whirlwind of claws, blades, and the bolts released from Steel's crossbow. With each strike, they were coated in ichorous blood. Squeals resounded with stark profundity, giving the impression of a disturbing cross between man and swine. Hopelessness wormed its way into their hearts; the defenders struggled with every ounce of willpower, casting the fiends back to the lowest hell imaginable. The Dreamstone siphoned their vitality, lighting every tendon and muscle fiber with its searing magic. Plegma slithered toward them, slamming against the barrier of magic force. The impact was intense yet somehow it held. What they hadn't noticed was a multitude of the fiends sneaking from behind. Those caught shrieked horribly. Mikka was mortified as she glimpsed behind, seeing human skin melding with their pursuers' flesh, hearing bones breaking and muscles contorting.

"Do not look back!" said Aedas. "Stay focused on what is in front of you!"

Mikka obeyed without question. The nightmare-kin pressed with its full weight. Bluish energy pulsed from the magic barrier, yet the monster advanced by small degrees.

"It's too strong," said Mikka.

"Just hold a little longer," the astromancer responded.

"But… I-" The barrier fell. In the end, it was Captain Helvia who faltered. The Ilgrathian woman collapsed, engulfed by a swarm of disfigured limbs. Mikka and Aedas dodged before they, too, could be swallowed. Helvia reached towards Mikka in desperation, but it was to no avail. Foreign flesh melded with her own, burning layers of skin and muscle. The captain of the guard screamed wildly. Mikka covered her ears, turning as the image of Helvia's disfigured face burned in her memory, mangled and bleeding, one half merged with the abomination. She heard the snapping of bones, the twisting of limbs and joints, as her master was forever silenced.

As they devoured Helvia, their attention shifted to Mikka. The girl fled swiftly before stumbling.

Aedas caught her just in time, dragging her to safety while the cultists fought their losing battle. Ava and Ida lingered near the altar as their subordinates fought, bled, and slew.

Only a half-dozen cultists remained; most were paralyzed as Plegma pushed on. A few mustered up the courage to fight, but this was to Plegma's advantage, for their sharp claws were singed upon contact, their swords snared by the thick matter of its form.

Those who did not retreat were consumed.

Steel and Stormbright fought relentlessly, their breathing heavy. Aurora crept silently as the thief was preoccupied with the nightmare-kin. She held a large stone, knowing deep down he would never relinquish the silvery chalice now that their lives were in danger. She would have to take matters into her own hands. All it took was waiting for the opportune second. He dispatched his foes as Stormbright was locked in his own battle, releasing magic towards a veritable horde of enemies. This left

Steel wide open from behind. Aurora acted in an instant, clubbing the side of his head with perfect execution. He fell to the ground, a trickle of blood rolling along his temple.

With a fanatic's haste, Aurora snagged the Moon Cup and fled to the central altar. Stormbright cried in horror as he realized his brother's condition. The girl stopped, panting as she offered the relic to Ava and Ida, her eyes pleading for salvation.

"Please, mothers! You must help us!"

The priestesses regarded her with shock. Their plans had been dashed so easily.

"Mothers, please…"

Ida spoke, "You would do anything to save our people, would you not?"

"Anything," said Aurora, although she was unaware what they meant.

They stepped forward, the serpentine dagger held as they stabbed downward. Aurora staggered as blood spouted from her lips. With what little life she had left, her lips formed so many questions, so many curses.

Desperately, she turned to Stormbright. The young sorcerer cradled his brother. The boy looked in her direction, his expression absent of hope.

"Hush, child," said Ava, the sorrow clear in her voice. "You have performed admirably for Amu'uth. May you be the first of many who joins him." They raised their arms, striking a second time. They carved through her chest as her body lay lifeless along the bloodied altar. Ava and Ida poured into the two chalices, squeezing whatever life essence remained from the girl's heart.

They held up both cups, one in each hand.

"Taldriath and Bruann—grant us salvation from these horrid demons! These sentinels of Old Man Darkness! Grant us a child, O lovers! Grant us a path to our future!"

In their fervor, they did not perceive the nightmare-kin's approach. Their surprise was cut short as teeth sank into Ava's neck.

Their cries rang sharply. Only when they had dropped the Moon Cups, Ida striking with her dagger so the nightmare-kin sloughed, did they fall in the dirt. White-hot fire assailed their body. Blood dripped and pooled underneath, as chunks of Ava's neck had been stripped away. There was nothing she could do for her sister; they were powerless, writhing meekly along the ground. Ava choked on her own blood. Ida groaned, bearing the pain she shared with her sister.

"Amu'uth…" Their hands strove for the cups that had spilt. "Give us our child. Give us Amu'uth…"

Around them, their followers fought and perished. Time was short; they would have to be quick.

"We are left with no other option," said Ida.

To her right Ava nodded, although she turned a light shade of blue. Climbing to their feet, they strove towards the two chalices, which held what little was left of Aurora's blood. It was not enough. They situated the cups, holding the dagger over their free palm. Metal flashed, with bright crimson flowing down their fingers.

This they poured into the cups.

"Amu'uth… requires blood… suffering…"

"Yes, Ava. Let Him taste our blood. We and Aurora have suffered this cruel world for long enough. Let Him live! We beckon to you, Sacred Twins! Let Him live! Let Amu'uth live!!"

They drank even as they bled, so the god in their belly might taste their blood, the life force of those who grieved at the hands of Fate. Their faces flushed as their organs failed. A smile played along their lips as all went cold. They laughed horribly, madly, sensing a kick along their stomach.

"There is hope for us," said Ida.

"Hope… Hope…"

The air permeated with aura—one exceedingly heavy. Those who stood near the twins perceived it—each kick of the unborn child bringing

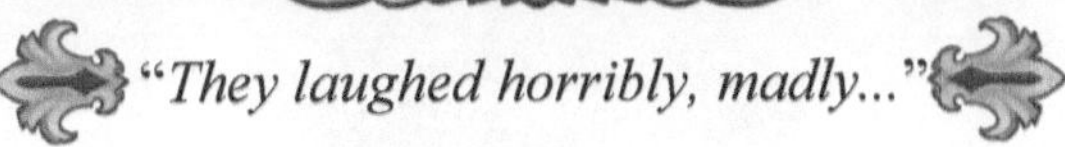

"They laughed horribly, madly..."

forth unimaginable torment. At this Stormbright lifted his head, having fought hard and tending to Steel. Suddenly, he realized the fate of Aurora and the priestesses.

"We must stay together," shouted Aedas as he lifted Mikka, shaking her awake. "For both our sakes, concentrate!"

Standing, Mikka groaned as another wave surged through them. Aedas gripped her hand, the Dreamstone augmenting her powers while she focused.

Instant relief passed over them.

"Quickly!" said the astromancer, pushing her to where Steel and Stormbright lay along the ground. The misery was undeniable as the young sorcerer tried protecting his brother, but when she moved close enough, it had ebbed.

By some miracle, Steel awakened as well. Stormbright held his brother tight as they rose. The act itself was strenuous enough. Around them, the nightmare-kin rippled with each powerful surge. As the frequency of knowing, presence, and power increased, they popped much like ticks. Plegma shifted, quaked, and screeched. Those present held their hands to their ears, and with a penultimate swell, the thing that was Plegma ceased to be, exploding in a hail of muscle, tissue, and bones.

Little by little, the agony abated. Then came serenity as the night sky shone a little brighter. A silvery glow permeated the air. The moons were no longer red, having well crossed and intersected by this point, parting their own separate ways. Ava and Ida gasped as they beheld the cries of their newborn child, an infant that would save the world from damnation.

"It is done." The twin sisters wept in that brief, wonderful moment. With a final, shuddering breath, they lay still, their body a mirror shade of the Sacred Twins above.

XIX

The Great Equilibrium

General Caerst reigned in her mount. The forest and its thick trunks surrounded her, the darkness cutting off vision but for a few cubits ahead. How many hours she rode along the trail, the Falconer could not say. She no longer spotted the twin orbs looming high and red in the sky, yet she knew Amu'uth wasn't far.

At that moment, searing agony shot through her skull. The roan foamed at the mouth as it swayed. The beast toppled, the Falconer barely escaping its mighty bulk.

The air pulsed and reverberated. General Caerst stopped her ears, resisting the presence which threatened to overpower her. The distress faded. At her side, her mount did not stir. She rose sluggishly, her mind swimming with terror.

Among the foggy distance ahead, she spotted a pale light.

Steeling her resolve, Caerst followed the tracks formed by dozens of nightmare-kin, not to mention the behemoth she had first encountered. The blackened trails converged at a single point. Pushing through a nearby thicket, the Falconer realized what the monstrosities' destination had been.

It was an ancient shrine.

She supposed this place was dedicated to the moons, the celestial bodies suspended high above the clearing. The scene was utter devastation: bodies lay in heaps of gore; myriad nightmare-kin corpses were situated in puddles of melted flesh and snapped, rotting bones. The stench of coagulated blood wormed into her nostrils. Glancing ahead she saw Steel, Stormbright, and Aedas, not to mention the servant girl she had encountered several nights ago.

Before her, the conjoined twins lay in tattered, bloodied robes, their body pale as tears dried on their cheeks, lips open while the newborn child writhed between their legs.

The babe's skin was a stark ivory, its head shaped back into an elongated point. To the shock of those present, silky phantasms of the dead were circling around the newborn. The infant expanded, stretching as its head, torso, and limbs took on an air of maturity. Muscles gained definition along its chest and arms. Dainty cherub cheeks changed to a gaunt, otherworldly complexion. General Caerst—as well as Steel, Stormbright, Mikka, and Aedas—had witnessed the babe's growth in an appallingly short amount of time. Amu'uth rose high overhead, towering at a height of what must have been five cubits.

Not a soul moved a muscle. Steel and Stormbright were unsure of what to say or do. Even the astromancer marvelled at the newborn deity. Amu'uth stood like a conqueror out of legend. Perhaps it was by instinct they were obedient to this new god; so transfixed were they by its aspect, light gait, and full, sonorous voice.

"So begins the dawn of a new age," quoth He, expression aloof as He stared at the twin moons, His creators, who had given the whitish figure solid form through the zealous priestesses. Amu'uth held out His arms, and from silvery moonlight coalesced a robe of regal make—bluish, white, and gold patterns befitting a king or the wisest of sages. His expression was one of curiosity, as the deity remarked at how easily reality bent to His whim.

Amu'uth sensed Steel's intent to kill. The young thief held up his moonsteel daggers, prepared for the worst.

"Did you think to harm me as I mourned for my parents?" The divine figure strode closer. Steel froze as the grass writhed beneath him. Wandering creepers trailed up his legs and arms, rooting him in place

while snatching up the two weapons. The vines holding the daggers twisted, undulating towards the god.

"Give it back, you fiend!"

Amu'uth smiled as a finger ran along the edge of one blade. *"You are most ungrateful,"* He said. *"I have not walked on this earth for five paces, and already you seek to end my life. I must admit I admire your tenacity. Soon, we shall be as one when I devour your life's essence, absorb what you have suffered."*

"Are you sure that's something you want from me?" Steel taunted.

The deity smirked, ignoring the question. *"I see my Queen has arrived,"* He said.

The others beheld the Falconer on the clearing's edge, one who marched in full-plate armor save for a helmet. The very object of her revenge lay within reach, but that faded as her admiration grew. Love was in those white irises—love, appreciation, and understanding.

Ilgrathié had never regarded her with such fondness; not her men she fought beside; not even her servants and fellow Ilgrathians whom she had known so intimately.

She walked in a dream. Halting, she made to kneel as the deity extended His hand, fingers lifting her chin so she stared directly at Him. Surprisingly, the god knelt also, mirroring her own emotions. Softly, tenderly, their lips met. Their fascination was clear as the passion endured. With a final, loving kiss, they stood together as one.

"What have you done to her?" inquired Aedas, a peculiar rage infusing his words.

"What have I done? My child, do you not recognize love when you see it? Ilgrathié has manipulated you, caused you to stray in lieu of a greater balance. This poor one was consumed with ending your existence. I witnessed her comrades falter, turning against the one they had so admired. Fret not, for no life is worthless under my new reign. She will embark on the true path of justice, and so will I anoint her as Queen."

"You are wrong!" exclaimed the astromancer. "What you speak of is nothing but lies! I can sense you are using magic to control her. You have her ensorcelled!"

The god smirked. "*She is a danger both to herself and those who would revere her. She is misguided. The world is misguided. That is why I was sent here—to correct the course of Fate and bring peace among the land. The gods have spoken—your incompetence will destroy you, unless I am to act.*"

"You do not speak for the gods!" retorted Aedas.

"*On the contrary,*" interjected Amu'uth, "*my plan is to reshape the world as was deemed fit by the Sacred Twins. To this effect, you will help me.*"

"No way we'll help you!" Steel raised his voice as he struggled against the powerful creepers.

"My brother is right," said Stormbright. "Calamtu awakened this magic within me for a reason, and I believe stopping your plans is a part of it."

The god merely chuckled as the Falconer lingered close, utterly fascinated with the radiance that was Amu'uth. "*Calamtu—such a reckless and petulant god. Did you not hear it from my mothers? Your souls are ones riddled with hardship. I can feel it inside each and every one of you. Through your trials and experience, I will become strong. But I will never forget you. I shall ne'er discard you as Ilgrathié has done with Her children. The End—which is a New Beginning—is inevitable. Old Man Darkness will cower before us—He whose estranged specter lies in the shadows between stars. I shall lay the foundation of a new earth. So it is foretold.*"

His hand stretched forth to Mikka. "*You possess great power, child. Come! Embrace one who would carry your soul to true Paradise. Worry not; for if you should die here, I will see you are given a new body, in a world that knows only happiness and fulfillment.*"

His eyes stared into hers as General Caerst held Him close. Mikka trembled.

"This is madness, Mikka!" said Steel. "Don't go through with this!"

"What do I have to live for?" she asked, seemingly in a daze. "My family and friends are gone."

"You have *us*," he said. Stormbright and Aedas joined him. With it, a vague recognition washed over her—a faint measure of control.

Mikka stopped beside him, giggled, albeit slightly. "You are peculiar," she said, planting an affectionate kiss on his cheek.

He noticed a peculiar glint in her look.

Steel understood her intentions. She walked forward, at the shock and bewilderment of the rest of them. The aura which the deity exuded was one of pure ecstasy.

She stared fully into Amu'uth. A benevolent grin crossed His features.

"Good, child. Do not worry, for I will make your joining quick."

She beheld fingers extending into claws, face darkening in a horrid mask. Amu'uth wrapped His limbs around her as His jaw stretched like a serpent. Mortal fear gripped them in a vise. Grasping the Dreamstone, Mikka unsheathed her dagger and stabbed with an overhead thrust. Black blood spewed from His chest while Amu'uth groaned.

General Caerst was quick to react. Steel and Stormbright witnessed Mikka collapse under the Falconer's rapier.

"Mikka!"

Steel wrestled with the binding creepers, tearing out several as Aedas cut at them with a dirk. Stormbright readied his magic, lightning flashing towards General Caerst. The Falconer evaded in the nick of time, though Amu'uth was hit square in the chest by the chaotic energy. He prepared another blast. Amu'uth waved His hands as the air stirred. Shapeless forms and wretched wights gathered around Him. Aurora, Ava and Ida, and Captain Helvia were among them in a swirling menagerie of souls.

Their lamentations went unheard as they bowed to the god's will and struck.

The sorcerer kept his distance as he dodged their sickly forms. At that moment, Steel had freed himself. General Caerst was surrounded by the dominated souls, her struggle evident as she ran towards Stormbright. At this, visceral rage bubbled inside the thief—fury at this mockery of a person and all she stood for. He loosed his crossbow. Instinctively, she pivoted, turning the deadly shot into a graze.

The souls shoved her away, prevailing in their struggle to face the young sorcerer. The Falconer shifted attention as she strove toward Steel. Tossing aside the crossbow and taking up the daggers along the ground, he charged as well.

The blades clashed against her rapier. Steel beheld stark raving lunacy as she parried and reversed his attack. Although her stabs appeared reckless—and perhaps to an extent they were—he realized they were executed with almost perfect technique.

"You will not resist Amu'uth forever!" she cried.

"You should listen to yourself. Don't you realize you're being controlled?"

She gave a wild howl, delivering a swipe that, if Steel hadn't dodged, he was certain would have sliced his head clean off.

He regained his composure. They fought on—*clash* after metallic *clang*. Just twenty paces to the thief's left, Stormbright fought against the wrathful spirits. He slashed fore and aft, cutting through phantasms though it affected them little. Amu'uth goaded the spirits into the fray as He tended to His wound.

The young sorcerer walked back, sheathing his sword. The spirits of Captain Helvia and Aurora lashed out, bringing deep gashes along his arms. He did not relent. Blue streaks of power interspersed among the specters. The magic tendrils danced around Amu'uth in a spherical arc, leaving Him unaffected. The ghosts of Helvia, Ava, Ida, and the traitorous

Aurora, however, were dispersed, free to wander towards the mysterious Great Beyond.

In that moment, he caught a final glimpse of the young initiate. Regret dawned on her sorrowful face as her form faded into thin air.

A clawed hand struck forth, sooner than he anticipated, grabbing him up by the throat. What stared at him was a distortion of life, much worse than Plegma and the nightmare-kin.

Perhaps it was more insidious than the Falconer!

"*Stop!*" He commanded.

Evidently the words were directed to his side. Myriad bruises and cuts ran along Steel's prone form. The Falconer held her rapier, poised for the finishing strike.

Despite her anger, she halted. Amu'uth's word was Law.

"*Bring him to me.*"

General Caerst swiveled toward Him, full of defiance.

"*Bring him to me, my Wildflower.*"

She hesitated before grabbing the thief by one boot, dragging him closer.

Amu'uth smiled as Stormbright was helpless in His grasp. "*As I have said, both of you will be the first to satiate my appetite.*"

The god's jaw stretched and unhinged. Stormbright froze as he peered into the abyss conjured by that horrifying deity.

So this was to be their fate. Stormbright peered into oblivion, deep into the maw where souls whorled and coalesced. He and Steel were to join them—become one with the great Amu'uth.

No, he would not let that happen.

A great howl resounded as the moon god released hold of him. He raised his head. Lightning streamed and crackled along his arms, bringing with it tremendous suffering. Strands of energy swayed and undulated; this inspired him to direct his magic towards the immortal. White ivory flesh cracked, blackened, and sizzled. Amu'uth bellowed his wrath.

General Caerst withdrew her rapier, readying a stab that would bring down the sorcerer for good.

Stormbright pivoted so his lightning blasted her directly. The Falconer flew until she landed at some distance, her head colliding with a nearby rock.

Aedas stood close, a faint issuance of color radiating from the astromancer's palm. The realization hit Stormbright, and he couldn't help but smile.

"Do not be fooled, young sorcerer; a god is weakest when they are newly born." Aedas indicated Amu'uth, who showed distress from Stormbright's lightning. "As you can observe, the Dreamstone has an effect on Him. Our time is short, but if we can manage to slay such a being, we must do so now." It was obvious the astromancer struggled to stand, yet Aedas did not falter in his conviction.

"Brother, are you all right?" Stormbright spun and knelt beside Steel. Although the lightning ceased along the sorcerer's body, curiously enough, his eyes glowed with power.

Steel coughed as he lay among the dirt. "I'm just wonderful…"

"Very good. We can finish it together!"

The thief grimaced as Stormbright helped him to his feet. "And here I was worrying about you. Damn it, Zolan."

Stormbright gave a strained laugh. "I can't channel much more," he said. "Aedas has got the advantage for us. Can you distract Amu'uth for me?"

"Aye—I can manage that."

"We can do this, Serithas. You and I, we are blade and lightning. Alone we are strong, but together we are unstoppable."

"Blade and lightning?" Steel chuckled. "I like the sound of it." He shoved his fist against Stormbright's shoulder with a smile, realizing what he had been missing this entire time. His brother would look out for him, no matter how grim the situation.

He nodded, his newfound determination granting him enough strength to run towards the wounded deity. The thief evaded Amu'uth's claws as he sought for an opening. As instructed, Steel feinted and maneuvered so the god was distracted. Stormbright hurried to one side along with Aedas, readying what little magic he had left. His vision blurred as energy coursed along his arms and fingers. The astromancer placed a hand along his back, and the surge of power was unmistakable. He felt for his center, directing his mind, body, and spirit into one as the lightning intensified, creating blazing strands which threatened to incinerate him.

Was he capable of this much power, or was it the Dreamstone?

The lightning cascaded, striking into Amu'uth's back. The deity bellowed like a demon. Steel hovered close, stabbing once the magic had ceased. The moonsteel daggers flashed silver as they reflected the twin celestial bodies above. Blackish blood streamed from wounds innumerable. The god strove as one might to strike back. Souls of the dead swirled around Him, trying as well to deter those who resisted. Alas, wherever the ghosts coalesced, Stormbright shot them down with lightning, thus releasing them from Amu'uth's control.

Steel did not falter as he slashed and dodged, cutting along muscles and tendons until the deity was brought to His knees.

"Now, Zolan!"

The sorcerer delivered one last burst of crackling energy before collapsing. Amu'uth howled as He faltered. Steel followed up with a guttural cry, plunging his daggers directly into the god's heart.

Steel panted. Traces of light crept underneath the deity's skin as He convulsed. The realization hit him while facing Stormbright, Mikka, and Aedas.

"Run!!"

Amu'uth gave a final cry as divine light dominated, culminating in an explosion of roaring celestial fire.

A low wind passed through the clearing. Bodies lay in heaps as not a soul stirred. The slow process of decay would come as the stench of blood and death diffused, and the corpses deteriorated, leaving naught but maggots and bones.

The moon god awakened. Amuuth's strength was fast fading, for His time was close.

How far had He fallen in such a short time? Wasn't He the one to bring a new age of prosperity—of love, hope, and joy—to those who needed Him the most? The deity pondered this in fury as He lay dying. To be undone by mortals, it was the greatest crime!

There was but one truth. The world could not be reshaped by one such as Him, yet perhaps another.

He pulled Himself across the battlefield. His body was a battered, broken mess. Amu'uth's limbs hardly responded to His command, with legs dragging limply behind as a single, unbroken arm carried Him onward. A thin trail of blood marked His passage. There at some distance, near the edge of the forest, He found General Caerst. The Falconer lay motionless, yet Amu'uth knew her life was intact, registering as a vibrant beating in her chest.

"My dearest Queen, you shall be my successor." The god held His hand over her face, black-bleeding fingers smearing her lips. *"If you would, take what is left of my life. I realize it isn't the whim of gods to shape this world, but instead that of mortals. Sleep, my love—my Wildflower. Sleep and dream of a brighter future. Dream until it becomes real. I will be watching from above, in the shadowy space between stars. I will be waiting for you. For you…"*

Amu'uth smiled as a trickle of His life essence passed into her. It was enough. He lay beside the one whom He had ensorcelled, her will bent to suit His own. The deity felt a strange love for the woman—her ambition, beauty, and potential.

After all, He had chosen her for a reason.

The god breathed deep. Next would come the risky part—the reliance on her to achieve His ultimate plan.

The irony wasn't lost on Him, and so Amu'uth died, laughing as His body faded with the coming dawn.

XX

After the Fall

Steel and Stormbright groaned as they opened their eyes. Their bodies were bruised and smeared in blood, though otherwise they appeared unharmed.

"I'm shocked we made it," said Steel.

Stormbright struggled to his feet. Stepping around the piles of dead, he was relieved to find Aedas conscious. He stopped next to Mikka, who was pale but still breathing. The puncture in her chest ran deep, but by some miracle it had missed her heart.

The thief stumbled beside him. "Mikka… Mikka, stay with us!"

Aedas approached, having well recovered his senses. Judging from the wound, the astromancer could tell it was serious. He held up the Dreamstone, its opalescent colors dancing around a perceptible crack.

"Move aside," he said, taking her hand and channeling the Dreamstone. As the stabbing wound mended across her chest, so too did the magic stone crumble. Little sparks crackled in the air, ringing with a tone of finality.

Mikka remained asleep as Stormbright inspected the injury along her chest. The wound had mostly healed, save for a scar underneath the right breast. There was still bleeding, yet it was slight.

With time, he imagined the wound might fully heal.

"Mikka. Please say something." Steel held his breath as he waited.

The girl opened her eyes, and the brothers eyed her with intense relief. Steel brought her close and laughed.

As Mikka was held by Steel, the young sorcerer rose, wandering over to what little was left of Plegma. The corpse was mutilated, with the greater half of its body decimated from the moon god's birth.

"Feel with your inner self," said Aedas, who walked beside him.

He did so.

"I don't sense anything," said Stormbright.

The astromancer hummed his approval. "The abomination is truly dead. Forsooth, I thank the gods this did not worsen."

"Speaking of worse, where is General Caerst?" Stormbright glanced around the clearing. He found no trace of her nor Amu'uth.

"I am uncertain…"

While pondering this mystery, Steel and Mikka limped to where they stood. The thief retrieved his daggers, gripped them firmly as he searched. His time spent in Captain Helvia's dungeon reemerged, searing like an unquenchable flame.

"Where is she?" Steel growled. He inspected the mounds of dead. He scoured the glade for any sign of where the Falconer might be. "I know General Caerst is alive. We must end her before it's too late."

"Steel, don't," said Mikka faintly, grabbing him by the shoulder. "We don't have time for this."

"You would be wise to heed her words," Aedas commented. "Can you not hear them?"

Steel listened, noticing the distant, thundering hoofbeats of riders heading in their direction. He grimaced, the object of his hatred just outside his grasp.

He turned to Stormbright.

"Help me find her," he said.

The galloping grew louder.

"Brother, we don't have time for-"

"I said *help me find her!*" he yelled, his voice filled with rage. "She ruined your life as well as mine! We must make sure she never returns! It ends right here!"

The youth took a step back. What happened to Steel while they were separated? The thief's harsh severity made his skin crawl, as he saw less of the man he knew, but something vaguely monstrous.

"I'm afraid the time for vengeance will have to wait," said Aedas. He ushered them back. "Do not forget your father, Steel. Is her life more important than his?"

At this, doubt registered within him. A visible hurt showed along his face.

Mikka tugged at his arm. "Come. It's time for us to leave."

Steel noted the softness in her expression. Confusion, melancholy, and anger whirled inside him. Steel wasn't sure what to do.

A push came from the astromancer. "You must leave! Meet me at The Black Quail Tavern, in the village of Shadevale by the week's end. Do not forget!"

Steel, Stormbright, and Mikka fled despite the thief's insistence to stay. Moments later, the cavalcade of soldiers emerged into view. Five armored figures rode atop their horses, all thanking their heavenly stars that the morning had come at last! As for the man in front, Aedas recognized him as Neto. Not only was he furious, but his armor was different, being a crude and rusted set from Candala's barracks.

"What in Her Radiance's name…?"

It was a scene of desolation. Bodies piled in heaps as the Ilgrathian soldiers uncovered the mangled forms of cultists and nightmare-kin. The lieutenant shook his head in dismay.

"It seems we've had to spar with a heathen deity," said Aedas casually.

Neto maneuvered his horse, scouting for any signs of life. He pursed his lips, almost having missed the trail of black blood. He pointed along the ground so the astromancer was aware of it. Neto dismounted, armor clinking as he crossed to an edge of the clearing. Aedas glimpsed the Falconer laying on her back. She was alive, though her lips were smeared with a black stain. At this Aedas cocked an eyebrow.

"I apologize," continued Neto. "General Caerst was my responsibility. You may punish me as you wish, sir."

The astromancer looked stolidly at General Caerst, then to Neto, who knelt at his side. "Are you aware of how she escaped?"

"Somehow, my soldiers betrayed me and fought one another. By the time I awoke they were dead. I must assume it was her doing."

"An eye for an eye." A low exhale escaped Aedas' lips. Alas, his plans would have to change. He loathed his predicament, yet perhaps he could leave a clue. "This time I will accompany you. I'm afraid the Dreamstone was destroyed, but it is a trifling matter. We have the Falconer, and now it is our duty to keep her from escaping."

"Aye," replied the lieutenant, gesturing for his men to retrieve the Falconer, the one person he had grown to respect amidst their defeat. He experienced a measure of pity, knowing the pressure from her duty must have shattered her sanity. "If I may ask," he said, "what was her reasoning for coming here?"

Aedas grimaced. "Lieutenant, our respected superior was swayed towards this 'other god', the result of which you see before you."

"Then it's as I feared," said Neto. "But enough talk. Let us be off while there is still time. Do you require medical attention?"

"Nay. Just rest, and I can fare as well on the road."

"So be it." The Ilgrathian signaled two of his men to dismount and restrain her. By the time they removed her weapons and armor, Neto realized she was awake. General Caerst said nothing as the rope was tied around her wrists. She wept softly.

"Gag her and put a sack over her head. This time she will not escape us. Take the armor as well, for it is mine she stole."

Aedas kept silent. He would have to find some way of contacting the brothers while departing with the Ilgrathians. An awful taste lingered in the back of his throat. He wasn't sure how, yet he shuddered at what was to come.

Dawn broke the distant horizon. Steel admired the majestic sight—the vibrant ochre hue that would sprout into a bright and clear day. The scent of roses and lilac tickled at his nostrils, an aroma carried from some distant valley below. He breathed deep. Off to the far edge of the escarpment, Stormbright was perched along the cliff's edge, his legs dangling as the wind carried its pleasing scents.

The boy sulked as he had these last several days. Steel knew he would have to speak with him soon.

Turning into the cave that was their habitation, his thoughts drifted to how their group had fared since fleeing Candala. They had found no shortage of food this high up, for Stormbright had stumbled across a bountiful patch of mountain berries early on in their journey. The two noted their vibrant red color and distinctive shape, remembering how they once picked raspberries with their fellow villagers. These fit the description well enough, and a studious glance of their color and stems showed no signs of poison. Chewing it revealed a taste both sweet and filling. Their eyes lit up as their intuition proved correct. Further exploring yielded dozens of hidden patches, and with Steel's resourceful trap-setting, they had netted themselves a grand total of four coneys. By the end of their first night, they were eating well with the hearty meat and sweet fruit—the fire burning warm whilst they cooked the rabbits and inhaled the wondrous scents. They smiled and talked as they feasted, often exchanging a laugh or two as the conversation meandered, the memory of their time within the Caprian Forest bleeding away, at least for the night.

Steel was glad for their fortune and, better yet, Mikka was returning to normal. He knelt beside her, seeing the girl was wrapped tightly in her bedroll. For the last three days, she had done little other than sleep and sate her hunger with the occasional handful of raspberries. The thief ensured her wounds were properly bandaged, with the occasional grimace being the sole reminder of such a grievous injury. He felt along her head, noting her fever had broken. That was good.

He was about to leave when she stirred.

"Steel… Is that-" She rose to a sitting position.

"You had me worried for a second," he interjected, holding her hand. He saw the warmth in her face, the earnest affection.

"You and Stormbright will be leaving soon. Off to meet with Aedas and your father."

Steel smiled. "We're so close, I can feel it."

"I'm assuming you wouldn't have room for one more," she said drowsily.

"Who said we were looking to add someone to our group?" He smirked. So did she; evidently his sarcasm wasn't lost on her. He rose to his feet and stepped toward the opening. "Are you sure you want to come with us?"

Mikka rose to a sitting position. "Why do you think I joined you in the first place? I can tell you and your brother care about rescuing your father. I bandaged your wounds after what happened with Captain Helvia and General Caerst. I suppose I should do the same for him."

"I suppose so." In truth, Steel hadn't imagined what state Kolthan might be in as a free man. Perhaps he blotted out the possibility? How could the man who protected them, raised them as adolescents, be anything less than sufficiently well? That said, Steel had been broken in just under a day; their father, by comparison, had endured for far longer.

"There is something about the two of you," said Mikka. "I can't quite explain it. I suppose it's a need for me to follow. A need to watch, and remember."

"You almost speak like a minstrel," he said.

"What, do you not like it?

Steel shook his head. "It's beautiful."

Taking a deep breath, he walked through the cave's entrance, the sunlight warming his skin. He saw Stormbright seated along the escarpment, the youth's legs dangling as he observed the panoramic view which their campsite afforded. To the distant southeast, he spotted Candala, that decrepit city of cutthroats.

Steel was glad to be rid of it.

The young sorcerer gave a fake smile. "Oh, hi Serithas."

"Hello, yourself." Steel sat beside him, letting his legs swing over the vast distance spanning below. The sensation was freeing, exhilarating. He could tell why Zolan enjoyed the spot so much.

"Still a little upset?" he asked.

Stormbright shrugged. "I guess so. It's just, she wasn't what I was expecting."

"Yeah. Women can be like that sometimes."

"What about you and Kitala? What about…?"

Steel glanced sidelong at his brother. "Crazy women are different," he said.

The young sorcerer paused. "I suppose you're right." The cool wind tugged at his golden locks of hair. Perhaps it was the fading heat of autumn, or maybe the wondrous vista that allowed him to be so talkative. Either way, it felt good.

"When did you realize she wasn't right for you?"

"Huh?" Stormbright noticed his brother's curiosity.

"When did you realize she was…?" Steel made a circular motion with his finger. "I knew when the bitch clocked me over the head with a rock."

"Aye, that is true. I believe she was someone who went through a great deal of anguish, yet… she didn't overcome it. Rather, she allowed the priestesses to change her into something she's not. So did the cultists, now that I think of it. I find that sad."

While saying it, a whirlwind of emotion stirred inside him. There was the same sense of betrayal—of disgust as well—but at the same time he wondered if he would have done any differently, had he been in her shoes.

Gods, he wished he knew.

"You didn't answer my question," his brother repeated.

Stormbright breathed slowly. "It was when… when she tried seducing me. I learned of the cult and who they truly were. She had almost taken advantage of me, though I pushed her away before anything happened." A wave of embarrassment hit him. The time was so distant, but he remembered how strange it was—the contradiction of desire and helplessness.

He had been so weak—so vulnerable.

He lifted his eyes, realizing Steel looked at him with discomfort.

"Are you okay, Brother? I know what I'm saying isn't pleasant, but I wasn't harmed. Brother?"

Steel cast a single glance, his eyes showing inner turmoil. "I'm sorry, Zolan…"

Stormbright frowned. "Something happened, didn't it? What I said must have struck a chord with you."

He noted his brother's discomfort. The idea of how he would have acted, had he been in Aurora's place, resurfaced. It explained so much—Steel's desperation, his uncontrollable anger toward the Falconer. He wasn't sure how, but Steel had lived through a similar nightmare.

"Tell me truthfully, Brother. What happened?"

Steel hesitated as he tried forming a reply—tried but failed to do so. "I was caught before I could steal the Moon Cup. Captain Helvia and General Caerst, they took their time getting the information they could. At first they hit me. Then they peeled the flesh from my fingers. Then," he swallowed, "there were dreams. They used the Dreamstone to get to me.

I'm not sure how they did it, Zolan. They dredged up my deepest, darkest fears. I saw you—Father—Kitala. All of you were slain in front of me. It was so real, Brother, I… I didn't know what to do. I didn't…"

Stormbright embraced him. He had never heard Serithas speak with such distress, not as he did now. He had seen him in tears, witnessed him stumble when his beloved Kitala had forgotten him as a star wraith, cursed to wander as a specter in the realm of the living. But this, it was like he sensed the wound inside. Those terrible memories would leave a permanent scar.

Compared to his brother, Stormbright never thought himself as much of a vengeful type. That said, he wished they had sufficient time to slay General Caerst when they had the chance. If only he had known. If only…

He held Steel tight as the young thief sought comfort in his arms, weeping quietly.

"That's it," said Stormbright, his tone low and full of emotion. "I'm here for you, Serithas."

Steel grew quiet until he regarded the sorcerer directly. "I sold you out," he said, his voice quavering. "I told them where to find you. I-I-I'm sorry, Zolan. I don't…"

The realization lit on Stormbright's face. "You mean the Ilgrathians who attacked? They were because of you?"

Steel nodded, his gaze sullen.

A stretch of time came and went before Stormbright spoke.

"I don't know what to say," he murmured. "You probably wouldn't believe it, but… you might have saved me. You remember when I mentioned Aurora? Her trying to seduce me?"

"Yeah?" Steel replied, confused.

"Nothing happened because we were interrupted. We were invaded by Ilgrathian soldiers. General Caerst was there, but luckily I escaped. You might call it an ironic twist of fate, Brother, but I really think you saved me."

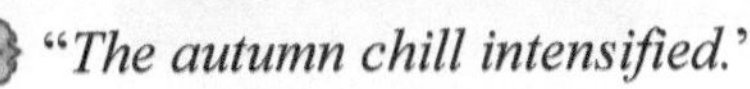

"The autumn chill intensified."

Steel shook his head, as if being spared a punishment he fully deserved.

"Zolan… I don't know what to…"

Again they embraced, and never had Serithas experienced such a deep measure of gratitude, of understanding, for what this young sorcerer—his brother—was capable of.

"You're my brother, Serithas. How could I not forgive you?"

Steel laughed slightly. He couldn't believe what he was hearing.

"We stick together, okay? For Father's sake… for our own sake."

"You're right, Zolan. We stick together—you and me."

"Besides," he said, "you should teach me a thing or two about how to talk to girls—ones who are agreeable."

At this he chuckled. Serithas, known also as Steel in the lands conquered by Alcaron, wrangled his brother by the shoulder, rubbing his knuckles atop the sorcerer's head.

"Ow, stop it!"

"Why should I stop when I'm teaching you the first lesson?" he said. "The first is to always show confidence! Show no doubt and stay relaxed, even when someone has you in a headlock."

"Ow-ow! Okay! I get it, I get it!"

Steel released his hold, the two of them laughing and teasing. A little while longer and the joking between them stopped. A calm serenity filled the air as they peered off into the grand horizon. The sun and sky, the distant smattering of clouds and grass and hills, the slight wind brushing at their hair and shoulders, all of it appeared so beautiful.

The autumn chill intensified. It was then Steel and Stormbright planned their next move.

Epilogue

The din of voices lowered. Those who drank and sang in The Black Quail Tavern wandered home earlier than was their wont, departing without so much as a good-bye, a handwave, or even a chuckle.

The occurrence was most unsettling to those who remained. Even Rabus thought this odd considering his usual clientele.

His hands scrubbed at one of the many tankards. A low rumble came from the back of his throat, hocking a globule of phlegm as he continued his cleaning.

It was eerie how rumor spread of two criminals near Candala, ones who had played a role in killing Captain Helvia, no less.

The tavern-keeper knew little more on the matter, though his instincts told him to focus on the supposed day of Aedas' return. He knew this was a pressing matter for his special guest, whom the astromancer had spent an exorbitant amount of drakons to keep hidden.

"Now's about the time, Aedas," he muttered.

The month's end was here.

Rabus observed Tela as the blonde courtesan gathered up tankards, plates, and utensils. The leftovers were strewn by a party of old drunkards—a bunch of brigands whom Rabus didn't like in the least.

"Be sure to keep a special eye out for our guests. If the astromancer's time is correct, they should be arriving this very evening."

"Aye, my lord," she responded, the sarcasm lacing her words. She waited for the inevitable beratement or insult, but this time it did not come. The aged prostitute regarded her employer with concern. "What is it, Rabus? Another one of your bad feelings?"

"Yes, something like that," he responded.

"It's pointless to worry," she said sympathetically. "I always keep a close watch. Our special guest is safe and sound above. I don't know what the Ilgrathians did to him, though thinking about it makes me shiver all over."

"Aye, just so. Even for one who's dealt with prisoners and fugitives, never in my life have I met someone so hopeless. It isn't that his mind is gone. It's like… like someone took a part of him."

He shut his eyes, grounding himself in the fragrance of cheap spirits, perfume, and sweat. A cold sweat clung to his brow. What was with him tonight? Perhaps it was the sparse business, save for the one table that had given him trouble? Surely that was the cause.

Tela placed a comforting hand on his shoulder. Normally Tela's gesture would have agitated him to no end. In truth, he found little attraction in his harlots compared to their male counterparts, and he suspected she was aware due to her constant jabs. Nevertheless, he was comforted.

"I'll go and check on him," she said.

"That's a good idea," was his response.

The tavern-keeper pinched the bridge of his nose as his business grew insufferably quiet. The faint rumble of thunder made the hairs on his neck rise. He stood alone as the gentle downpour grew in intensity, the howling winds and sheets of water thrashing along the tavern roof.

A knock sounded at the door. This time Rabus answered it himself, noting his maiden prostitutes were imminently preoccupied. Opening the metallic grille, he counted three hooded figures. The one nearest him bore the look of a scoundrel, perhaps even a killer. The other two were smaller in stature, with one being female.

"What's your business?" he asked.

"We have special orders to meet with a human named Aedas," said the man closest to him. Although he tried to hide it, Rabus caught a glimmer of green irises underneath a head of wild brown hair.

"Aedas?" the tavern-keeper feigned ignorance, as if hearing the name for the first time. "What sort of business do you have with this person?"

The hooded thief glanced at his surroundings, assuring they wouldn't be overheard. "He sent us to find someone—a person who's very dear to us. We wanted to make sure he's safe."

"Oh? And what is this person's name, praytell?"

The figure did not immediately respond. The tavern-keeper pictured these visitors being imposters of some sort, perhaps the fugitives who had robbed Helvia Manor, until the name "Kolthan" was whispered.

Rabus grunted in approval, sliding the grille closed. He turned the latches and locks which normally barred less savory figures, thus permitting them entrance.

"You may seat yourselves as you like."

Steel, Stormbright, and Mikka drew back their hoods as the wind and rain pounded from outside. The brothers' hearts beat more rapidly than normal. Their father, Kolthan, was here!

"I honestly don't know how I should feel," said Stormbright, an earnest smile dawning on his lips.

"You and me both." Steel rocked him by the shoulder, giving a low laugh. Mikka snickered as she, too, basked in their joy.

It was the next that she fell silent.

"Something isn't right," she said.

After a while the tavern-keeper returned, with Tela bringing in their esteemed guest. First Stormbright peered in their direction, then Steel as well. The man wasn't Kolthan—nor was Aedas anywhere to be found. The blonde-haired, fair-skinned Ilgrathian gave them a blank stare. Drool collected along his chin, which Tela promptly cleaned with a kerchief.

"This," said Rabus with a grimace, "is your father."

"What in the name of-" Steel did not hide his disbelief. "How can you expect us to believe such lies? He's not our father. That isn't Kolthan!"

Upon utterance of the name, a hint of recognition lit within the Ilgrathian. Stormbright noticed as much from the man standing across them.

"Brother…" Doubt lingered in his voice.

"Did you expect to get away with this? Tricking us into thinking this was the person we were searching for?"

"Now wait just a minute. I had no part in this deal other than granting him shelter. The astromancer informed me this 'Menthus' was the real Kolthan."

"Like hells it is! You must have tricked him into leading us here. You will not fool us, Tavern-Keeper!"

Rabus paced back as Steel felt for his daggers.

"I demand you show us our father!" he persisted.

"Brother…"

"What!" The thief realized Stormbright was tugging at his shoulder. His murderous intent relaxed as the sorcerer gestured to the Ilgrathian. Steel shifted his gaze to the man whom this tavern-keeper labeled as Kolthan. The man was staring at them.

Perhaps it was an inclination? No—his eyes were the same. How could they be the same?

"I can feel with my *inner sense*, Brother," continued Stormbright. "I don't know how, but that's… that's…"

"Your father," said Mikka.

Steel inhaled. He wasn't sure how it had happened, though the truth was too much to deny. How had Kolthan ended up like this? He inspected the man's arm and saw it was fully healed; that was one worry dealt with, as he recalled the grievous wound General Caerst had made.

Epilogue

It was the strangest impression, yet he believed only the gods could guide them—show them the way. At least to Steel, it seemed one chapter of their life had ended while another was starting to take form.

"Father?" he murmured.

END

Under the Shadow of Twin Moons, a new world is born.

Glossary

A

Aedas (ay-dus): A human that was captured and conditioned to serve the Ilgrathians, following the realization that he has a talent for astromancy. Aedas acts as an advisor of sorts, as he is one of the few human sorcerers that's allowed to practice his magic. He has grayed ebony hair and a somewhat scrawny build.

Aeromancy: The magic school of manipulating winds, clouds, and lightning. Stormbright is an aeromancer himself, although he specializes in lightning.

Alcaron (AL-kuh-RON): The golden empire of Ilgrathié. Alcaron is ground zero for the goddess' vision of Paradise. These lands are wild and teeming with sweet fruits and chirping birds. At least on the surface, it appears like everything one could desire is here; yet there are many dark secrets lurking underneath.

Amu'uth (ah-MOOTH): A recently-born deity that is revered by the Children of the Sacred Twins, Amu'uth is a moon god who aims to spawn a new age of prosperity. First and foremost, this involves the driving away of the Ilgrathians. The human deity is gaunt in appearance, with pale-white skin, a muscular build, and an elongated forehead. He stands at a height of approximately 5 cubits (7.5 feet).

Ancients, the: A forgotten race who constructed the grand city of Candala. It is believed by some that its original purpose was to create a massive citadel warded by various magicks, as the horrific form of Plegma remained sealed underneath. Scholars believe that time was approximately 1,500 years ago. The reason for the Ancients' departure remains a mystery, however.

Astromancy: The magic school of peering into the past, present, and possible futures. As one might expect, this talent is highly coveted, as astromancers are quite rare in the world. Aedas and Ida are both astromancers.

Aurora (oh-ROAR-ah): A young initiate of seventeen years, Aurora is a believer in the Children of the Sacred Twins and acts as an agent of sorts. She has flowing black hair, dark eyes, and an alluring figure, carefully accentuated with dark makeup and eyeshadow.

Ava (ay-vah): One of the two conjoined priestesses leading the Children of the Sacred Twins. Ava is benevolent, joyous, and empathetic, specializing in oneiromancy. Both she and her sister have flowing silver hair and blue eyes.

Awakening: When learning the art of sorcery, it is possible to have one's potential awakened in a few different ways: The first is through years of hard work, training, and discipline, whereas the second is being "called" by a powerful entity. Oftentimes this is through a deity, but it can also be achieved by others.

B

Berrin (bear-in): A member of the Children of the Sacred Twins who keeps a protective eye out for his fellow brothers and sisters.

Black Quail Tavern, the: The one and only tavern located in the village of Shadevale. The structure stands at two stories, with the interior being clean and quiet. Tavern-keeper Rabus runs the place, and is helped out by his own harlots.

Blood: It's widely known that, in magic, blood is what links humans and the various races together. The closer one's blood bonds are, the greater the chance that a sorcerer can affect a person vicariously, such as through a sibling, parent, or other close relative.

Brevus (breh-vus): An Ilgrathian guard patrolling Helvia Manor. Both he and his fellows love to jest and spread rumors.

Bruann (BROO-ann): The second of Zirvonia's two orbiting moons. Bruann is farther out among the skies, though most scholars and sorcerers have agreed that it's the larger of the two.

Brugmar (broog-mahr): A large humanoid beast standing at three-times the height of a regular human. These creatures most resemble a hybrid mix between a lion and a wolf, showing several rows of teeth like a shark. Brugmars are savage beings who are widely feared among Zirvonia. Only the bravest would dare to stand against them.

C

Calamtu (KUH-lam-TOO): The god of storms and fury. Calamtu is a deity to be feared as much as admired, and thus His worship is practiced from afar. He is rarely if ever seen, as He's been spotted only a handful of times throughout the centuries.

Candala (can-DAH-lah): A city built and abandoned by the Ancients. This is a place that was first reinhabited by humans, then invaded approximately 50 years ago by Alcaron. The metropolis is rife with crime and permeating smog. Not only this, but an ancient corruption seeps outward from underneath its sewers—strange nightmare-kin and other malformed beings. It is a hive of thievery, betrayal, and strange magicks.

Candala Depths: This comprises both the city sewers as well as the interconnecting tunnels below it. The city depths are immense both in their size and layout, as it seems the intent was to seal away the ancient horror known as Plegma, one of the grand sentinels of nightmare-kin. Over the centuries, the nightmare-kin presence has only increased as Plegma's seal has weakened. This has caused the walls to become suffused with an awful meaty substance, and even the layout appears like it's been irrevocably altered.

Caprian Forest, the: A dark forest where it's said that terrible beasts stalk about at night. Some have speculated that the place is cursed, but Alcaronian officials have largely denounced this claim. Despite this knowledge, those who know of the area give it a wide berth.

Captain Helvia (hell-vee-ah): An Ilgrathian serving as inquisitor and captain of the city guard in Candala. She makes do with the fact that she is not a Falconer, seeing it as an unnecessary advantage. Captain Helvia may not be an official leader as far as city politics are considered, but her position is feared by all Candala's residents. She has raven black hair and dark eyes.

Children of the Sacred Twins, the: A cult centered around the worship of Taldriath and Bruann, the twin moons looming high in the night sky. Perhaps at one point their method of worship was peaceful, but over time the cult has adopted the practice of sacrificing Ilgrathians to their gods. This, along with their penchant of hosting ritualistic orgies, has led to their bad name and reputation. Even those who sympathize with the cause of repelling the Ilgrathians have shunned this group of fanatics.

Cubit: Measuring unit that's more familiar to ancient history in our world. 1 cubit roughly translates to 1.5 feet, or 0.5 meters.

D

Demon: A type of imp covered in fiendish black scales, with crooked beaks, sharp talons, and tattered wings. Demons are highly efficient killing machines, even though they're far weaker when divided. Together, however, demons can dispatch even the toughest of prey. They have a penchant for slaughter and are capable of slaying their allies just as quickly as their enemies.

Divnarost (DIV-nuh-ROST): A once-mighty kingdom that has fallen into ruin over the last century. Nearly all of Divnarost's cities have been overtaken by the curse of the star wraiths, with Miracor serving as the last bastion for the Islirians - the nation's original founders. This is a culture that values omens and knowledge above all else, as they're the very first astromancers to hone their craft.

Drakon, Coin: The Alcaronian gold coin. Drakons are so named after Alcaron's first lieutenant, Mirios Drakon, who paved the way for Ilgrathié's rule nearly 500 years ago. His profile is printed on one side, whereas the other has the symbol of a falcon.

Dreamstone: A miraculous type of gem which glimmers with opalescent colors. Dreamstone is capable of making the impossible possible, amplifying one's ability to use oneiromancy and shape the world around them. Even those with a casual knowledge in the magic arts can wield such a stone. The tradeoff, however, is that the effort is highly taxing.

Driftwind: A lonely village that is two days east of Candala, skirting the edge of the Caprian Forest. The settlement was just recently destroyed by Captain Helvia and her soldiers, as this was one of two places where the Children of the Sacred Twins had hid their moon cup relics. Now it's completely bereft of life, almost haunting as all traces of bodies were wiped away by nightmare-kin.

E

Enlightened, the: Some creatures, either through their natural state of being or rigorous magical study, will become enlightened. This is an altered state of mind which corresponds directly with their abilities, oftentimes manifesting as a field of altered reality. The more powerful the creature is, the larger the radius is and the more fantastical this reality becomes. Beings such as the Faunus, Amu'uth, and Ilgrathié all hold this ability.

F

Falcon: The standard Alcaronian soldier. Their garb is either brass or polished moonsteel, with spears and longbows as their preferred weapons.

Falconer: An elite female soldier personally chosen by Ilgrathié, one who's given a drop of the goddess' blood. This grants them enhanced strength, cunning, and dexterity, but does little to alter their appearance. This is one of the highest ranks of Alcaron's military.

Faunus (fawn-us): A magic beast that dwells in glades or along abandoned roads. Fauni are generally seen as benevolent creatures who are eager to help. Some individuals such as the Children of the Sacred Twins see them as holy emissaries, as they will oftentimes sing, play, and dance under the light of the twin moons.

Fields of Man, the: A vast series of rolling plains and acacia trees. The Fields of Man is the cradle of human civilization in Zirvonia, one that's given limited autonomy by Alcaron. The lands are shaken by storms that come and go in mere moments, leaving devastation and heavy mudslides in their wake. The Fields of Man serves as an effective buffer between Alcaron and Divnarost, hence why the humans are given a certain amount of freedom.

G

Galvos (GAHL-vos): A sturdy, bald-headed innkeeper who runs The Golden Leaf Inn. The human chooses not to say much, although it's said he holds sympathy for those who would resist Alcaron and the Ilgrathians.

General Caerst (kayrst): An esteemed Falconer who failed in conquering Divnarost, General Caerst is now on a quest for vengeance against Steel and Stormbright. She is 47 years of age, although by Ilgrathian standards, this is fairly young. She is slim and beautiful. Her eyes are blue and her hair is a vibrant gold, with a long braid stretching down her back.

Geomancy: The magic school of manipulating earth and the forces of nature. Those referred to as druids are often geomancers.

Ghost of Helvia Manor, the: A vaguely humanoid figure with glossy eyes and a hunched figure. This creature is purported to have once been a priest for the Children of the Sacred Twins. It's also rumored that he sought their aid when the Ilgrathians invaded approximately 50 years ago. Perhaps his wish was granted?

Gillaskar (gih-LAH-scar): A mountain region that is almost completely isolated from the rest of the world. Gillaskar is a loose conglomeration of tribes made up by the giant-like race known as Gillaski. These tribes are scattered among the Dreaming Mountains, and each is led by its own Enlightened.

Gillaski (gih-LAH-skee): A humanoid race who dwell in the mountainous regions of Gillaskar, otherwise known as the Dreaming Mountains. Gillaski are taller than regular men, with some reaching up to 8 cubits (or 12 feet) in height. Contrary to their appearance and tribalistic nature, Gillaski are a rather spiritual folk, revering powerful creatures which they have found in their domains over the centuries. Some are revered as gods, whereas others merely play a role as dutiful guardians. This has led to the belief that there is nothing at all beyond the Dreaming Mountains. Such is supported by the axiom, "As one in the earth, so too are we undone."

Golden Leaf Inn, the: A tavern located in the Beggar's District of Candala. Despite its dubious surroundings, the inn has a decently good reputation to hold. Beds are kept clean and the ale is fresh, even if the customers are more than a little shady.

Great Beyond, the: A vast realm of seemingly infinite possibilities. The Great Beyond encompasses a host of worlds outside Zirvonia. Under normal circumstances, only trained sorcerers are able to explore these wide, fathomless regions, and even that comes with great risk. It is an ethereal realm, and it's believed that the secrets to life, death, and the meaning of existence may be found here.

Great Equilibrium, the: Also known as the bi-lunar eclipse, this is a time of convergence when the twin moons appear as if they're crossing over and becoming one. Not only is this event rare, but there is a spiritual connotation as well. Those who worship Taldriath and Bruann believe that such an event marks a new era for the world—a time of new beginnings. Often they are instructed on how this age might come to pass, and so believers work tirelessly to see that their will is carried out.

Gulizar (goo-lih-zahr): The head shaman of Harskul and brother to Aedas. The man is short, bald, and lanky, with green eyes.

H

Harskul (HAR-skull): The destroyed home of Steel, Stormbright, and their father Kolthan. This was once a quaint village with an honored history of celebrating the old ways. Settlements like these are usually overseen by a shaman who, by the power of potent narcotics, is able to peer into the future and predict the seasons, along with potential signs and omens.

Helvia Manor: Located in Candala's Wealthy District, this is the abode of Captain Helvia. It's a vast estate comprising dozens of rooms, hallways, and a height of three stories. This is where Helvia keeps her vast collection of literature, her harem, and also a private vault containing her wealth. There are currently legends of a ghost that wanders the manor's cellars, as a few servants have gone missing over the years. Little more has been found, however, despite there being rigorous investigations.

Human: A fairly young race in the world, humans first migrated to Zirvonia from the western jungles known as the Obsidian Wilds. For centuries, they have lived in various states of tribal hierarchy. The first major signs of civilization began to develop, yet they were destroyed by the armies of Alcaron. Now they're little more than a subservient race, subjected to their Ilgrathian masters. Humans can live for around 90 years. Their average life expectancy is 25 years.

Hydromancy: The magic school of controlling water, steam, and ice. Ice magic, in particular, is one of the more famous talents in the world. As such, hydromancers are highly coveted.

I

Ida (ee-dah): One of the two conjoined priestesses leading the Children of the Sacred Twins. Ida is cold, viperous, and melancholic, specializing in astromancy. Both she and her sister have flowing silver hair and blue eyes.

Ilgrathian (eel-GRAY-thee-IN): A race that has existed in the world for several thousand years. The first Ilgrathians were descendants of the people hailing from Kuhstra (COO-strah). Now, they are united under their goddess Ilgrathié. They have light-bronze skin, with hair colors ranging from gold to brunette to steely gray. Even the most normal of Ilgrathians appear like heroes out of legend, that is, until one learns of their lustful appetites. Ilgrathians can live for around 180 years. Their average life expectancy is 60 years.

Ilgrathian Heroes: Legends such as Tiliana (tih-lee-ah-nah), Dekaro (deh-CAR-oh), Shalatar (shah-lah-tar), and Mideus (mih-dee-us) are known far and wide for their deeds of expanding Alcaron's borders. Not all of them are Falconers or military generals, however, since Alcaron's influence has also spread through the arts of poetry and song. These, too, are celebrated for furthering Ilgrathié's cause.

Ilgrathié (eel-GRAH-thee-AY): The Holy Falcon who will guide the world unto Paradise. Ilgrathié is a pleasure goddess in nature, though Her doctrine requires that the world be cleansed of all other heathen beliefs. Taking its place is nothing short of debauchery. Atrocities such as rape, pillaging, and torture are all permitted, so long as it furthers Her cause. Above all, Ilgrathié's mantra is "pain and pleasure."

Initiate: One who is accepted into the Children of the Sacred Twins but is not a full member. Initiates are treated as ones who are still impure, having limited privileges compared to their peers. An initiate must first seduce another in the name of the Sacred Twins. Sometimes the partner in such an affair becomes an initiate themselves, whereas the prime initiate is promoted to a proper member.

Inner Sense: A sorcerer's ability to sense magic. More accurately, it's a way for one to enhance their five senses, detect signs and simulacra that normal beings would likely miss. It should be noted that, over time, this can serve as quite the mental strain.

Islirian (is-LEER-ee-IN): A gray-skinned people who live near the southern edge of the world. Islirians are cursed, doomed to transform into star wraiths upon dying. The only known countermeasure has been to burn the dead shortly before this process can occur. They were once highly respected and feared, but they have since fallen into ruin. Islirians can live around 120 years. Their average life expectancy following their curse is 20 years.

K

King Telinor (teh-lih-noor): The last monarch of Divnarost before the star wraith curse. Like other star wraiths, he appears like a specter with a starry veil for a body. Only in this case, he wears the old crown of Divnarost, as he holds some air of authority with his subjects.

Kitala (kih-tah-lah): The former queen of Divnarost that was slain by General Caerst. Kitala was the youngest ruler since the nation's founding. She is 23 years old, and when she was human she possessed raven black hair, green eyes, and smooth gray skin. Kitala is now reborn as a star wraith, and has no memory of her ventures with Steel and Stormbright.

Kolthan (kohl-than): The father of Steel and Stormbright, as well as husband to his deceased wife Tana. Kolthan is a burly giant, with flowing auburn hair, rippling muscles, and a stony demeanor. He was the chief warrior of Harskul before its razing. Kolthan is now a battered husk of his former self, clinging onto his own humanity after years of torture in the Soul Cistern. He speaks only in fragments, but he is still capable of thought and emotion.

L

Lieutenant Neto (net-oh): An Ilgrathian lieutenant who aids and guides General Caerst in her pursuit for revenge. Neto is perhaps loyal to a fault, but he is also quite dependable. He has tufted brown hair and blue eyes.

Listener: A type of information broker that's almost exclusive to Candala. These individuals make it their habit to eavesdrop and spread rumors for a price. Not all of these rumors are true, however.

M

Menthus (men-thus): An alias used for Kolthan while he is disguised as an Ilgrathian.

Mikka (MEE-kah): A former prostitute who is now Captain Helvia's personal advisor. Mikka is well versed in the arts of magic, particularly oneiromancy and the harnessing of dreamstone, and has since taught Helvia what she knows. She has curled auburn hair and azure eyes.

Miracor (MIH-rah-KOR): The last city of Divnarost that hasn't been overtaken by star wraiths. The Islirians here are a battered and broken people, clinging on to the last vestiges of life. The settlement is in an advanced state of ruin, with much of its knowledge and culture lost to the ages. The city was under siege by Alcaron, but was saved by Steel, Stormbright, and an alliance made with the star wraiths.

Mirungel (MIH-run-GEHL): The capital city of Alcaron. Also referred to by the Ilgrathians as the City of Chimes, Mirungel is the epicenter of all that goes on under Ilgrathié. It is a place that's nestled alongside Aerie Mountain, and here the Ilgrathians indulge in all pleasures imaginable.

Moon Cup: A type of relic that is revered by the Children of the Sacred Twins, being constructed of ivory and silver. There are two of these relics in total, and both are required to complete the ritual corresponding to The Great Equilibrium.

Moonhaven: A village situated less than a day's journey southwest of Candala. The area was swarmed some time ago by nightmare-kin and a corrupted Faunus, all of whom devoured its residents before creeping back into their otherworldly lair. This is a place where one of the two sacred moon cups was held, yet it was stolen away by the nightmare-kin. The village is now little more than an empty husk.

Moonsteel: A metal that's nearly ten-times stronger than steel. However, the deposits found in the world are notably rare. Moonsteel is highly valued for its beauty, durability, and tolerance to heat. It can withstand extremely high temperatures, with some claiming that it can even weather a dragon's breath.

N

Natural and Unnatural Properties of Dreamstone, the: A tome detailing the intricacies and risks that come from using the substance known as dreamstone. The book is equal parts a scientific dissection of its physical nature and magical capabilities, as well as being a manual on how one might best make use of it.

Necromancy: The magic school of reanimating the dead in order to do one's bidding. This is quite different from the school of sciomancy, primarily because the magician is returning the dead's souls to their bodies. Those who are raised can recall what they went through in life, though they're under the sorcerer's complete control.

Nightmare Corruption: In addition to devouring their victims, some nightmare-kin have the ability to corrupt their prey and use them as sentries. It is unknown how this is done, exactly, but it seems that this is reserved for beings with some form of magical potency. The Faunus that Stormbright and Aurora encounter is one such example.

Nightmare-Kin: A horrific race of amorphous monsters bleeding in from the Great Beyond. Unlike other species, nightmare-kin seem bent on the assimilation of all life, morphing their victims into something twisted and otherworldly.

O

Old Man Darkness: The primeval lord of death and the unknown. Old Man Darkness is believed to rule the infinite realms of the Great

Beyond. Even so, very little is known about Him. It's speculated that He created the nightmare-kin, although evidence for this is somewhat lacking.

Oneiromancy: The magic school of warping the laws of physics. Perhaps the most archaic of sorceries, oneiromancers use their power in conjunction with other spells, reshaping the world as they see fit. Whereas most magic is temporary, oneiromancy is permanent. Flying cities among the stars. Volcanoes spewing torrents of liquid ice. Vast underground spaces where the sun shines eternally. All is possible when utilizing this form of magic. The lair of the Faunus is an excellent example of oneiromancy being used.

P

Palace of the Sacred Twins, the: A subterranean lair located within Candala's depths. This is where the Children of the Sacred Twins hide away in secret, atop a mighty tower that has long been abandoned. The tower acts as a spring of sorts, though it's more of a byproduct of Ava and Ida's dream magicks than premeditated design.

Parcel, Coin: The Alcaronian copper coin. These were collectively named by couriers, as coppers were exchanged for sending parcels and packages throughout the nation. The courier's image is printed on one side, whereas the other has a symbol of a falcon. Ten parcels make up a single sylph.

Plegma (PLEG-mah): An exceptionally powerful nightmare-kin that was sealed away 1,500 years ago. It is said that Plegma once laid waste to entire settlements, rapidly growing as it devoured everything in its path.

Plegma's Seal: An ancient vault door constructed of stone at the deepest level of Candala's tunnels. Although the door has been warded with ancient spells, they have since weakened over the centuries. At some point Plegma must have broken through, as the stone door now lays in a pile of rubble.

Pool of Desire, the: A chamber locked away in the lower levels of the Palace of the Sacred Twins. It's made up of a spring where clean, warm water is piped through. The chamber was originally constructed before the cult's habitation, but it has since been restored by Ava and Ida. Oneiromancy is capable of many miracles, and the restoration of this place is but one of them.

Pyromancy: The magic school of harnessing and manipulating fire. Pyromancers are somewhat rare in the world, as most of them don't live for terribly long.

R

Rabus (rah-bus): An obese tavern-keeper who runs The Black Quail Tavern. Rabus is known as quite the shady dealer to many, yet he and Aedas share a strong connection as friends. Rabus is dark-haired with green eyes.

Rukh (rook): Large warbird bred by the Ilgrathians, with a wing span of ten-cubits across. They are horrific and aggressive predators, with a fondness for mutilating their prey.

S

Sciomancy: The magic school of summoning spirits from the Great Beyond. Unlike a necromancer, a sciomancer communes with the spirits he commands. One can conjure vast hordes out of thin air, binding them to the sciomancer. Some spirits are more easily controlled than others, and if the magician's focus lapses, then these beings can potentially free themselves and go berserk.

Shadevale: A small, decrepit village located just a week's journey north of Candala. Most of the buildings are formed out of hewn stone or sculpted mud. Its human denizens live meager lives, as they are almost entirely dependent on the Ilgrathians and their military presence in town. To the nation of Alcaron, this is a valuable checkpoint between Candala and the Ilgrathian capital.

Shariz'lan (shar-iz-LAHN): The head chirurgeon of Miracor, as well as the most experienced astromancer of the Islirians. Following the death of Kitala's parents at a young age, Shariz'lan has acted as a guardian for the child. Until the queen's death, she aided Kitala by gazing into the future, predicting details and possible outcomes of battles. Her appearance is almost hag-like, with a wrinkly face and long, bony fingers.

Silken Dove, the: A high-class inn located in the Wealthy District of Candala. The interiors here are well-furnished and -cared for. The owner, in particular, has proven sympathetic to humans who are desperate for help.

Silver Hearth Inn, the: A tavern located in the Merchant's District of Candala. Comparatively speaking, the alehouse is quite functional and decently well-kept. It has three stories in total, and the clientele have a tendency to be rowdy.

Slave Pits, the: A series of tunnels and caverns running underneath Mirungel, spanning the different corners of Aerie Mountain. This is a place where humans are beaten and broken: they're whipped, tortured, and defiled so that they might serve the higher castes of society. Only the strong can survive in such a horrific place, as cannibals are allowed to prey on the weak, thinning out a slave population that's already bursting at the seams.

Sorcerers: Also referred to as magicians. Sorcerers in Zirvonia are very powerful. However, they require hard work and discipline to use their magic effectively, even those who are awakened by higher powers. Sorcerers can master only one school of magic, which is based on their personality and talents. It is possible for one to dabble in other schools, though the results are often less than satisfactory.

Soul Cistern, the: A mysterious place where strong souls are taken and extracted. Little is actually known about this section of the Slave Pits, only that it's spoken about in hushed whispers, and with more than a tinge of fear.

Star Wraith: A strange spectral being somewhat akin to a ghost. Their bodies are like rifts in the fabric of space, displaying starry vistas as if they were a portal to the cosmos. This is what becomes of Islirians following their deaths, assuming their bodies aren't burned.

Standing Stones: These make up certain landmarks around the southern reaches of the Fields of Man. Their only known purpose is that these sites hold religious significance, as they are speculated to be places of power. It is here where the Children of the Sacred Twins guard their moon cups at night, as it's said the chalices draw power from the twin moons.

Steel: Also known as Serithas (seh-rih-thus), Steel is the older of the two main brothers. He is tall and slightly muscular in build, with brunette hair and green eyes. He is 17 years old.

Stormbright: Also known as Zolan (zoh-lin), Stormbright is the younger of the two brothers. He has blue eyes and dirty-blond hair flowing down to his shoulders. He is 15 years old.

Sylph: A type of spectral fae that glides along the winds, perching themselves atop mountain ranges. It's well known that most sylphs have allied themselves with Ilgrathié, though it's been speculated that a few have defied Her over the years. Sylphs typically emerge from strong gales of wind, and if one is reckless enough to be caught off-guard, they can be torn to shreds in mere seconds. Many sylphs have since developed a taste for bloodshed, thanks to their bond with the Ilgrathians. In cases like these, they will sing a magic song which causes the victim to mutilate themselves before expiring.

Sylph, Coin: The Alcaronian silver coin. These are named after the sylph race, the majority of whom guard Ilgrathié in Her chamber. The swirling image of a sylph is printed on one side, whereas the other has a symbol of a falcon. Ten sylphs make up a single drakon.

T

Taldriath (TAHL-dree-ith): The first of Zirvonia's two orbiting moons. Taldriath looms much closer in the heavens. It's believed that, eventually, these celestial bodies will collide and wreak untold devastation on the world.

Tela (tay-lah): A harlot sporting blonde curls and a somewhat aged complexion, although this has done little to turn away her customers. Tela currently works for Rabus in The Black Quail Tavern and makes the most out of her quiet life.

Thayden: A town situated nearly a day east of Candala, leading onward to Driftwind. The town is currently under siege by Captain Helvia, as once she learned its denizens might be holding one of the moon cups, the settlement closed its gates and refused to cooperate. It is now half-destroyed, with much of its walls and structures being burnt to cinders.

V

Vana (vah-nah): Aurora's auburn-haired companion. She, too, was a fellow initiate before she was unfortunately devoured by nightmare-kin.

Z

Zirvonia (zer-VOH-nee-AH): A wild land inhabited by sylphs, shadow hounds, and other varieties of monsters. In recent centuries, it has been colonized by humans and Ilgrathians, a semblance of order forming over its many plains, rivers, and forests. Many ancient secrets lurk in hidden places, hinting at truths far wilder and more fantastic than one could imagine.

Afterword

From the bottom of my heart, dear reader, I cannot thank you enough.

Despite taking far less time to outline and draft, this story was anything *but* easy. A great deal of time was spent editing, balancing, and fine-tuning the more delicate subject matters of this book. The process proved more time consuming than I had hoped, but I am pleased with the result.

Greater trials for Steel and Stormbright lay ahead. With that said, I hope this remains the darkest tale shared by the two brothers. Steel and Stormbright both mean a lot to me, and so I wanted to test them on a truly personal level—not only through physical conflict, but with an emotional facet as well.

I hope I achieved just that, and even more so, that it made for a gripping story. As always, planning is underway for the sequel. I look forward to the feedback this book will receive—both the good and the bad—as I continue to hone my abilities as a writer. My instincts are telling me this will be a quadrilogy, or at least this section of the brothers' life. Brighter prospects lay beyond for the thief and sorcerer, and I hope you will join me for their redemption.

God Bless,
The Lord Otter

About the Otter

The Lord Otter was born and raised in the mountainous countryside of Tennessee, deep at the heart of Appalachia, where Rocky Top and the Smoky Mountains dwell in all their glory. It is here he cultivated a love for all things otherworldly and fantastical. From reading an illustrated copy of *The Time Machine* at an early age, pulp adventure has fascinated this young water weasel for most of his adult life.

Otter lives quietly in Central Florida, where he conjures up new and exciting stories while weaving through the great maze known as Life. He wishes you the best of tidings, and a sincere thank you for the support.

He also asks that you give him lots of fish.

Links:

Substack: downstreampulp.substack.com

X/Twitter: @The_Lord_Otter

YouTube: the_lord_otter